Death

A LIFE

Death

A LIFE

with
George Pendle

THREE RIVERS PRESS

NEW YORK

Publisher's Note

The names, identifying characteristics, and taxonomic rank of the persons, species, and supernatural beings included in this book have been changed to protect the innocent, the guilty, and those beyond all human conceptions of ethical responsibility.

Library of Congress Cataloging-in-Publication Data
Pendle, George, 1976–
Death : a life / by George Pendle.—1st ed.
p. cm.
1. Death—Humor. I. Title.
PN6231.D35P46 2008
813'.6—dc22   2008011069

ISBN 978-0-307-39560-3

Printed in the United States of America

Design by Nancy Beth Field

10 9 8 7 6 5 4

First Edition

"And in those days shall men seek death, and shall not find it; and shall desire to die, and death shall flee from them."

—Revelation 9:6

INTRODUCTION

For someone who is set to play such a pivotal role in each of our lives, it seems strange that we know so little about Death. A deeply private figure, never interviewed or photographed, Death has been content to let his vast body of work do the talking. Now, for the first time, Death speaks out.

Death: A Life is a highly personal chronicle that not only provides insights into the upbringing and character of one of our planet's most interesting and unusual beings, but also sheds a fascinating light on the world in which we die. Up until now the sheer dearth of information on Death has meant that rumors and gossip have long been left to fill the factual void. Sensationalism and prejudice have triumphed; sobriety and accuracy have fallen by the wayside. As such, the Death that has been handed down to us through the generations is a monstrous and unfair confabulation of superstition, hearsay, and deep-seated instinctual fears.

Death has been variously described as the humorless Grim Reaper and the benevolent Father Time; as a destroying angel and a dancing skeleton; as Thanatos, son of Night; and Anubis, son of Ra; but who is he really? Where did he come from? And why does he do the things that he does?

Within these pages such questions will be laid to rest, for in this book, Death finally reveals to us the skin above the skull. He recounts his childhood in the lowest pits of Hell; the mental and physical cruelty he suffered at the hands of his demiurge parents; the insecurity and neurosis that wracked him at the Dawn of Time; his friendships with the great civilizations of antiquity; his enmities with the mythical gods; and his gradual, blithe descent down the shelving beach of curiosity into the deepening sea of addiction.

Readers will find it hard not to be shocked and amazed by the revelation of the "lost weekend" he spent with the Horsemen of the Apocalypse, or his magnificent but ultimately doomed rebellion against the Grand Scheme of Things, not to mention his wrenching institutionalization at the hands of angelic rivals, and his slow and painful recovery. The unsettling honesty, shocking candor, and mordant humor that characterizes his tale sheds a bright new light on the darkness that lies at the end of our lives.

But why, you may ask, has Death decided to write his book now? Who can fathom the mind of the world's first truly omniscient narrator, but certain hints are provided throughout this book. First, there is the need to set the record straight, to answer some of his detractors' taunts, and to correct the narrow-minded bigotry that has grown around his name. Second, there are the undoubted therapeutic benefits to be gained from recanting his travails to an audience. Third, and perhaps most important, is the chance to redress what Death sees as the fundamental misconception of Creation—that it is not Death that should be feared, but rather the dreadful possibilities of Life.

It is hoped that *Death: A Life* will provide not merely an interesting record of one of the world's most famed personalities but also a constructive perspective to those struggling with similar problems of self-doubt and addiction. It can safely be said that no one has touched more lives, more deeply, than Death. Through this devastating memoir, it is hoped he will touch many, many more.

As for my own role in bringing Death's remarkable memoir to light, I can only say that it stems from a long-seated attraction toward the lives of others, undoubtedly prompted by my own unremarkable existence.

Unlike the vast majority of memoirists, I was the recipient of a happy childhood. My parents, it seems, loved me. They fed me, clothed me, and schooled me in precise accord with prevailing morality.

My dealings with my relatives were equally avuncular. I feared none of their visits and even under hypnosis could not manage to unearth a single false memory of abuse at their hands. I slept soundly at night and did not wet the sheets.

As I grew into my teens I became an outgoing child, not insular in the slightest. I did not pull the wings off flies or cut myself with broken glass. I found existentialism dull, and the works of Edvard Munch gloomy. I performed well at school, if avoiding scholarly distinction, and neglected to become addicted to alcohol, drugs, or even masturbation.

My summer jobs did not consist of turning tricks as a truck-stop prostitute or being the experimental subject of a disbarred doctor of medicine. My friends, of whom I had many, often remarked on my well-balanced character and all-round reliability, and my girl-friends were neither members of occultist groups, nor addicts of crack cocaine.

As I grew I discovered a singular lack of skeletons in the familial closet. Everything was exactly as I thought it was. By the time I entered adult life I could class myself as fit, happy, content, untroubled, and willfully ignorant of the many troubles that can befall humankind.

Ironically, however, I longed to write about myself. I yearned to put the real "me" down on paper for the world to see. But who would read such a memoir of contentment? By the time I realized my calling, it was too late for me to endure a terrible upbringing, too late to be scarred by childhood abuse. I knew that no one was looked down upon more in memoirist circles than the wrist-cutting arriviste. A certain pedigree of mistreatment was demanded—sustained, brutal, and given by those who should have loved one most. Here, as within the aristocracy, one's family was all important.

Yet my wish to be a memoir writer did not dim. Of course, it was too late for me, but with so much suffering in the world, why couldn't I live vicariously through another's misery? So I placed advertisements in newspapers and magazines, calling on people with stories of personal tragedy to come forward. Together, I explained, we could transmute their leaden suffering into bestselling gold.

I was immediately contacted by a forty-five-year-old man who told me a horrifying story that would become my first book, *Case 463/E>9*. The only child of experimental psychologists, the subject had been referred to throughout his youth by his case number, and his every move had been studied and recorded. When he had found a wounded pigeon in his garden, his parents had bludgeoned it to death in front of his eyes to gauge his reaction. On Christmas Day, after he had unwrapped his presents, his parents had forced him to take them into the garden and set fire to them. In both cases his response, his parents recorded, was "negative." Case 463/E>9 told me that his terrible upbringing had led him to loathe the laughter and happiness of children, a crippling phobia that he finally learned to manage by becoming the successful headmaster of a prestigious boarding school. The ensuing book was a minor bestseller and was excerpted in the *New York Review of Books* and *People* magazine.

With that the floodgates opened, and I was subsumed under a tidal wave of other people's misery. I became expert at mixing the horrific detail of tortures suffered with touching recollections of lost innocence, and for many of my subjects, my house became a home away from broken home.

So good was I at my job that, with each new commission, I felt that I was understanding my subjects' suffering somewhat better than they were themselves. Each inappropriate medical treatment, double-murder orphaning, and unjust consignment to a lunatic asylum was like a dagger through my own, unbroken heart. Soon I developed a tolerance for man's inhumanity to man. My subjects' stories began to seem pedestrian and formulaic. A childhood abduction by religious fundamentalists barely raised a shiver. A single mother's drunken alcoholism and descent into prostitution left me yawning. I was suffering from a trauma glut.

I was thinking of packing it all in and returning to my university thesis topic—a study of the similarities of the even-numbered presidents of the United States—when I was awoken late one night by a strange telephone call. It began in silence before a voice that was barely there at all spoke my name, referred to one of my advertisements, and said he wanted to tell his story.

The man's voice was so peculiar that I thought he must be a foreigner. This boded well. Tales of cold Slavic upbringings or African child-soldiering inevitably led to the subjects finding their way to a Western metropolis and a good, uplifting, profitable ending. But as I gazed at the magnificent statue I had recently installed in my bedroom of an unconscious Thomas De Quincey, I sensed there was something about this voice on the telephone that seemed to have greater depths of sorrow behind it than even the Albanian white slave trade could offer. I agreed to meet my subject the following week.

I was somewhat disappointed, upon arriving at the designated address, to find myself at a run-down apartment block located in one of the less salubrious areas of the city. This would seem to preclude any hope of a happy ending. But already I began fitting this story into one of my many formulas—"A Promising Life Ruined" perhaps, with a dash of "Survival Is the Greatest Achievement" tacked onto the end.

Picking my way around the overturned shopping carts and broken glass, I took a urine-scented elevator to the thirteenth floor. I was just about to knock on apartment number 66F when the door swung open as if of its own accord. I edged inside.

"Sit down," I was told.

The voice seemed to come from the far corner of the room, which, despite all the lights being on and the sunlight streaming through the south-facing windows, was draped in a funereal darkness. Throughout our subsequent talk, no matter how hard I squinted, I could barely make out a distinct shape.

"I want you to tell my story," said the voice. This was promising. It usually took hours of cajoling and sympathy for my subjects to open up. "For centuries I've been mistreated, abused, had tales told about me that are quite untrue. Now I want to set the record straight."

I presumed this was just exaggeration and started jotting down notes. Then he said something that made me stop in my tracks.

"I'm Death, you see."

What an unusual name, I thought to myself. Was it Belgian? When I asked him his first name, he shook his head and repeated it again, more slowly this time.

"I . . . am . . . *Death.*"

I put down my pen, took off my glasses, and began polishing them with my tie. I had faced crazies before, all desperate to tell you how they had been raised by devils and were in fact lords of the eighth level of Hell. These people usually had suffered some sort of abuse, of course, but they were generally incoherent and presented certain libel situations—Oprah Winfrey sinisterly controlling their minds from the television set was a particular favorite—that I could not afford to deal with. I thanked "Mr. Death" for his time, looked at my watch, regretted that I had another appointment, and got up to leave when my body was gripped by seizures and the lightbulb over my head began to bleed. As my body pinballed from wall to wall, the voice continued to speak.

"For millennia I've had to listen to your pathetic human suffering. The same old stories, time after time, 'I'm so miserable!' 'Life is unfair!' 'I don't deserve this!' Well, let me tell you that being Death is no picnic either. I've suffered heartache, cruelty, maltreatment, neglect. I've wanted to end it all, but suicide's hardly an option. I've read what you believe me to be. I've seen the pictures. You think I'm all grins and dance macabres, and interminable games of chess on deserted beaches. Well, it's not like that. I didn't always want to do this, you know? I have feelings too."

I slammed back into my chair, and the dark shape in the corner seemed to stand up. I gulped. But the darkness merely leaned over and picked up a bucket, which it placed beneath the still-bleeding lightbulb. It then got me a glass of water and an aspirin. My mouth filled with steam as the liquid hit my red-hot fillings.

"Comfortable?" he asked me as he sat back down.

"No," I replied.

"Good," he said. "That is probably for the best."

"Why don't you start at the beginning?" I suggested, as I tried to steady my shaking hand over my notepad.

"Oh," said Death, "I'll start before that."

So began the most horrific story I have ever heard.

George Pendle
February 2008

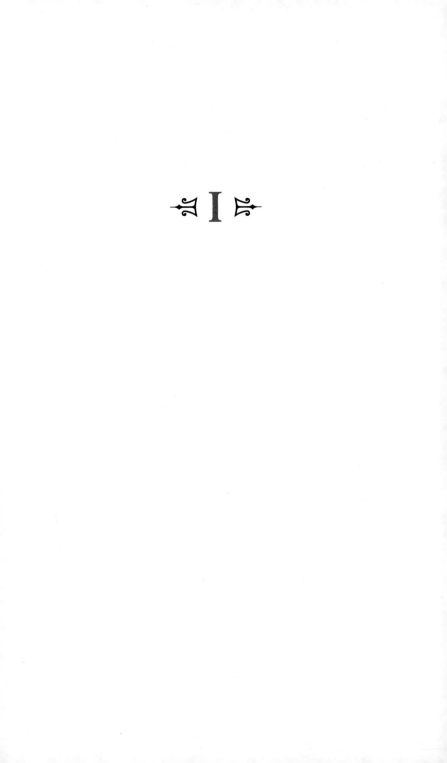

I

The Beginning
of The End

‑‑‑‑❧‑‑‑‑

My **earliest** memory is of my mother. She was a heavyset lady, the size of a small mountain. Everyone knew her as Sin.

I remember her standing in front of a glistening pool of molten rock, making sure that her scales were oozing and slime covered. "I look horrible," she would say, turning to me confidingly, "quite, quite horrible." She would go back to combing through her snakes and vomiting bile down her chest, and I would watch enraptured. Fangs glistened in her mouth, empty eye sockets brought out the sickly pallor of her skin, the familiar odor of decay hung heavy around her. That was Mother.

My father was Satan. He was Mother's father too, which led to some awkward introductions at parties. This never bothered me too much. It was, after all, the Dawn of Creation, and exotic family trees were fairly commonplace. I recall Father explaining to me, once I had reached a certain age, that the options for a sincere and honest relationship before time began were severely limited. The cherubim and seraphim were prudes who kept their legs crossed, Night was available but impossible to find, and Chaos was a total wreck (and I mean *wreck*).

My mother's pregnancy with me had been difficult. There was the morning sickness, the swollenness, the aching joints, and the fact that I was gnawing on her entrails constantly. Mother would sometimes look at me, and then down at the gaping holes in her belly, and I knew she was wondering whether it had all been worth it.

Of course Father was never around. Today you would call him an absent father (and husband). I only got to see him on the occasional eon when he'd fly by, all flames and bluster, with a red-lipped demoness in tow. Mother put on a brave face—she had plenty of them lying around—but I knew something wasn't quite right in our home.

The one day in my childhood that I remember spending with Father was when I helped him mirror Hell's firmament. There I was, passing him slabs of glass, desperately seeking his approval, and all the while he kept looking at me as if he couldn't quite place who I was, or what I was doing there, or what, ultimately, I was for. There are things that happen to you in your existence that you just don't question, maybe because you're afraid of what the answer will be. Father's abandonment of Mother and me was one of those things. I never dared asked why.

As a result, Mother and I were very close. One might almost say too close. No sooner had I been born than we began rutting. For me there were no glimpses of her getting changed in the bathroom stirring strange and complicated feelings. There were no ambivalent memories of being spanked, or of dressing up in her clothes while she was away. No. For me it was simply wham, bam, thank you Mom.

I know what you're thinking. We're only two pages in and already we've covered rape, incest, mutilation, and abandonment. But in my family's defense you should remember that we were in Hell, Mother was the embodiment of Sin, and Father was Satan, Master of Misrule and Lord of Lies. Finger painting wasn't really an option.

It's true that if Father had been around, he might have stopped

Daddy.

me from doing what I was doing. But he wasn't around, and from the get-go I struggled with the concepts of right and wrong. Maybe it was Mother's influence on me. Whenever anybody spent any time around her they would always end up doing something very, very bad. Anyhow, with all the rutting it wasn't long before Mother gave birth to a pair of monstrous dogs. Well, I was quite surprised too. Now I don't know if I was responsible or whether Cerberus had something to do with it—he was always humping anything that moved—but the dogs kept running back and forth into Mother's womb causing her no end of problems. Is it any wonder, I ask you, that I grew up to be somewhat suspicious of intimacy?

I was an only child. In fact, I was *the* only child. Hell wasn't considered a particularly good place to raise children at the time. Playgrounds were specifically designed to grind up those who played in them, babysitters were required by hellish law to actually sit on babies, and the schools were just terrible. When I asked Mother why I was the only being who had actually been born in Hell as opposed to being exiled there, she admitted that I had been a mistake. She had forgotten to wear protection one night—her spiked suit of armor—and Father had leapt on her.

I was left largely to look after myself, but Hell was an interesting place in which to grow up. I recall crawling around the Palace of

Pandemonium playing with my demonic toys—sharp, flinty combustible objects that burst into flame whenever I held them close—while around me the Dukes of Hell plotted and schemed new ways to revenge themselves upon Heaven. Sometimes, when the Dukes were being particularly devious in their machinations, I was ushered outside to feed the Ducks of Hell who floated in a pool of acid, having been damned for their pride in their plumage and their refusal to quack on command.

Feathered Fiend.

This isn't to say I was completely alone. I had a number of paternal substitutes to wile away the hours before time began. I used to play hide-and-seek with Uncle Abaddon, captain of the Furies and leader of the Seventh Infernal Order. I remember one game going on for incalculable moments as I hid at the bottom of the Bottomless Pit and the poor old devil went into a rage, hurling thunderbolts, scouring canyons, frantic to find me before Father returned. Of course he needn't have worried. Father was never home.

Lucifuge Rofocale, prime minister of Hell, was another guardian I clung to. An elderly demon, with fifteen wooden limbs and seventy-seven eye patches, he had fought bravely in the Battle of Heaven, and would often tell me stories of how he had been hurled headlong, flaming, from the ethereal sky.

"Clamor, such as heard in Heaven till then, was never!" he would splutter, swinging his rusted sword back and forth at his imagined enemies before collapsing into his throne of coal. Then again, everyone had a story to tell in Hell. The battle for Heaven had been a matter of principle, despite its eternal consequences, and the devils were proud of their role in it. "A chance to stand up for what was undeniably wrong," recalled Lucifuge, absentmindedly crushing an imp in his massive hand and proceeding to bite off its head.

As well as being veterans of the same campaign, these guardians of mine had a tremendous respect for Father. It was a respect that I could never entirely understand.

"Your father was the brightest and best of us all," I remember Sargatanas, the brigadier general of Hell, recounting. "He was forever putting down the angel Gabriel. Oh that Gabriel, no one liked him. Always a little too keen, if you know what I mean. Anyway, your father was the one who thought we should try to instigate an Angelic Workers Republic and replace God with a Central Seraphic Council composed of an amoral proletariat and auxiliary cherub brigade. Ah, such foresight! We owe him everything."

"But you've all been damned for eternity in the fiery pits," I couldn't help but say.

"Very true, young Death, very true," croaked Sargatanas. "But, as your father says, 'Better to rule in Hell than to serve in Heaven.' "

"But surely you don't like eternal damnation?"

"Why of course I do, my boy!" he replied, sucking in his chest. "There's nothing finer than awakening to the dreadful din of hissing, followed by a dip in a pool of burning magma and a good exfoliation in the scalding steam vents, before lying down beneath the fiery sky content in the knowledge that you're subject of the eternal ire of the All-Powerful."

"But didn't you have feathery wings in Heaven," I protested, "not these horrid scaly ones? Wasn't that better?"

"Feathers!" spluttered Sargatanas. "Feathers are for the birds, my boy. Flaking, peeling, scale-ridden wings, now that's what real beings wear. I'll tell you a secret," he said, and drew me closer. "The eternal pain at having known Paradise and lost it is priceless. I wouldn't swap it for anything."

"Really?" I said. "You really wouldn't want to be back in Heaven?"

"Never. Not without my pool of burning magma."

"But if you wanted pools of burning magma in Heaven, couldn't you get them?" I asked.

"Oh no," said Sargatanas, rubbing his chins. "Well, maybe. But not like the magma down here."

I had always been a bit confused about the devils. They were always crying out in pain and anguish, yet when you tried to console them they always said they wouldn't want to be anywhere else. I remember Sargatanas taking me to the highest tower in the Palace, as the gorgons and hydras screeched below. He proudly swept a claw over the hellish landscape, which was, as usual, completely obscured by a thick, choking fog. "To think," he said, "without your father we wouldn't have all this."

The Palace of Pandemonium: "Disorder! Disorder!"

Being Satan's child did have its perks. I could torment any of the Dukes of Hell without so much as a smack. They would just waggle their talons at me as I clawed their faces and look at one another and say, "Just like his father." I remember one day Beelzebub, whom I liked very much for the swarm of flies that perpetually surrounded him, took me to one side and said that great things were expected of me. At the time I hadn't a clue what he meant.

As I said, I wasn't an easy child. I tortured my poor mother. Literally. With fire and hot irons, every night. And in Hell it was always night. But what did I know? I was young, dumb, and full of the emptiness of the void. Looking back on it all, I realize that the person I really blamed was Father. All the time I was drilling into Mother's skull I was wondering what had happened to him. Where was he? Why didn't he write?

When I wasn't beating Mother, or setting her aflame, or stretching her out on a rack, or running her through with spikes, or throwing her onto sharp rocks, or hammering her head flat, I helped her guard the Gates of Hell. Mother insisted on keeping the gates sparklingly clean. This was harder than you might imagine since they were entirely constructed of splintered bone and cartilage. I never got along with the gates. The doorknob screamed at me whenever I touched it, and the hinges were always making unsavory remarks about my skin. Mother never told me why she had decided to start guarding them. "I just did," she'd say, as her long forked tongue licked the gates free of soot, sending the keyhole into moaning ecstasies.

I remember watching her at work and marveling at her certainty. She was so thorough and absorbed in what she was doing. I suppose everyone finds their true calling in the end, but at the time I didn't know what I was meant to be accomplishing. On some days I'd pretend I was a demon. I had made myself a pair of horns and a tail out of the horns and tail of a smaller, weaker fiend, but the real demons would see through my disguise and tease me, saying that I was a good-for-everything, always-do-well. Other times I'd pretend I was the embodiment of some moral transgression, like Rape or Murder, but deep down I knew I wasn't, and Mother would tell me to stop being silly and to pass the duster.

Infernal devils being what they are, there was an unending line of imps and demons trying to sneak through the gates. But Mother was impervious to both threats and flattery. I remember when Buriel, one of the many Princes of Hell, said he needed to pop out for a minute as he'd forgotten his keys somewhere in the void. Mother ate him. Or when that charming roué, Asmodeus, put a long tentacle across her shoulder and tried to woo her with his piscine charms. Mother ate him too.

Asmodeus: Devil of Many Parts, Few of Them Matching.

Yes, we heard the whole gamut of excuses: how they had fallen by mistake, or taken the wrong turn and ended up in Hell by accident. In the case of the strangely delicate devil known as Reginald, I was almost inclined to believe him.

Reginald always wore a tunic that shone brilliantly despite the soot and dirt that clung to it. His face carried a permanent look of consternation. Every day he would appear at the gates and repeat his story—it never varied. He had arrived at the Battle of Heaven late, he explained, and had rushed headlong to fight on the side of good when a strap on his sandal had come loose and he had tripped and fallen headlong into Hell. He even had his damaged sandal to prove it. He thus insisted that he was not a fallen angel, but rather an angel who had fallen. It was an interesting semantic distinction.

"I assure you, madam," I remember him saying to Mother, "I am telling the truth." This always caused the surrounding devils, who always turned out in great numbers whenever Reginald tried to argue his way out, to burst into fits of laughter.

"But no one tells the truth in Hell, Reginald," said Mother, who I think was secretly quite fond of Reginald.

"But I'm not a devil!" said Reginald, his voice rising in pitch. "Look at my wings." Reginald's wings, although in need of a good comb, seemed distinctly more feathery than the usual scaly fare.

"Ah, Reginald," said my mother, "but no one in Hell looks like they should. We are all dissemblers here."

"Oh, but this is ridiculous!" said Reginald. "Look, I've got a halo! I'm a bloody angel!" It was true that hovering over his head was a ring of effervescent light, albeit one that had seen better days and now spun atop Reginald's head on a slightly rakish orbit.

"Reginald, Reginald, Reginald," said my mother, her eyes gleaming, "are you saying the Creator made a mistake?"

"Well . . . I . . ."

"Are you saying the Lord God Almighty, in all His infinite wisdom, somehow made a blunder?"

"Well, I wouldn't go so far as to call it a mistake . . ." spluttered Reginald.

"What kind of an angel, Reginald," said Mother, gleefully sensing the endgame approaching, "would doubt the infallibility of the Creator? Surely that's the kind of thing that could land a person in Hell, isn't it, Reginald?"

"But . . . but . . . ," said Reginald.

"Nice try, Reggie dear," said my mother soothingly, putting an arm across Reginald's slumping shoulders, "but not today. Why don't you come back tomorrow and we can talk this over again."

Arguments with Reginald always seemed to end this way, and to the jeers of the onlooking devils, he would trudge back to his gleaming cave, scrape off the obscene graffiti that had invariably appeared during his brief absence, and pluck sadly at a rather battered and out-of-tune harp. I often visited Reginald there and talked to him about Heaven. Unlike all the other devils he really seemed to want to return.

"I tell you, Master Death, I would do anything to get back," said Reginald. "Anything good that is, of course. Of late I've been tempted to try and steal your mother's keys. A little voice in my head is always telling me that only then would I be able to go back to Heaven."

"That would be Uncle Puruel," I explained. "He's very small but quite persuasive." I heard Puruel shout a high-pitched greeting to me from out of Reginald's ear.

I felt a strange affinity for Reginald, because I too didn't quite fit in. Neither demon nor god, my self-esteem was shot. I just wanted to belong, to be approved of. But while the other devils were always plotting or torturing or cackling, I preferred doing nothing. Nothing at all. I would sit far away from the burning flames, in the Bottomless Pit, or the Endless Abyss, or the Black Gulf, and there I would feel settled and comfortable. As the Darkness rushed around me I didn't talk, or breathe, or think. I just reveled in the eternal blackness and in the deep silence that persists forever. The older I grew—the closer I came to being a fully grown-up unchanging perpetual—the more I liked feeling the edge of Creation just slipping by.

I remember it had been a quiet day at the Gates of Hell. Reginald had come and gone, a note stuck to his back reading TORTURE ME, when suddenly an overwhelming aura of evil swept toward us. There was the flap of mighty wings, the succubae vanished, and Father appeared in front of us. He was wearing fleur-de-lis velvet slippers the size of aircraft carriers, an immense dark purple dressing gown with three interlinked sixes embroidered tastefully on the chest, and a vast black towel hung over his shoulders. He had just come back from bathing in a volcano.

"Hello, Sin," he said to Mother, a smile lingering at his mouth.

In Hell, Silence Is Leaden.

"Hello, husband. I mean, Father. I mean . . ." Mother giggled. She was always thrown into a blushing confusion by Father's presence.

"Just call me Satan, darling," he said, casually looking around him.

"But it sounds so awkward," said Mother, girlish now, smiling coquettishly and twirling her snakes around a finger.

"Would you mind letting me out for a moment," said Father, raking a long talon across Mother's cheek and motioning toward the gates.

"Well . . . I . . . ," said Mother, torn between sexual attraction, filial respect, and duty.

"I won't be long, I promise," sung the Master of Mendacity as he reached for the keys.

"Well, I really shouldn't," said Mother, lowering her eyes. "What would the others say?" She gestured around but Father's presence had scared everyone away.

"I'm sure they'd understand, baby," said Father. Hooking the keys in his hand, he savagely kissed Mother, leaving her swooning, and strode toward the gates.

Well, that was about all I could stand. I leapt in front of Father and refused to move.

"And you are?" he inquired, pointing at me. There was an awkward silence. It was not the first time Father had forgotten who I was. There had been the time in the Palace of Pandemonium when he had almost eaten me whole, before dear old Sargatanas had hurried over and reminded him who I was.

Admittedly, Father and I did not look alike. He was an imposing creature, with huge scaly wings, a dark red face, and giant horns reaching up to the vaults of Hell, whereas I was as ugly as Mother.

The Annual Family Engraving Was Always a Fractious Affair.
(from left) *Me, Mother, Father.*

This time, however, I was older, and angrier. So the bastard didn't even recognize me? Well, I'd make sure he never forgot me. Needless to say, there was a fight. I leapt at him and began gouging at his insides with my dart, a sharp little instrument I had created out of the spine of an escaping fiend and some string. As I attacked, I realized I hadn't been this close to Father in years. Mother said he used to be the most beautiful angel of all, and from a distance he still cut a dashing figure, but close up you could see he was getting soft about the middle and his flames were receding above his temples. Looking back on it, I realize that despite the egotism and bravado, Father had confidence issues. Here he was, damned for all eternity, with every demon in Hell looking to him for guidance, while he was feeling that his best years were all behind him.

Mother eventually slithered between us and broke up the fight and explained to Father who I was. He nodded his head, as if he wasn't entirely convinced. "And as for you," she said turning to me, "you shouldn't attack your father like that."

"He's not my father," I cried. "I hate him!"

"I hate you too, son," said Father adoringly. "I hate you both."

It was difficult to show displeasure to a father whose entire being was devoted to doing wrong. When I refused to do his bidding, he seemed even happier than when I carried it out.

Beaming broadly, Father took Mother to one side and whispered in her ear and after some time she came and spoke to me. She said Father had found something out about one of God's new projects called "Earth," and he wanted to explore it. I was initially very suspicious. After all, you don't get a nickname like the Lord of Lies for nothing. But Mother still had a soft spot for him and wanted to let him through. They were asking me to look the other way.

"If you don't do it for him, do it for me," she cried, and persuaded by a son's natural guilt, I let Father pass through the gates unmolested, smiling that cocky smile of his.

I was in a foul mood. As the doors slammed shut, I heard a cough behind me. Not the usual rasping, hacking, beetle-and-phlegm-laden coughs that permeated Hell, but a polite, neat little cough that signaled a presence rather than a pestilence.

"Er . . . Master Death. I couldn't help but notice that you just let someone out. I was wondering, could I . . ."

"Oh, fuck off, Reginald," I said.

Earthly Desires

Mother and I sat around for ages, literally. We didn't talk much. I was confused and angry, but I had to admit that for once Father's lies sounded plausible, if not terribly promising. God was always getting involved in new projects, creating worlds that didn't quite work. I knew this because the results usually ended up in Hell, which at the time acted less as a place for eternal damnation than as the bottom drawer of a dresser in the spare room of Creation.

Everyone in Hell was familiar with the world known as "H'trae," which now lay cooling over in the Field of the Damned. God had populated it entirely with deities who worshipped a being completely lacking in supernatural powers known as "Dog." Dog had issued his people two commandments: first, he demanded that bones be sacrificed to him on a regular basis. Second, he demanded that his worshippers should play fetch with him until he was too tired to wag his tail. When Dog eventually tore H'trae apart in a happy frenzy, God had brushed the planet's remains under the carpet. Dog too ended up in Hell, condemned for all eternity to chase after an ever-floating Frisbee that remained always just tantalizingly out of his reach. Perversely, this made him very, very happy.

With thoughts such as these I wiled away the time waiting for Father's return, and eventually we heard a rather tired knock on the

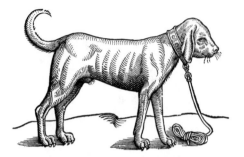

Dog: Depicted Wearing the Holy Lead of Walk.

Gates of Hell. He was back, a gleam in his eye and lipstick on his collar bone, thighs, and soles of his feet. But before we could say a word, before the gates had even slammed shut, he announced that we should pack our things and get ready to go—we were all moving to Earth. Mother raised herself on her scaly tail and slithered over to him in confusion. I distinctly remember that day. Father had molten tears in his eyes. He declared we were going to be a family again. Gathering us up in his arms, he roared that we'd have so much fun.

To my utmost surprise he was absolutely right.

So we packed our things and left. I had few possessions to carry, but I had carefully collected some of the Darkness from the deepest depths of the Bottomless Pit. In the depths of the Pit, the Darkness would wrap itself around me, filling me with a veritable ecstasy of emptiness, but when I tried to take it with me, it ran through my fingers like water, spooling into a puddle and extinguishing the perpetual hellfire at my feet. It took some coaxing, but by the judicious placement of a flaming coal in my bag, I managed to get the Darkness to leap inside to extinguish it. I quickly zipped the bag shut. It made me feel comfortable knowing it was there.

Father had suggested we try to raise as little fuss as possible in

The Darkness (profile): The Puppy Fat Would Soon Go.

leaving so as not to alert the rest of the damned. However, since secrets cannot physically exist in Hell, where all plots are public knowledge, all conspiracies well known and familiar, and all cabals openly recruiting new members, our whispered words soon drew a numberless horde of imps and succubae flocking to the Gates of Hell. With one flap of his immense wings, Father hurled them back, and Mother and I swatted frantically at the multitude of mischievous sprites who were desperately trying to force their way into our clothes and luggage.

Just as we were edging our way out of the gates, who should come running toward us but Reginald, his toga on fire, being pursued by a hundred imps with pitchforks.

"But what about me?" he cried. "What's going to happen to me?"

"I'm sorry, Reginald," I replied, tearing the last of the sprites from my pockets and flinging them back toward the fire, "but rules are rules."

Little did I know then how those words would come back to haunt me. When I think what I could have spared myself by listening to them! If only now I could tell my younger self to stop and heed the wisdom I spoke then without knowing it. But I can't, and I didn't. I slammed the gates shut, turned the key in its lock, and as the bolt slid home heard Reginald's familiar screams begin yet again.

❧✦❧

It was the first trip we had ever taken as a family, and the first time I had ever left Hell. But as we swam, sank, waded, and crept across the unbridgeable void separating the damned from the saved, I barely noticed the vast expanses that stretched out before us. Instead my eyes were locked firmly on my parents as we moved relentlessly as one, toward the coast of Earth.

Father was at his most charming, and Mother giggled and blushed. I noticed she had shined her scales and covered her chest in a particularly loathsome shade of vomit especially for the journey. Every now and then she would wiggle her tail in delight, and Father would pinch and slap her playfully and let out peals of laughter. It is a joy for a child to see his parents so deeply in love, and as they passed exploding supernovas arm in arm they seemed like the perfect couple. My animosity toward Father was gradually slipping away, and although I noticed he could not stop himself from ogling any black holes we passed, he was putting on a good show. He kept turning to me and telling me how excited I would be when we got to Earth.

The Universe (detail).

But it was a long trip. The epochs ticked by, and the conversation subsided. The farther from Hell we went, the more anxious Father became. I didn't know then what his relationship was like with God, but I did know the Gates of Hell were there for a reason, and we were meant to be on the other side of them. Looking back on our journey now I feel certain that Father had come to some kind of arrangement with the heavenly powers. How else to explain our unperturbed progress through the hollowness of pre-Creation? I even seem to recall that our way was lit, at several points, by thunderbolts that looked suspiciously divine. Yet knowing what I know now, I realize making a deal with God did not necessarily mean He was going to hold to it.

Our tempers began to fray. Father kept insisting that we were approaching the Beginning of Time, but Mother began to nag him to look at the map—a large, mostly empty chart that, since it was made in Hell, only told you where you weren't. Bored, I kept asking "Are we nearly then yet?," which caused Father to scowl all the more. It was beginning to seem as if this was another of Father's doomed schemes, as when the nine-fathom deep water bed he had installed in Hell had evaporated.

As we made yet another wrong turn, I sighed loudly. Flames burst out of Father's head and he swung around terrifyingly.

"Do you want me to leave you here?" he roared. "Do you want me to leave you here in the middle of the void?"

I shouted back that yes, he could leave me here, I didn't care, and I never wanted to go to Earth in the first place. Well, Father paused, surprised at my response. But then, gathering my protesting mother in his arms, he flapped his wings and in a moment the two of them had disappeared.

I was left all alone.

"Mother?" I cried out, but there was no reply. Without Father's flames, the utter blackness of the vast emptiness seemed to grow even dimmer. Yet I wasn't scared. I had always been attracted to absence, to lack, to want, and there was something about this infinite oblivion that was comforting. As the dark crept toward me invisibly, reaching out to envelop me imperceptibly, filling my being impalpably, I felt remarkably . . . perky. With a spring in my step, I began striding across the vacant expanses of the yet-to-be, and felt a slipping of my hellish chains. A new figure inside me was awakening. All thoughts of Father, Mother, and Earth disappeared. In fact, all thoughts disappeared. Nothing filled my mind.

I was so enraptured by these new and strange feelings that I stumbled headlong into a large white angel. He was a vast creature, easily as big as Father, but he was dressed in gleaming white robes. Atop his head buzzed a pristine halo, as bright as a fluorescent bulb, and when his wings flapped together, feathers of the most shimmering softness imaginable fluttered from them. He was wildly swinging a fiery sword around his head while making loud screeching noises. Nevertheless, there was something ungainly about him. His sandals looked much too big, and his sword swept through the air haphazardly. At one point he dropped it so close to his foot that he squealed and leapt back in horror. It was at that point he noticed me. He screamed again.

"Who goes there?" he screeched in the voice of a thousand startled sparrows.

"Just me," said I.

"Oh! Please forgive me, my Lord. If I had known it was just You I would have begun the hosannas." And then the angel cleared his throat and began singing a hymn. It was woefully out of tune. I just stood there, very confused, shuffling my feet. After a while, the angel peered at me out of the corner of his eyes and slowly stopped singing.

"You're not Him, are you?"

"Er, no," I foolishly replied, "I'm me."

"Me?" said the angel. "Or me?"

"Just me," I confessed.

"Oh." There was an awkward silence. I leaned over and picked up the sword, whose flames immediately expired. I handed it back to the angel.

"Hold on!" he said. "Are you from Earth?"

I felt my head begin to spin. I had inherited none of my parents' natural deceptiveness. Now, however, I needed to dissemble.

"Yes?" I said, thinking that as long as the angel didn't know I was from Hell I would be safe.

The angel dropped his sword again, slicing a sliver off his sandal.

"I knew it! I knew it!" yelled the angel. "I'm Urizel," he said as he extended a soft, heavily moisturized palm in my direction. I shook it. "What are you doing here?"

"I . . . got lost," I decided.

"Oh, don't worry," whispered Urizel conspiratorially. "I get lost all the time. I mean, how can you keep up with Creation? One minute there's nothing, then there's something. It's simply impossible to keep track." He stepped back and looked me up and down. "So are you a sheep? Or a human? I can never tell the difference. In either case, I thought you didn't have wings?"

"Oh, we do for now, but it's just to begin with," I said, flapping my scaly wings nonchalantly. "Apparently we're going to evolve out of them soon."

"Evolve?" said Urizel, turning the word round in his mouth. "Is that one of His new projects?"

"Yes," I said. If only Father could have seen me, he would have been proud.

Suddenly however, a loud trumpet sounded, and from out of the ether appeared three more angels. They looked a lot fiercer than the one to whom I was speaking. One was blowing a silver trumpet, one was cloaked in a thundercloud, and one was wearing shining white armor and had dazzling golden hair. They surrounded me in an instant. The trumpeting continued.

"Israfel," boomed the angel clad in white armor. "Israfel! When you've quite finished ravishing our ears, will you please be quiet?"

Israfel, looking pink-cheeked and a little out of breath, lowered his trumpet. The trumpeting continued.

"Israfel!"

"Sorry," said Israfel and hid the trumpet beneath his robes, where it continued to sound.

"What's going on here, Urizel?" said the angel in the white armor as he shook out his golden hair. He had a medal pinned to his chest that read CHAMPION OF THE FAITH, and another below it that read RUNNER-UP, DISCUS.

"Hello, Michael," said Urizel. He swallowed nervously.

"That's Archangel Michael to you, Urizel," roared the angel in the thundercloud, "you miserable excuse for a heavenly being."

"Yes, yes, of course Gabriel, I mean Archangel, Gabriel, sir. Sorry. I was just inquisiting of this being from whence he cameth."

"Really?" proclaimed Michael, looking down his perfectly aquiline nose at me. "We have heard whispers of beings in the wrong places, and you know how He hates beings in wrong places. From whence cameth he?"

"From Earth, sir, Archangel, sir."

The faces of the three archangels darkened.

"We don't like your sort round here," Gabriel spat at me.

"Now, now, Gabriel," said Michael, before fixing an unconvincing smile of piety to his face. "All His creatures are beloved to us."

"Oh really? Is that so?" said Gabriel, turning his thunderous aspect to his colleague. "Well, what about the creeping things?"

"I told you we're not talking about the creeping things anymore," hissed Michael.

"You said you didn't like the creeping things," said Gabriel, unpleasantly warming to his theme. "You said they kept getting in your hair."

"Listen," said Michael, "what I may or may not have said is unimportant right now." He turned his visage toward me and reaffixed the smile that had slipped somewhat in the previous conversation.

"So are you a sheep, or a human?" he said.

"Oh, I'm a human," I responded, furling up my wings as tightly as possible.

*Archangel Michael: **Do Not Touch His Hair**.*

"Prove it!" Gabriel leered.

"Yes," said Michael, glad to be on the offensive again. "Yes, I think you *shall* have to prove it. It's the only way."

"But how can I prove I'm human?" I complained. I began looking frantically for a suitable piece of nothingness to hide in.

"Well," said Michael, "He said that He made you people in the image and likeness of Him, although I personally can't see the similarity. So go on then."

"Go on what exactly?" I inquired.

"Do Him," said Michael, as if the answer should have been obvious. "Do God." So there I was, separated from my parents, in the middle of the void, surrounded by a group of rather surly angels, being asked to do an impression of a deity I had never met. My earlier enthusiasm had all but vanished, and I suddenly became aware of what a sheltered existence I had led, and how little I knew of the ways of Creation. Here was I, a simple being from Hell, who thought he knew everything there was to know about existence, and already I was at a loss as to how to proceed in this sophisticated and perplexing Universe. Truly such moments are humbling to a young supernatural being. But I had no time to bemoan my fate.

I hadn't the slightest idea of what God was like. All I could imagine was that He was the exact opposite of my own father. Clinging to this belief, I spread my arms, as if in a warm embrace, and boomed in a high, unthreatening voice, "I . . . I love you . . . my child?"

"Oh, he's very good, isn't he?" interjected Urizel, clapping his hands together.

"Not bad," said Michael, a little disappointed.

A deafening trumpeting gave Israfel's answer.

"Oh, give it a rest," moaned Michael. He seemed to have lost all interest in me. He opened a small mirror and began combing his blond locks.

Only Gabriel didn't say a word. He just stared at me.

"Haven't we met before?" he growled.

"Not that I know of," I said as I desperately tried to look as un-Satanic as possible.

"No, we have. Now where was it?" continued Gabriel. "Heaven?"

"Oh, I don't think so," I replied desperately. "I've never been there."

"Your face," continued Gabriel, looming closer toward me now. "I've seen your face somewhere before."

"Come on, Gabriel," said Michael, snapping shut his mirror. "It's hosanna time."

Gabriel took a long final look at me.

"Humph," he said.

"Okay then, human, on your way," said Michael. "Don't forget. We know if you've been bad or good, so be good for goodness' sake. Urizel, as you were."

"Yes, sir, Archangel, sir. Thank you, sir," replied Urizel as the three archangels flapped their wings and disappeared into the void. When they were out of sight, I collapsed, exhausted. But what exhilaration swept through my body! I had done it! I had lied my way out of trouble as if I were Father himself. I felt a shudder of nondread, of unpain, of antiagony, of what I now know can only have been the first inklings of Joy. It was some time before I realized that the angel next to me was crying.

"I'm going to be stuck out here for all eternity," he sobbed. "No more hosannas for Urizel. It's just blackness and guard duty and . . ." he gestured at me, "sheep."

"Human, actually," I responded, much more confident now that the archangels had gone. "And I think you're doing a splendid job."

"Really?" said Urizel, lifting up his head.

"Oh yes," said I. "I bet very few angels would have spotted me wandering by."

"I suppose so," said Urizel, wiping the diamond tears from his cheeks.

"In fact," I continued, "I wouldn't be at all surprised if you were made an archangel yourself one day."

"You think so?" said Urizel, brightening considerably. "*Archangel Urizel* does have a nice ring to it . . ."

"Well," I said, slapping his feathered back. "I should be on my way."

"Of course, of course," said Urizel happily. "It was Earth you wanted, wasn't it? Just go past that inscrutable piece of blackness and take a right and you're pretty much there."

I thanked him and was just about to leave when Urizel raised his lily-white hand and cried, "Wait!" If I had had blood in my veins, or veins in my body, they would undoubtedly have frozen. After all my evasions, was I about to be caught?

"Before you go," said Urizel, "what do you think of this?"

He swung his sword over his head in a frighteningly unstable elliptical arc, before whirling it beneath both wings and arms. He leapt in the air, let out a high-pitched yelp, and ended crouched before me, holding his sword quivering above his head, a small bead of angelic sweat dripping down his forehead before evaporating into a cosmic mist. A flurry of feathers fluttered down upon us. Urizel looked up expectantly.

"Well," I said, feeling every inch the spawn of my father. "That's just brilliant."

꒦꒷꒦

Slowly nothingness became somethingness and I found Mother frantically searching for me behind a crab nebula. As I approached I heard Father insisting that I had probably returned to Hell and that they should carry on without me. I cleared my throat and Mother rushed across to hug me, swearing that she'd never leave me again, while Father avoided my looks of reproach and said we should be getting on.

Earth was like nothing I had ever seen before. For a start it was smooth and round. Nothing in Hell had been smooth and round. There was a famous saying in Hell that went: "If it isn't spiky and it isn't painful, it isn't Hell."

As we flew closer we could see that instead of being a scorched wilderness of fire and smoke, the ground was covered in a lush blanket of green, a color I had previously only seen on the festering wounds of the damned. I was amazed to see that the oceans of Earth did not consist of roiling slicks of brimstone, but of a nonacidic liquid that swept calmly into the shore in gentle translucent waves. What's more, the trees were not knotted and bent, nor were their branches impaling the screaming bodies of fallen angels. The air did not choke; the sky did not sag; the lakes and rivers were not filled with sickening, oozing, teethsome creatures, or indeed any of my relations. In short, it was nothing like Hell. At least not to begin with.

Upon arrival, Father stood arms akimbo surveying the new land, while Mother was all aflutter, slithering back and forth across the lush grass, perplexed as to why her scales were not being hideously scraped by jagged stones. After a few minutes of frolic she stopped and turned to Father excitedly.

"So where are the gates?"

"What gates?" said Father.

"Well, what are we meant to do, dear, if there aren't any gates to guard?"

"Whatever you want," said Father, with an expansive gesture.

"Oh," said Mother, and stopped her slithering. I could see she was confused.

"The same goes for you . . . you," said Father pointing at me, his brow knitted as my name once again eluded him. I didn't know what to say.

That first night we sat around Father's flames and held one another close. It was all so new and strange, and I had a feeling that while I had been Satan's son in Hell, here I would have no special dispensations. I was to be a nobody, a nothing, a nonentity. That night I let the Darkness of the Bottomless Pit out of my bag. It shook itself out and looked at me with a vacant stare. I patted it and it curled around my feet. For the first time in my existence I felt totally free. It felt terrible.

The next day I began to explore this new world. I found Father already hard at work tempting. He was lying on his side trying to convince a hovering mosquito that it should drink blood rather than tree sap. The mosquito was putting up a fight, but Father was quite strong willed when he put his mind to it.

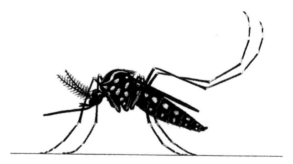

Mosquitoes: Guileless.

"You know what the other creatures of the forest call you," whispered Father.

"No," said the mosquito with its antenna flapping.

"They call you a sap-drinking sissy."

"I don't believe you," said the mosquito indignantly.

"Oh, but it's true," said Father, all open-faced and honest. "I heard them myself."

"Why? Why would they do that?" said the mosquito, tears shining in its tiny little eyes.

"They think you're pathetic. I heard one of the horses say that all that sap has made you stupid."

"But I get on so well with the horses," said the mosquito. "I cool them down with the beating of my little wings."

"Oh no," said Father in mock surprise. "The horses hate you. They say you're worthless. So do the rabbits."

"Not the rabbits!" cried the mosquito.

"Yes," said my father. "Those rabbits are two-faced monsters. They say you were a mistake of Creation."

"Well," said the mosquito, wiping its dripping proboscis with a minute leg and drawing itself up to its full, tiny height. "I may only be a mosquito, but I am a proud mosquito. Henceforth I shall drink nothing but the blood of living creatures!"

"That'll show 'em," said Father, before turning his attention to a *Tyrannosaurus rex* who had been peacefully munching on leaves.

It was little wonder that Father had been so keen on moving us here. No creature on Earth had built up an immunity to lies yet. It was the golden age of gullibility. All of Creation were sitting ducks for his fabrications.

Mother was also finding that her own innate skills were blossoming in this new, innocent environment. I found her in a sumptuous glade with a smile on her face.

"I've just made gray squirrels envy red squirrels," she said.

I had never thought about it before, but Mother must have been extremely frustrated in Hell. As the personification of Sin among the already damned, she had never really had a chance to show what she was capable of doing. But here, for once, she was looking fit to burst with pride, not just maggots and pus.

"It just feels right to me to be here at this point in my existence." She beamed as a red squirrel and a gray squirrel began wrestling on the ground in front of her. "*So* right." The grass on which she was standing began to wilt out of sheer laziness.

Nutsradamus, Famed Red Squirrel Seer and Demagogue, Whose Oblique Utterances Begat Many Apocalyptic Squirrel Cults and Belief in an Eternal Hibernation.

You may at this point be wondering just how it was that Mother, Father, and I knew the names of all these creatures, having just arrived on Earth. Well, each animal, vegetable, and mineral on Earth had a laminated card attached to it. On this laminated card was typed the phrase HI, I'M . . . with the creature's name spelled out beneath it. Of course, such a system had its problems. Many of the smaller creatures could not move because of the weight of the cards attached to them, and a great number of the cards became lost or mixed up. I have it from a good source that "bananas" were originally meant to be called "cycloparaffin," but Father must have switched the cards without anyone noticing. Once the wrong card had been worn for any amount of time, the name stuck. In fact, back then, if you looked at Earth closely, you could see that it had been finished in a rather ramshackle way. The basics were pretty solid—gravity, atmosphere, sound—but there was still plastic wrapping on some of the trees, and crumbs of manna laced the garden floor from where the Creator had eaten while He worked.

As it was, my first days on Earth were somewhat anticlimactic. Mother and Father seemed so happy tempting and corrupting that I didn't want to interrupt them. But the fact was that I hadn't the slightest clue what to do with myself. I tried to convince cows to take over the world, to rampage across the fields slaughtering all in their wake, to start a new religion of udder worship, to build cities devoted to the consumption of grass, their aqueducts running with fresh milk. I even prepared a pictorial presentation of cows traveling into outer space aboard butter-powered space churns, but the cows seemed unconvinced, and soon returned to wondering how many stomachs they had. The current belief was seventeen.

Cows: Unambitious.

I thought maybe I should try something a little smaller and spent an entire morning pouring water on Gold, trying to get him to react. But he just sat there staring at me, completely nonplussed by my suggestions that he should fizz wildly and explode. Things got worse when I tried convincing Helium to get some color in her cheeks, and maybe a little odor. She simply yawned at me languorously and explained that she was a noble gas and, as with all nobility, preferred the inert life.

By my second day on Earth I was disconsolate and had retreated to a cavern and enveloped myself in the comforting embrace of the

Darkness. I was blissfully doing absolutely nothing when I heard the sound of grunting coming from a small copse opposite the cave entrance. I crept over to investigate, curious as to what new horrors my parents might be instigating, but was greeted by the sight of two very strange-looking creatures. At first I thought they were angels, or devils, but they were much smaller and had no wings. Instead they had large protuberant brows that lent them an air of immense stupidity that I would soon find out was thoroughly justified. It was my first sighting of humans.

The two creatures, who were seated before a large mound of laminated name tags, seemed to be engaged in a fierce debate.

"Me Adam," said the larger, hairier one of the two, whom I took to be the male, attaching a card that read ADAM to his chest, before jabbing his finger at the other. "She Adam."

"No," grunted the smaller, less hairy one. She attached a card to herself that read BRACHIOSAUR. "Me Eve," she said, before pointing her finger at the other. "You Eve."

"No!" retorted the large one. "Me Adam. You Adam."

"No!" rejoined the smaller one, pointing at herself. "You Eve. Me Eve." This went on for some time.

Eventually I plucked up the courage to introduce myself.

"Hello. I'm Death. Wonderful day, isn't it?"

They looked at me uncomprehendingly, then at their pile of laminated cards, and then back at me.

"You Adam?" said the male one.

"No. You Eve," said the female one.

They looked at each other and suddenly began pulling out each other's hair. They fought for a bit, and before I knew it they had begun rutting on the floor in front of me. I stood there amazed. I learned later that humans had been created out of dust. It showed. It was hardly any surprise to me that they would go on to eat the Forbidden Fruit. They ate everything—apples, leaves, bark, grass, each other's feces. They were repulsive creatures.

Just as I was musing on what I could possibly get them to do that

Adam and Eve: Dumb As a Box of Rocks
(If the Rocks Were Really, Really Dumb).

they weren't already doing, an incredibly bright orb of light filled the sky above me. I had never seen such an intense brightness before, not even when Reginald had been thrown into the Lake of Phosphorous in Hell. It seemed to cut straight through me and sent the Darkness scampering back into the cave. Of course I knew instantly that this was God, because the light had on a large laminated badge that read HI, I'M . . . GOD. I hid behind a shrub.

"Adam," boomed a voice as loud as any I had ever heard.

"Me Adam?" responded the female.

"No, you're Eve, dear," boomed God.

"Me Eve," interjected the male.

"No. No. You're Adam!" boomed God in frustration. "Anyway, how are things going? Do you like the place?"

"Er . . . ," said Adam and Eve.

"Well, look, I don't have much time," boomed God, "but I don't want you to eat from the Tree of Knowledge, all right?"

"Er . . ."

"That's the big green one over there."

"Er . . ."

"The one with the big laminated card on it reading TREE OF KNOWLEDGE."

"Er . . ."

"I just planted it the other day," God boomed. "It's over there and I think it really pulls the garden together." The light pointed to its right, or rather it seemed to point to its right because orbs of light can't really point. Nevertheless, it made it perfectly clear that despite being completely round, it was favoring one direction over another. Such are the privileges of divinity.

"Er . . ."

"Because you've already eaten my Bush of Anticipation."

"Er . . ."

"And I really wanted to see how that would turn out."

"Er . . ."

"So don't touch it!" God paused. He cleared His throat. "For in the day that thou eatest thereof thou shalt surely die," He boomed. "Or something."

"You Adam?" ventured Adam, shading his eyes with his hand.

"I separated the light from the darkness for this?" boomed God, and the orb of light and its laminated badge receded into the sky. Adam and Eve blinked their eyes and shook their heads as if they had awoken from a bad dream. I stepped out from behind my shrub.

"Who Die?" said Adam.

"You Die," said Eve to Adam.

"No, me Eve," said Adam.

"No, me Eve," said Eve.

They both looked at me.

"You Die?" they grunted in unison.

"No," I said. "Death. I'm Death." But the incident had piqued my interest. I felt something stirring deep inside of me. What was this "die" God spoke of? There seemed only one way to find out.

First Blood

The Tree of Knowledge lay in the Glade of Discernment, which was situated in the Woods of Awareness, deep within the Forest of Understanding at the heart of the Garden of Eden. In the glade stood thousands of trees whose fruit all contained some intrinsic facet of experience as well as a healthy dose of vitamin C. There was the Tree of Laughter, its crop shaking mirthfully on the branch; the Tree of Terror, whose shriveled grapes retreated shivering from one's grasp; and the Tree of Amateur Dramatics, whose fruit sometimes completely forgot what they were meant to taste like and started crying.

When I got to know the trees better, I found out that God had originally planned on populating the Earth solely with trees, but His ardor for arbor had cooled somewhat when He had discovered the joys of creeping things.

Creeping Things: Creepy.

As it was, the history of trees would end up closely paralleling that of humans, with the trees even having their own wooden Messiah; a humble olive tree, whose sap, it was alleged, could heal oak wilt, Dutch elm disease, and spike phytoplasma. But the tree Messiah was betrayed by flora envious of its powers, and it suffered horrible tortures; being whittled, sawed, and carved into the shape of a cross, where, in a remarkable twist of fate, it found itself nailed to the back of the human Messiah. Many orthodox deciduous trees still blamed this terrible episode on the Yews.

A Yew to a Kill.

I eventually found a tree with a laminated tag reading TREE OF KNOWLEDGE and grasped one of its rosy fruits in my hand. I could hardly remember seeing anything quite so round, except once when Uncle Lachador had knocked the head off an imp, sandpapered its face off, and used it as a bowling ball at Hell's popular Rack and Bawl. I bit into the fruit and was greeted by a familiar flavor I could not quite place. Immediately my mind was filled with images of Hell, of the Bottomless Pit, and of my favorite dark chasms of yore. I was once again guarding the Gates of Hell with Mother, and in the distance I could see Reginald being chased barefoot across fields of broken glass, but the more I chewed, the more the images faded away and a bitterness entered the fruit's taste. I swallowed uncomfortably and was disheartened to find myself back on Earth.

"Did you like it?" said the tree. "Wouldn't you like to have another bite?" By now the bitter taste had disappeared and the sweet aroma of the fruit was once again tantalizing me, but I felt none the wiser.

"Are you really the Tree of Knowledge?" I asked.

"Oh no," said the tree.

I looked at the laminated tag. It distinctly read TREE OF KNOWLEDGE. I pointed this out to the tree.

"Ah, yes. Happy were the days when I had the correct laminated card pinned to my trunk. Would that I could go back to those days! Ah, but that was far away and long ago."

"What are you?" I asked.

"I am the Tree of Nostalgia," it replied, "although I'm not what I once was."

"But you've only just been created," I exclaimed. "What have you to be nostalgic about?"

"Once upon a time," droned the Tree of Nostalgia, "all this was nothing. Nothing as far as the eye could see, long before Creation and all this modern nonsense. I tell you they don't do nothing like they used to do. Now it's all 'this,' and 'that.' I remember the morning sun coming up earlier today. So bright and hard it was! Now it's all soft and watery. And don't get me started on the temperature. How I long for the early morning cool, instead of this warmish noon."

The tree was clearly mad.

"Oh, what a thrill I got when you bit into my apple. How important you made me feel. Now everything's so uncertain, but back then you could be sure of things."

"But that was about twenty-five seconds ago," I exclaimed.

"Oh, you were so precise and articulate when you said that last sentence," continued the tree. "Not like now where you're all wordless. Standards have slipped, I tell you. Things were much better before I started speaking this sentence . . ."

The tree went suddenly silent.

"What is it?" I asked.

"I just ran out of things to remember." It began to wave its branches around frantically. "Help, I'm stuck in the present. It's horrible! Everything's new and contemporary! Get away, horrible bright colorful now! Come back sepia-tinted, half-forgotten then! Help! It's everywhere!"

The tree was a pitiful sight, so I stepped forward and kicked it hard in the trunk. There was a yelp, followed by a pause. And then, "Oh, that really hurt! You really hurt me! But it was a good pain. An honest pain. I wouldn't be the tree I am today without having been kicked around a little, let me tell you . . ."

As the Tree of Nostalgia yammered on I noticed that the tree next to it sported a laminated tag reading TREE OF NOSTALGIA. Reckoning that they must have simply swapped tags, I picked one of this tree's fruit and bit into it. It had a sugary, syrupy flavor, and my mind was immediately filled with an image of a small kitten hanging from a clothesline. As the kitten swayed in the wind, it turned to me with its large eyes and squeaked, "Hang in there!" I spat out my mouthful in disgust.

"What are you?" I cried, my hopes beginning to diminish.

"I'm the Tree of Sentimentality," said the tree. "Didn't you like my ooky-wooky fruit?"

Behind me I could hear the Tree of Nostalgia droning on, ". . . such a nice conversation with that person, wasn't it? You don't get conversations like that anymore. . . ."

I heard something clear its throat behind me. The sound came from a small lean tree, whose knots and whorls made it look as if it were wearing a pair of spectacles. It wore a laminated tag declaring it the TREE OF DISMEMBERMENT.

"The Tree of Knowledge is over there," it gestured with a branch, "in the Dell of Enlightenment."

"What's this place?"

"This is the Copse of Schmaltz," it responded.

"And what are you?" I asked. "You don't look like the Tree of Dismemberment."

"No, I'm the Tree of Fortuitousness."

"No, he's not," shouted a tree from across the copse.

"In that case, who is he?" I asked.

"He's the Tree of Deception," yelled the other tree. "Don't listen to a word he says."

"Actually," said the bespectacled tree, "I *am* the Tree of Fortuitousness. That tree over there is the Tree of Spiteful Interjections."

"Oh, you *would* say that, wouldn't you! He's so cunning. . . ."

The two trees waggled their branches at each other, causing a soft breeze to waft through the copse. I would later learn that such arguments were responsible for much of the Earth's wind, hurricanes being formed after particularly violent clashes of arboreal opinion.

Fallen Trees After Debating the Sonic Consequences of Uprooted Vegetation in Uninhabited Woodland Areas.

I heard a heavy panting noise and saw Father rushing toward me, his arms full of laminated name tags.

"You haven't seen me, right?" he said, before hurrying off again.

"You see?" exclaimed the so-called Tree of Fortuitousness. "That was fortuitous, wasn't it?"

"Pure coincidence!" shouted the other. The breeze was freshening, and I was surrounded by foliage of questionable sanity. I began to despair of ever finding the Tree of Knowledge. I was about to follow after Father to ask him if he knew where it was when a painfully bright light appeared overhead, rooting me to the spot. Its laminated name tag now read HI, I'M . . . GOD.

"Where's your name tag?" boomed God. "If I've told you once, I've told you a hundred times; if you want to be part of Creation you have to wear a name tag."

"I don't have one," I replied.

"Why ever not?" boomed God.

"I don't know," I said. I didn't.

"What's your name?" boomed the light, taking out a pen and pencil.

"Death," I said meekly.

"Death? Death? Death? Aren't you Satan's son?"

"Yes."

"How is he?" boomed God.

"Fine." I didn't know what else to say. The conversation was getting a bit strange.

"Such a naughty, naughty thing," boomed God playfully.

There was another awkward pause.

"Well," boomed God, "what are you doing here?"

"I've been trying to work that out myself," I said. "I feel that I have important things to do, and important things to say, and I want to share them with all Creation, I just don't know what they are exactly. But I can feel something. My true calling is buried deep inside me, I know it is! I just don't know how to get at it. Can you tell me? Can You help me understand my true role in existence? Can You tell me what I'm doing here?"

"No," boomed God. "I mean, what are you doing *here*? The Forest of Understanding is strictly off-limits, you know?"

"Oh," I said. My enthusiasm had been lanced. "I was trying to find the Tree of Knowledge."

"You stay away from that tree," boomed God. "Why does everyone want a piece of that tree?"

"But God . . ."

"Call Me Lord."

"But Lord . . ."

"Actually maybe God's better. Or maybe Sir. What do you think about Sir? Too formal?"

"Well, they're all very good, Sir. Lord. God. But what *am* I meant to be doing? What's my role in Creation?"

"Oh, you'll find out sooner or later. Don't worry."

God hung in the air, shimmering. If a bright orb of blinding light could be said to be examining its fingernails, that is what it was doing. I decided I might as well ask Him my question directly.

"Lord God Sir? What is 'die'?"

"Well," boomed God, suddenly full of enthusiasm, "die is the plural of dice, and dice are small cubes with marks on them, which you roll. I like to think they impart a certain arbitrary mood to Creation because I didn't want it to feel that it was too, you know, staged. I've been trying to teach the Universe how to play but he is a stubborn fellow and keeps on throwing them down black holes. I think he prefers cards. Perhaps we can play together when you come and visit."

"I'm coming to visit?" I asked.

"Oh yes," boomed God. "Ta-ta." And the bright light vanished into the trees. I looked down at my chest and saw a laminated card pinned to it. It read HI, I'M . . . DEATH.

I felt inordinately depressed, and I had a terrible headache, which I would soon learn were the side effects of being talked to by God. I trudged out of the forest to loud jeers from the Tree of Provocation.

≒⊹≓

I was just reaching the outer edge of the forest when a white four-legged creature with a bonelike growth on its forehead trotted into view. It was not like the horse or the bull or the wolf or the deer that I had seen wandering Earth before. It seemed special somehow. It looked at me with large round eyes, thick with eyelashes, and shook its blond mane playfully. It had a laminated tag attached to its horn reading UNICORN. Each letter of the word "unicorn" was written in a different color of the rainbow. Seeing this creature suddenly and inexplicably lifted my spirits. Its sheer loveliness seemed to restore my faith that everything in Creation had a purpose. I went to pat it on the head, but just as my hand reached out to smooth its tousled blond forelock, the Unicorn snapped at my hand with surprising venom.

I was so shocked that I stumbled backward, tripped, and crashed into a tree. Steadying myself on the tree's thick trunk, I noticed that it was shuddering all the way up its huge height. Suddenly a threatening, groaning sound emanated from deep within it, transfixing both the Unicorn and me. A laminated tag fluttered to the ground. I picked it up. It read TREE OF MISHAP. I looked at the Unicorn. It was ambling toward me. It seemed to be smiling in a rather sinister fashion, its surprisingly sharp white teeth glistening in its mouth. I felt inexplicably nervous. I heard a snap from far above me in the tree and a hard fruit, the size of a boulder, plummeted down onto the Unicorn's head. There was a loud crack.

Well, I couldn't help but laugh. The moment reminded me of Uncle Hiniel's Tuesday night skull-crushing sessions in Hell. However, unlike the tortured imps, the Unicorn did not get up and stagger around comically with a completely flat head. Instead, after a few less than droll convulsions, it lay completely still, its legs splayed out beneath it, its tongue lolling out of its mouth, and a dark, viscous liquid oozing from one of its ears. I shouted to it, but got no response.

It was at that precise moment, as my words faded into the air, that I suddenly felt irresistibly drawn toward the Unicorn, like an iron

Unicorns: Unifriendly.

filing is drawn toward a magnet. It was a compulsion like I had never felt before, but it felt natural. Before I even knew what I was doing, I found myself leaning over the Unicorn's body. My hand was reach-ing toward its chest, being drawn closer and closer, when I heard an irritated voice say, "Well, that's just great, isn't it?"

The spell was broken. I looked around me to see whether the Tree of Sarcasm was anywhere nearby, but the voice seemed to be coming from the Unicorn itself.

"Pardon?" I ventured.

"I said that's just fucking marvelous," repeated the voice, louder now. It was definitely coming from the Unicorn, but its mouth wasn't moving.

"Hello?" I proffered.

"Oh! A 'hello'! That's what I get, is it, after crushing my skull in with a bloody great fruit."

"I'm sorry," I said. The Unicorn was still not moving, but the voice was getting louder and louder.

"Oh, you're sorry, are you? You're sorry! Well, doesn't that make everything better! I'm sorry too. Sorry I ever laid eyes on you!"

The dark liquid continued to spill out of the Unicorn's ear. It was so dark and rich, it transfixed me.

"What happened?" I asked. I had never seen anything like it before.

"You've only gone and killed me."

The word "kill" sent a flush of excitement coursing through my body.

"I've what?"

"You've killed me, you prick! I've died, I'm dead, passed away, terminated. I am an ex-Unicorn and you're the reason why, you nonce!"

There it was again. The word "die." So this is what God had been talking about with Adam and Eve. I felt warm and fuzzy inside.

"Oh," I said, spinning in the enormity of my discovery. "Is there anything I can do to help?"

"Oh no, thank you very much. You've done quite enough already."

"Has this ever happened to you before?" I ventured.

"No, you fucking idiot," replied the Unicorn. "It's never happened to anyone before."

And he was right. At this early stage of Creation nothing had died—not a fallen angel, not a blade of grass—everything was bright and shiny and new.

"Well," I said, vainly trying to placate the creature, "at least you're the first." The Unicorn mulled this over.

"Yes, I suppose that's some consolation. I'll probably get in the record books, won't I? I mean, God did say this was all going to end someday. I just didn't think it would be the next fucking day."

"Look, I'm sorry," I said. But secretly I was thrilled.

"Listen," said the Unicorn, "I'm getting a bit uncomfortable here, why don't you help me out of this body?"

"How do I do that?" I asked.

"How the fuck should I know?" cried the Unicorn.

I took a deep breath, cleared my mind, and the compulsion took over once again. My hand reached over to the Unicorn's body and suddenly slipped straight into it without leaving a mark. I heard a slight popping noise. Instantly I felt as though I had done something right, something truly right, for the first time in my existence.

"About time!" said the Unicorn, as a thin gleaming luster drifted up from the body. I realized instinctively that it was the creature's soul. The Darkness, which had been nipping at my heels excitedly, leapt forward, spreading in size, enveloping both me and the Unicorn's soul within itself. The earth began to slip away, and I was left at the center of an utter blackness. Everything receded, became nothing, and I was now gripped by an ecstasy that threatened to overpower me and wipe me from existence. But something held me back, a curiosity about what else I might learn on Earth, and I steadied myself and fought my way out of the Darkness. From inside it I heard the sound of a spectral hoof tapping impatiently.

"Well, I would say it's been a pleasure," said the Unicorn's soul as it slowly dissolved from view, "but it hasn't."

"Where are you going?" I gasped. I was giddy with revelation.

"I see a light," said the Unicorn, its voice growing softer and softer, "a bright light . . . it's spelling out a word . . . two words . . . the words say . . ."

"Yes," I said encouragingly.

". . . the words say . . ."

"What do the words say?"

". . . the words say . . . Fuck . . . You."

There was a brief whinny of mocking laughter, and then nothing. But I was hardly paying attention. I felt as though a bottle of black ink had been spilled inside me, coating me in a wondrous gloom that shaded my whole being. I had arrived at a moment of illumination, or rather its opposite; a gloaming of wisdom.

The Darkness sat in front of me looking rather pleased with itself. A strange tingling pervaded my essence, the thrilling chill of my first transmuted soul. The Unicorn's body lay cold and still on the ground. The edge of the forest surrounded me. Everything seemed to be the same, but I had changed. I could see now that I was not a misfit, that I truly belonged, that I was one with all living things. I could see all of existence balancing precariously on a tightrope above me. My role, I realized, was to catch it. At last I had found my calling.

I'd be the Death of you all.

Dead Man
Talking

From that moment on, I was hooked. If this was dying, I wanted more. For the first time in my existence, I knew what I was born to do: not torment, or tempt, or even rend asunder, but to usher, to escort, to shepherd others into the Other.

Admittedly it took some practice before I became proficient in my trade, but fortunately the fatalities in Eden from accidents alone were tremendous. Trial and error was the defining principle in those early days—after all, it's hard to live by your instincts when you're the first of your kind ever to exist. Millions of totally pointless and often contradictory creatures had been created who were quite unsuited to survival. There were root vegetables with claustrophobia, rocks that cried after avalanches, fish that were allergic to water, and vain insects who were so revolted by the way they looked they couldn't bring themselves to reproduce.

Self-loathing and stupidity swept through Creation like a plague. Phoenixes forgot to flap their wings, griffons overlooked eating, leviathans beached themselves while sunbathing, and small furry creatures with soft paws picked fights with big scaly creatures with sharp claws. Such literally mindless bloodshed gave me plenty of schooling in my nerve-racking new profession. There was a certain

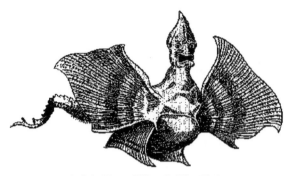

It Didn't Know What It Was Either.

technique for ejaculating souls out of bodies that was not as easy as it seemed, especially when combined with the performance anxiety I felt so acutely during my early days. When dealing with souls, I tried to be as friendly as possible—after all, this was a new experience for us both. But many of the souls were suspicious and peered out at me through the mouths of their dead bodies.

"What?" they'd say. "Afterlife? What's wrong with this life? No, no, you go on without me." I'd then have to point out that they had drowned in quicksand, or been torn apart by bears, or otherwise convince them of the hopelessness of their situation before they would agree to come out.

Most souls, however, were not so much obstreperous as impatient. If I took too long, or if there had been a particularly localized slaughter, say in a meteorite shower, or forest fire, the souls would start to back up, and I'd be harangued by dozens of plaintive voices all telling me to hurry up. Some of the older creatures, such as the mayflies, who had lived full and rich lives, were gentler. "You just take your time, sonny, and don't listen to them others," they'd say, as I sweated to find their tiny souls.

Toughest of all in my early days were the dinosaurs, who were rife with design faults. No sooner had you scooped the head and neck of their massive souls out of their body and finally worked your way down to the tail, then you'd find the head and neck had popped back into the body. What's more, as their life flashed before their eyes they would often become convinced that they were alive again. Their souls would get up and lumber off, and I'd have to ask the other dead in the vicinity if they'd seen which way they went. I rarely got a straight answer.

"I'd like to help you, son, I really would," said one field mouse, who had been killed when a stegosaur collapsed on top of him, "but I don't think it would be fair."

"He did kill you, you know," I reasoned. "He squashed you flat."

"I know, I know," said the field mouse, "but one must have solidarity with the living on these occasions."

This puzzled me a little. I didn't like to think that it was "me" against "them." In fact, in my early days, I tried to make dying as pleasant as possible for the recently deceased, before whisking them off into the Darkness as quickly as I could. "Whisk them away to what?" you may ask. I never really thought too much about where they were headed. It was beyond the scope of my job. Sure, there was talk of Salvation and Damnation, but I was hardly going to pay much attention to that now, was I? It was only later when I was shown the Grand Scheme of Things that I found out that everyone was initially supposed to have gone to Heaven, but the place got so overcrowded that half the afterlife was outsourced to Hell. There were complaints at first, but one afterlife is very much like another, give or take an infinite amount of torture.

When it came to my relationship with the dead, dogs were the exception to the rule. They always seemed to like me, and I liked them. They never argued or complained, but their souls did have a tendency to bound out of their bodies, tongue lolling, tail wagging, and run in and out of the Darkness barking wildly. I'd try to catch them, but they'd think it was a game and dash away from me every time I came close. This happened so often that during my early days on Earth I was constantly surrounded by the souls of ten or twelve dogs who I just could not subsume into the void. They'd all peer at me while I worked, their heads cocked to one side, one ear bent backward, and bark madly when I had freed the soul.

"Not very dignified, this," said the diminishing soul of a disgruntled deer, as the dog souls ran around him yapping wildly and snapping at his incorporeal heels. "I mean it's hardly the blinding light, is it?" I had an idea. I waited until the deer's soul had disappeared, and checking both ways to make sure no one was watching, I tore off one of the legs of the deer's body and, waving it at the pack of dog souls, threw it into the heart of the Darkness. The dogs bounded after it, disappearing one after the other, the sound of their barks growing distant and disappearing. There was only the faint sound of the deer's soul shouting "Hey, that's my leg!" before silence once again descended on the void.

Soon my name was on all Creation's lips, maws, and other vocalizing orifices. I became a blur, zipping from body to body like black lightning. I could deal with thousands, millions, of souls in a day and not feel overworked. But I distinctly remember wondering when I would meet my first human soul.

Before I carry on, I think I should attempt to clear up a major misconception about my role. I don't actually kill anyone. I don't rip out the heart, or squeeze out the brains, or suck out the blood. I don't pull the trigger, or push the button, or put sharp things where they're not meant to be. I'm not responsible for you and your loved ones dying. No, you living do a great job of dying without my help. I just turn up once the convulsions have calmed down and the pulse has stopped, and I move the souls along. Yes, some humans are unhappy when they die, and at such moments most are unwilling to admit that they might have been responsible for their own passing in some way. Hence I get all the blame. But it's not as if I deserve it.

Admittedly when I hear the same plea for clemency for the millionth time, I may well stifle a yawn, but I do a good job, a necessary job. Call me callous if you like, but it's difficult to make friends when you're the point of contact between time and eternity, between the now and the hereafter. Everything, except for me, is just passing through. Yes, of course, there may have been times when I turned up a teensy bit too early to collect a soul and perhaps spooked some of you in your last moments on Earth, but in those situations the worst I can be accused of is impatience. Tapping my hourglass and whistling may not be particularly sensitive, but I've got a job to do.

Suffice it to say that during these early days I didn't hate Life at all. I had no axe to grind, no sour grapes to squeeze. I was a natural force of Creation. If I seemed unwilling to care about your human feelings of despair and pain, it was simply because I could not feel them. At least not to begin with.

With all the new experiences I was having, I barely noticed the Fall of Man. Adam and Eve had eventually found what they thought was the Tree of Knowledge. Alas, thanks to Father's machinations, it turned out to be the Tree of Prudery. They immediately became very resentful about being unclothed, as well as generally disapproving of the nakedness of all Creation. They had begun to clothe all the creatures—great and small—in waistcoats, pantaloons, and gaiters made out of twigs and leaves. But when the animals had begun to eat their garments, Adam and Eve had stopped, offended by what they saw as the animals' ungratefulness. A nibble on the Tree of Disenchantment, followed by a long luncheon beneath the Tree of Superciliousness, soon saw Adam and Eve find the whole idea of being created by someone else distinctly *infra dig.* So they absconded from the Garden of Eden in clothes stitched together from laminated tags. God was quite upset. He came to me in a blinding light one night.

"Er . . . Death," He boomed.

"Yes?" I said.

"You haven't seen those humans anywhere, have you?"

"No. No, I haven't."

"Oh," boomed the voice unhappily. "Do you think something could have eaten them?"

"Not that I know of," I said. "There's been some ingestion over in the Copse of Erudition, but I think that's largely due to the Tree of Hunger being placed between the Tree of Sharp Teeth and the Tree of Putting Two and Two Together."

"Ho hum," boomed God. "Well, where on Earth could they be?"

God always struck me as a strangely impotent omnipotent. You could often catch Him humming uncertainly to Himself as He floated through the Garden, sometimes stumbling on the odd root, apologizing frequently, desperately trying to make friends with the animals, who out of a sense of obligation nodded their heads, but whose impatience with Him was clear. I felt quite sorry for Him at times. Creation was all too busy being alive, chasing and being chased, and, of course, rutting like wild animals. It simply didn't have time to deal with some lonely supreme being.

As it was, I soon came across Adam and Eve. The fairies that had lived at the bottom of the Garden of Eden had been torn apart by a horde of hungry dachshunds, and I was spiriting their fey souls to the nether, when I heard voices coming from a well-appointed cave overlooking a charming swamp. A sign at its entrance read DUN-FALLIN. I peeked inside and saw Adam and Eve, but the clueless Neanderthals of my first acquaintance were long gone.

"Fairies are all very well," I heard Adam say as he stoked the fire that roared in the cave, "but not in my backyard."

"Yes, dear," said Eve, bending down to pat the head of one of the pack of dachshunds that swarmed around her. "Who's a good boy?" she said to the dog. "We shall have to start feeding you again."

"No need," interrupted Adam. "Fairy meat's good enough for them."

Adam and Eve had gained language, and with it snobbery and entitlement (I noticed the laminated tag from the Tree of Conceit woven into their clothes). When I introduced myself, they looked me up and down with cold, judgmental eyes, and when I tried to explain how despondent God was, they said that that was no concern of theirs. Well, I didn't know what to say. I stayed for a while,

*Dachshunds: The Reason There Are
No Fairies in the World.*

pleading my case, but they virtually ignored me, and then started making fun of the Darkness, calling it "vacuous" and "dim." I left before its feelings could be hurt.

When God eventually caught up with them, it was extremely awkward. I was in the neighborhood collecting the last of the gnomes who also had been savaged by Adam and Eve's dog pack. God said that He felt injured by their behavior. Adam and Eve said they regretted God's unhappiness in the most formal of tones. God said He loved them, but Adam and Eve declared that they thought His love for them was rather vulgar, and certainly not fitting for one who aspired to the divine. In fact, they said, they were beginning to wonder if paying homage to Him was really the best use of their time. Could He, they asked, show them any proof of His divinity that would make Him worthy of their worship? So it was that God decreed a parade of Creation should be put on for the pair. It did not go well.

I remember Adam rolling his eyes at the elephant, calling it "shallow" and "insubstantial," and Eve laughing unkindly at the lions and tigers, declaring, in a hushed tone just loud enough for God to hear, that they were "deliciously kitsch." When He showed them the vast pools of magma surging red-hot beneath the earth's crust, Adam affected a yawn, and when He showed them the bluest of blue skies, Eve simply checked her sundial and said they should be getting on. Finally, when God laid bare for them the vast expanse of the Universe, the dark firmament lit with gleaming and wandering stars, the wondrous vastness of Creation, the couple pretended to be distracted by a rock. "That's mine too," boomed God, a little too eagerly, allowing Eve to say that they were sure of it, considering how hideous it was.

Returned to their cave, Adam and Eve went inside without a second look at their Creator. He waved to them forlornly from the entrance.

"Pray to Me!" He boomed. "I'm always around!" But His gravitas was undercut by what sounded like a choked sob.

Slowly Eden began to empty out of creatures, most of whom had eaten from the Tree of Restlessness, or the Tree of Leaving Home Without a Backward Glance. The grass picked itself up and germinated to pastures new, and the trees that remained withered and died. Urizel, the angel I had met while traversing the void, was sent down to act as a sort of night watchman, guarding the remains of Eden, although I wasn't quite sure what there was left to guard. He greeted me fondly, still wielding his fiery, ever-turning sword, and I congratulated him on his reassignment.

"Just like you said, I'll be an archangel one day! A definite promotion! Look at all this matter! Ah, to feel something under your feet again instead of the abysmal void." I don't think he realized quite how far from Heaven he was.

I didn't see God for months, but I soon saw Adam and Eve again. They and their dachshunds were being attacked by a pack of sabertoothed tigers still smarting from their comments about the tastelessness of their stripes. As I came upon them they were complaining bitterly about being eaten.

"It's just too, too much," said Adam as a tiger tore off part of his shoulder.

"I agree," said Eve, her back being clawed to ribbons. "Tooth and claw is so, well, so prehistoric."

"Simply stone age, dear," said Adam, his head now fully inside one of the tigers' jaws. And so the first humans on Earth died (their dachshunds survived, however, and could be seen hunting woolly mammoths alongside the saber-toothed tigers for years to come).

I found human souls required special attention. Their toes and fingers make them particularly tricky to pop cleanly out of their bodies. In fact, many of my early human souls went into the void missing a digit or two. Being my first, Adam and Eve caused me all sorts of trouble.

"Oh, *do* come on," they cried as their souls slipped and snapped out of my grasp. "I mean, if this is dying, what hope for the hereafter?" After much grunting and pulling, I finally worked them free and hustled them into the Darkness. If the truth be told, I was glad to see the back of them.

At that moment I heard a booming sneeze come from behind a boulder, and a bright radiance suddenly burst forth. God had obviously been watching the whole time.

"Well done, Death," He boomed. "Good work. Those two had definitely overstayed their welcome. And well done, you," He boomed to the saber-toothed tigers, who pointedly ignored Him as they settled down to feast on Adam and Eve's innards. "I shall honor your work," He boomed. He seemed desperate to ingratiate Himself with the animals, who paid Him no attention whatsoever. "I shall make you all . . . extinct!"

"Are you certain?" said I.

"Why yes! All good deeds should be praised, so sayest I."

"But extinct?" I queried.

"Yes." boomed God.

"Well, I don't think it means what you think it means."

At that moment a high-pitched cry came from Adam and Eve's cave. God looked at me and I at Him, and we both peered inside. There, on the ground, were two small creatures, bawling and screaming.

"Ah," boomed God. "So they were not so proper after all."

Murder in
Paradise

⊰✦⊱

The years passed, and I kept an eye on the two boys. They had been named Cain and Abel because they had been found lying close to two laminated tags that read SUGAR CANE and ABALONE. Thankfully, they showed none of the haughtiness of their parents; indeed, they seemed quite the opposite. They prayed to God constantly and were always going on about how much He liked them. In fact, they could often be found lording it over the other animals, calling them "stupid" and "unloved" and boasting that the two of them were God's favorites. It didn't make them terribly popular.

But God did like them. He was forever fooling around with them, playing hide-and-seek, laughing and singing with them. It was quite a sight to see the three of them—the two muscled young men and the all-powerful oscillating light—walking arm in arm across the earth together. Sometimes the three of them would disappear for hours and come back rosy cheeked and panting, as if from a long journey.

I thought nothing of this. I was happy for God, so I simply continued with my work. I collected the souls of dead crickets and dead cauliflowers, dead rocks and dead sticks, dead tigers and dead elephants, dead everything. Every day a new creature would die, and I would make its acquaintance. To tell the truth, I liked meeting things and finding out how their lives had been, listening to what regrets they had and what they hoped for in the afterlife. In fact, all seemed well with the world, until I felt myself being drawn irresistibly toward the brothers' fields.

Cain and Abel: Games of "Uncle" Dragged on Forever
Since Neither Knew What the Word Meant.

Lying there on the ground, with blood streaming from his head, was Abel. A lamb was charring on the altar, a sacrifice to Him no doubt. Knowing how much the Creator thought of the boys, I began to feel slightly uneasy.

"Speak to me, Abel," I said, crouching down and resting his head on my lap. "What happened?"

Abel coughed up a mouthful of blood and weakly whispered, "It was . . ."

And then he died.

I leaned over him, popped out his soul, and continued to listen.

". . . too dark to tell. I was busy tying up one of my stupid animals for sacrifice, and then nothing. Maybe I tripped." He gestured toward his lifeless body. "Aw, look at me, my hair's all mussed up."

I had already seen enough dying to know when foul play had occurred.

"This was no accident, Abel," I said. "Someone killed you."

"Killed me? But who? Why?"

Whenever anything died there were always questions. Questions I couldn't always answer.

"Look at your skull," I said to Abel, motioning him toward his former body. "That's no accidental wound. Somebody hit you over the head with a rock, or some kind of club."

"A club?" Abel gaped. "What's that?"

The poor sap never even knew what hit him. I looked around and saw a thick branch that had been carved into a smaller, more manageable shape. Blood stained its tip.

"That's a club, Abel. I'll start making some inquiries. In the meantime you'd better get going."

The Darkness began to envelop him.

"Wait!" he cried. "You mean I don't get to see who killed me? That's a bit unfair."

Abel had a point. It was against the rules, sure, but this was a special case. Four humans had existed on Earth, and the murder rate was already 25 percent. I allowed him to tag along with me.

Who would want to kill Abel? I asked myself. Who but everything in Creation. They all had a reason to dislike him. My first suspects were, of course, his animals. Abel had been a shepherd, and the bleating in the pasture said he was a harsh one. I had recognized the lamb being sacrificed—I had transmitted him into the great beyond only that afternoon, just another in the boy's long line of sacrifices. He was called Cyril. He had been popular.

My first stop was the cliff face above Abel's farm. It was where the goats liked to sit.

"Any of you kids know what happened to Abel?" I asked.

"Get lost," said a Ram, "We don't want to hear about Abel. He's always telling us where to go and what to eat. We're sick of him."

"Sick enough to kill him?" I asked.

That got their attention.

"What do you mean? He's dead?" bleated the Ram. I couldn't tell whether he was feigning surprise or not.

"Don't play patsy with me," I snapped. "The big man's going to be disappointed, and I'm not going to be the one taking the heat."

The goats looked at one another. I had them rattled.

"Okay, okay," said the Ram. "It wasn't us, but we were told to look the other way, if you know what I mean."

"Maybe I don't," I said. I didn't.

"Look, we were pretty sick and tired of being part of Abel's herd. Some of us had started thinking of branching out, of becoming an agrarian collective. And after all the sacrifices recently, who could blame us?"

"But what did you mean by looking the other way?"

"Well, Gary here—step forward, Gary—Gary says that he wakes up in the night to the sound of somebody telling him to stay away from the altar before sunset. Now, none of us particularly liked hanging round the altar for obvious reasons, so we do as we're told. We never thought he'd actually be killed, just roughed up a little."

"Who spoke to you, Gary?" I asked. "Was it the dinosaurs? Was it the lettuce? Who was it, Gary?"

"Me and the lettuce don't get on," said Gary, a young goat. He looked smart, but not too smart. "And it didn't sound like a dinosaur. There was no mention of red meat, or tenderness. Dinosaurs are very picky about what they eat."

Tyrannosaurus Anorexic.

That was true. Dinosaurs were such picky eaters sometimes they'd starve to death rather than eat anything that wasn't done just so.

"But what did he look like?"

"I couldn't see," said Gary, blushing a little. "The thing grabbed my forelock and pulled it over my eyes."

"What did the voice sound like?"

"Well, the funny thing is, I thought it was Abel, Death, I swear."

"Stupid goats," said Abel's soul, before I could stop him. I knocked him halfway into the Darkness.

"What was that?" said Gary, tilting his head at me. He had stopped chewing.

"Nothing, Gary. Nothing. Well, thanks for your help."

Gary walked off, looking sheepish, which was odd for a goat. He knew he had been talking too much. Most goats were taciturn, obeying a code of silence known as "the omeeeerta." I wondered if he would get into trouble. (He did, as it turned out. I found him at the bottom of a tar pit three weeks later, his hooves encased in heavy terra-cotta.)

"It needed to have been something with hands," said Abel's soul, hurrying behind me as we left the goats. "How else could they have grabbed Gary's forelock? Perhaps it was one of the great apes?"

"Or one of the not-so-great ones," I murmured to myself. "That would be consistent with the club theory. Only someone with opposable thumbs could operate such advanced technology. Let's try the gorillas."

By the time we got to the forest in which the gorillas lived, it was pitch-dark. I heard wild shrieking and beating of chests as huge numbers of apes engaged in their favorite occupation, the oldest sport in existence—thumb wrestling.

The other creatures of the jungle looked on enviously as two giant silverbacks clasped each other's hands and attempted to pin their opponent's thumb down with their own. Both apes were baring their teeth as they tumbled back and forth across the jungle floor, with the crowd of animals around them hooting and screeching encouragement. It was not the cleanest of matches.

"Bunch of bananas!" grunted one of the gorillas as he found his thumb trapped, distracting his opponent momentarily and allowing him to wriggle his thumb free. There was much use of the index finger, a common trick, and only through sheer exhaustion was the match finally settled.

I went to speak to the losing knuckle walker. He was sucking on his mangled thumb.

"Hello, Bonobo," I said. "You'd better watch that doesn't get infected."

"Oh, hi Death," said Bonobo. We had had a run-in a few months before when he had fallen from a tree and lain in a coma for a few days. I had played a few hands of pinochle with his soul while we waited to see the outcome.

"Any of the apes have a grudge against Abel?" I asked.

"Abel?" said Bonobo. "That spoiled brat? Why do you ask?"

"Because he's dead, and someone with opposable thumbs did it."

"Well, look," said Bonobo. "None of us liked him, it's true. Or his brother. I mean they spent so much time with God they thought they were better than us."

"Stupid monkeys," said Abel's soul.

"Did you say something?" said Bonobo. I cast the Darkness thickly around Abel. Perhaps the brothers were not so different from their parents after all.

"They refused to thumb-wrestle with us," continued Bonobo. "They said it wasn't what God's chosen should be doing. God's chosen! Pah! We know what they were chosen for. But what motive would we have to kill them?"

"Pride. Greed. Hunger. Boredom," I said.

Bonobo shifted on his rock uncomfortably.

"Hey, I'm not saying we're as good as gold, but come on, Death, we're vegetarians."

Vegetarians with a grudge, I thought to myself. "Do you know what a club is?" I asked Bonobo.

"A club?" Bonobo mulled the word over. "A club? Is it a long yellow fruit with a peelable skin?" The look of stupidity was too real to have been faked. It would be some time before the apes got into tools.

I told Bonobo I'd be back and warned him not to leave the jungle. But I was pretty sure it wasn't him or any of his ape friends.

Apes of Wrath?

I returned to the field in which Abel's body lay. It was thick with flies.

"Hey, Death," they buzzed. "You want us to save you a piece?"

"No thanks, fellas," I said, and leaned over the body. My work habits coincided with their eating habits, so we saw quite a lot of one another. I picked up the bloodstained club and examined it. It was too complex to be the work of the animals, and too simple to be the work of Mother or Father. I was mulling over this dilemma when a tall brunette walked over to me. It was Cain.

"Why hello, Death," he said, cool as a cucumber.

"Hello, Cain," I replied. "Sorry about your brother."

"What brother?" said Cain.

"Abel," I said pointing at the dead body.

"Oh. My. God!" screamed Cain.

"Yes, darling?" boomed a voice. A blinding light enveloped us.

"There's been a problem," I interjected quickly. I didn't want things to get out of control.

"Me in Heaven above!" boomed God. "What's happened to Abel?"

"He's been murdered, God. I'm trying to find out who did it."

"Hello, God!" said Abel's soul excitedly from within my cloak. "I've missed You. I was in the middle of making You a sacrifice better than any You'd ever had before. Much better than Cain's."

"Oh, you . . . !" screeched Cain, spinning around wildly, trying to locate Abel's voice. "Your sacrifices are unhealthy, greasy, meaty things, all high in polyunsaturated fat. And God doesn't want to get fat, do You, God?"

"No," boomed God bashfully. "No, I don't. But there are only so many greens you can have sacrificed to you, Cain."

"What are You saying?" cried Cain. "You don't like my sacrifices? I knew it, I knew it!"

"That's not what I said, Cain," boomed God.

"You've always preferred Abel," continued Cain. "That's why I . . ."

"Go on," I said. This was getting interesting.

"Oh!" cried Cain. "You just don't understand."

"I do, Cain," I said. "I do."

"Abel said You didn't love me," implored Cain as he swung round to face God.

"He doesn't!" piped up Abel's soul from the edge of the void.

"I love all things," boomed God.

"But some things more than others, right, Lord?" said Abel's soul. His face beamed with smug self-satisfaction. It had been a mistake to bring him along.

"Do you know what this is, Cain?" I held up the club.

"It's a club," cried Cain, in tears now. "The club I used to murder my brother, Abel!"

There was a shocked silence. I thought it best to leave so God and Cain could work things out between them and was doing so when I heard Abel's voice pipe up.

"Hold on, Death, I want to see this. I knew it was him, I just knew it! Hey, where are you going, Death? I said turn around, I *said . . .*"

With a shrug of my shoulders I sent his soul cascading into the Darkness.

The Dawn of Time was very much like this. Enmities commencing, relationships forming and breaking, blood spilling. Everyone was a little crazy, and as the years sped by, the holes in Creation began to show. God was a big-picture guy. He had been fine with the light and the darkness and the oceans and sky, but when it came to the details, like individual creatures, He was hopeless.

Take Methuselah, for example. Through some bookkeeping mistake Methuselah had not been given a time to die. For years he followed me around with a pleading look in his eyes. I would find him waiting for me at plague pits pretending to be dead. I'd see him screaming and rolling around on the ground during battles, feigning fatal injuries, but he never had a scratch on him. Even when he threw himself into flaming buildings, he would invariably come out the other side, a little charred, but alive. He would often stare longingly at me as I removed the soul from a body.

"That's it, my boy," he'd say, licking his lips. "Ease him out, send him off now. Off to the afterlife."

The fact was that after a hundred years or so, Methuselah had done everything that a postprehistoric, antediluvian world had to offer. He had walked about, and whittled, contracted innumerable diseases, whittled some more, lost all his teeth, whittled new ones, and finally lost most of his sanity. Without a time to die scheduled, he was invulnerable. He could stand beneath an avalanche, and somehow the boulders would miss him. He could swim far out to sea until he was exhausted, only for the waves to wash him back to

Methuselah: "Kill Me."

shore. He could smear himself in butter and dance in front of the carnivorous animals, but they would not lay a claw on him. Even when he resorted to taunting them, pulling their tails, and slapping their faces, they merely walked away as if he was not there.

After a while he started making running dashes at the Darkness.

"I'm going home!" he'd whoop as he leapt toward it, but I could normally stop him from slipping through. One time, however, he was so desperate in his charge, and I was so busy dealing with the complicated soul of a dinosaur, that he knocked me over, splashing the Darkness everywhere. By the time I'd pulled myself together, Methuselah had gotten up to his waist in a small puddle of the void and was wriggling from side to side, desperately trying to force his belly through. I pulled him out and told him he had to wait his turn, and he trudged off disconsolately. He eventually died in the year of the Great Flood, when a lot of the loopholes in Creation were closed. By then he was 969 years old, yet curiously he didn't seem all that excited at the prospect.

"You know it's funny, Death," his soul told me as his body grew white and swollen. "When you want it, you can't get it, and when you've got it, you don't want it." I thought it was an odd thing to say, but then I was still growing used to the strange inconsistencies of the living. At the time, I remember thinking how lucky I was not to have been born mortal. The traumas of a finite existence were horrific. The glut of emotions one had to endure, the almost certain painful ending. Time and again I saw the living becoming the dead, yet I was always surprised how many showed regret for the passing of that cruel and inhuman punishment called Life. I just could not understand it except as a kind of psychosis in which people grew to like the miseries heaped upon them.

Little did I know then how completely I would change my mind.

Following the Methuselah debacle I was issued the *Book of Endings,* a large black tome that listed within it the exact time, date, and place of everything's designated end. It helped immensely in ushering souls into the void, as having one's name in print seemed to make dying much more official than my appearance ever could. When I met with resistance, I'd point at creatures' names in the *Book* and they'd just nod their heads and say, "Oh, I see," and hop into the Darkness.

But even without the *Book* I could tell the Great Flood was coming a mile off. God's mood had been increasingly changeable. Ever since Abel's murder He had been growing more and more disappointed with Creation, and I could hear Him walking across the earth booming to Himself, "Wrong . . . quite wrong." He had always been the uncertain sort, creating hundreds of different types of the same snail with only minor differences, or repeating trees over and over again. Only one thing seemed to make Him happy and that was the antics of Noah, a raving nutjob of the highest order.

I wasn't quite sure how Noah had got into this state. Some talked about an insatiable appetite for animal dung, others of a wasted youth sniffing tar. Whatever the reason, Noah was so mad he had married a rhubarb plant, whom he named Mrs. Noah. (Mrs. Noah would later claim that it was *she* who had instigated the interkingdom marriage in an attempt to escape her provincial, bourgeois life.)

Mrs. Noah (right) and Her Cousin, Joyce.

Between them they had three sons, three small pebbles known as Bacon, Sausage, and Ham, whom Noah would arrange in picturesque tableaus of familial bliss within his cave. After a while, however, even Noah's antics couldn't change God's mind.

"Death," He boomed to me one day, "I have decided I will blot out from the earth the men whom I created—men together with beasts, creeping things, and birds of the sky—for I regret that I made them."

It wasn't the first time I had heard such talk—God had a terrible habit of regretting things the mornings after the seven days and nights before—nevertheless, the situation required some delicacy.

"Very good, Lord God Sir, but surely You will save the creeping things? You've always loved the creeping things."

"Yes, it is true, I have always liked the things that creep," boomed God. "Maybe I shall spare the creeping things, but certainly I will destroy the men, and the beasts, and the birds of the sky."

"But beasts are so difficult to make," I reminded Him. "Remember all those hours you spent on the hooves and horns and quadruple stomach chambers?"

"Yes, yes, you're right. It would be a shame to get rid of the beasts. Awfully hard work, the beasts. In that case, I will just rid Creation of the men and the birds of the sky."

"But who keeps the beasts company if not the birds?" I said. "The beasts would be awfully lonely without the birds twittering above them. I have often heard it said by the beasts of the field that were it not for the birds of the sky Life would hardly be worth living."

"Which animal said that?" boomed God.

"I believe it was the koala bears, Lord God Sir, and the giraffes have also registered their appreciation for the birds. They do get awfully depressed now that there aren't any dinosaurs to talk to. 'Feathered ribbons of the sky' I believe they called them."

"Hmmm," boomed God. "Well, all right then, I shall save the birds and the beasts and the creeping things, but the men will certainly be destroyed. All except Noah. He does make me chuckle so."

There was an immaculately conceived pause.

"Unless," boomed God, "you should have some reason for Me not destroying all the men?"

"Well," I said, "it's just that it's going to be a lot of work for me. I've told You about the finger and toe problem before and with every man and woman dying all at once. . . ."

"Oh, very well," boomed God, "I'll call the whole thing off. But what about Noah?"

"What about him," I asked.

"Well, when I told him the Deluge was coming and that he alone would survive, he seemed so happy. He kept on saying that finally he'd be rid of Mrs. Noah and his ungrateful sons."

"I see."

"When's he due to die?"

I looked in the *Book of Endings*.

"Not for a few years yet."

"Can't we make an exception?"

"Well, You're the one, O Lord God Sir, who said that the *Book* should be immutable."

"Did I?" boomed God. "What a stupid thing to say."

"Perhaps," I said, as inspiration hit, "we could *pretend* the flood was coming. What do you think?"

"I think it's a marvelous idea," boomed God, "and I'm glad I thought of it."

So, for the next few weeks, as Noah built the giant wooden ark he believed was necessary for his survival, Urizel and a few other angelic helpers and I carefully stowed every living creature out of sight. God conjured up a few raindrops, and at the first sign of them, Noah leapt into his ark, leaving his wife and sons behind him, but bringing along a harem of potatoes. We slowly pushed the ark into a small pond, and Noah ran around it naked for forty days while a light drizzle fell. At the end of the "Flood," Noah's ark beached itself on the pond's shore, where he was amazed to be reunited with his wife and children whom, he grumbled, he never knew were such strong swimmers.

The "Deluge": Nothing Like This.

Many of God's favorites in the early days straddled the border between sanity and shoe-eating lunacy. The stupid creatures—those who had to concentrate extremely hard just to chew—rarely went mad. But when even a modicum of intelligence was bestowed on something or other, it usually sent them off their rocker. Take cockles, for instance, to whom God had gifted an inordinately high IQ and who—having perceived as intolerable their situation as one-footed hermaphroditic bivalves—had gone immediately out of their minds and had begun to pretend they were mussels. Fortunately this hadn't stirred things up too much.

Which Is the Cockle and Which Is the Mussel? Wrong.

The humans were another matter altogether. Take Abraham, for example, who soon succeeded Noah as God's favorite. If you'd have passed him in the fields, you'd have thought he was quite normal. But behind that genial bearded countenance was a man addicted to sacrifice. Abraham couldn't lay his eyes on something without wanting to lay his hands on it, tie it to an altar, and stab it repeatedly with a knife. Not a day went by without some small bird or lizard falling victim to Abraham's strange, insatiable lust. No sooner would Mrs. Abraham, a peaceable sort, come home from the market than that day's supper would be immediately hacked to pieces and offered up to the divine. Mrs. Abraham didn't mind this so much. It was rare, she said, for a man to help with the cooking. Nevertheless, she often confided in me that she could feel her husband's eyes on her, sizing up how much rope he would need to truss her down and how many buckets would be required to catch her blood. It was little wonder that Isaac, their only son, was something of a neurotic.

"He's going to kill me," Isaac would weep to me. "I just know he will. He keeps telling me to prepare myself for the greatest gift a father could give a son. And I know he doesn't mean a bicycle because they haven't been invented yet."

Nevertheless, I knew I shouldn't be angry with the man. During slow periods, Abraham was a constant provider of work for me. I always knew that at some point in my day I'd be drawn to his incessant slicing and dicing.

Abraham: Devout Patriarch, or Serial Killer?

"Ah, Mr. Death," he'd say jovially, as I came to pick up the lamb, badger, or apple he had just sacrificed. "Am I not your greatest benefactor? Do I not send more into the void in the praise of our Lord than anyone else?" I concurred, and thanked him, and went about my business, but he was sacrificing so abundantly that eventually God came and had a word with me.

"Can't we get him to stop?" God boomed. As with so many of His enthusiasms, His affection for Abraham had soon waned. "I mean, I appreciate it and all, but the infinite is only so big."

I tried to have a word with Abraham, but there was something about the gleam in his eye that troubled me. It spoke of something quite terrifying, not so much a love of dying but a hatred for Life that, while understandable considering Life's arbitrary nature, made me feel ever so slightly uncomfortable. I remember thinking to myself that even I didn't mind Life that much. In fact, I found it rather jolly. After all, I could hardly exist without it, and it could hardly exist without me. Of course, I see now that this was the beginning of a fateful codependence that would threaten my very existence, and that of the world, too. Looking back on it, I should have recognized my uneasiness with Abraham as a warning. I had been getting too close to Life. Much too close.

The Age of Myth

By now I had begun to identify a typology of the dying. There were the protesters, who believed their deaths to be a mistake, who'd complain and argue and demand to call their coroners. There were the romantics, who thought they were dreaming and tried in vain to pinch their spectral bodies with their ghostly hands. There were the optimists, who believed they were finally going to be rewarded for a lifetime spent growing their hair in a certain way, and there were the pessimists, who believed they were finally going to be punished for *not* growing their hair in a certain way. But by far the largest proportion of the dead were the confused. A characteristic conversation with one of the recently deceased would go something like this:

"Where am I?" they'd say.

"You are Not at all," I'd reply mysteriously. I had discovered that a mixture of non sequiturs and melancholic insinuations was the best way to avoid confrontation, and it usually didn't take too many unfathomable comments for the souls to realize what was going on. Nevertheless, some were very stubborn.

"Who are you?" they'd ask.

"I am the End of All Things."

"What kind of a name is that?"

"Pardon?"

"What kind of a name is the 'End of All Things'? What do people call you? Mr. All Things?"

"No. They call me—"

" 'You know who we're having round tonight, dear?' " they would mock. " 'The End of.' 'The End of who, dear?' 'The End of All Things, you know, he lives down the road with Mrs. All Things.' You should change your name, that's what you should do."

"My name is Death!" I'd reply.

"Well, why did you say it was Mr. All Things then?"

This went on for some time.

Keeping the dead from jumping back into the world of the living was another serious problem. "Do you mind if I just blow out that candle?" they would ask, as I held their immortal soul in my hands.

"There is no going back," I'd intone as grimly as possible.

"Oh, I'll just be a minute. It's just that it's an awful waste of wax."

"No. It is impossible."

"No, it's not," they'd say. "Look, I can almost blow it out from here." And they'd immediately begin huffing and puffing.

"Stop it!"

"Look," they'd reply, "I didn't ask for this, you know. How was I to know that I'd drop dead from a heart attack just after I'd lit it? What's more, think of the symmetry—I die, the candle goes out, it's very poetic."

"Oh, very well," I'd say, and waft the Darkness at the candle, expelling its light immediately. I was always a sucker for the elegiac.

"Now that wasn't too hard, was it?"

"No," I would say. "No, I suppose it wasn't."

"Well then, do you mind if we stop off at my sister's hut? She's expecting me for supper tonight and I don't want her waiting around on my behalf."

The problem was that in my attempts to be nice to the recently departed, they walked all over me. And it wasn't just me. God had grown so tired of people calling on Him for the most ridiculous things—smaller noses, longer fingers, giant chickens—that He'd begun to grow quite aloof from the world. I hadn't seen Him in years when suddenly that old familiar orb of dazzling white light appeared before me.

"Death, I need to speak to you," He boomed. "These people are driving Me crazy. Samson is obsessed with his hair, Solomon is cutting everything in two, and I can barely speak to Job with that persecution complex of his."

"Well, Lord God Sir," I said, "You have been rather rough on Job."

"What do you mean?"

"Well, You had the Sabeans kill all his servants."

"Many suffer misfortune, Death."

"Yes, but then lightning killed all his sheep."

"A mere coincidence," boomed God.

"And the Chaldeans ran off with his camels."

"Who can answer for the Chaldeans?"

"Well, who can answer for the mighty wind that blew down his house and killed all his children?"

"Do you have a problem with My ways, Death?"

"Oh, don't get me wrong, O Lord, I don't mind. It's all grist to the mill. But were the boils really necessary?"

"The man should have washed."

"And the all-over body rash, that was a bit nasty, wasn't it? I mean, he was scraping himself with shards of crockery. Crockery that had been broken when a mysterious earthquake destroyed the cave he was hiding in."

"Look," boomed God, "Job was such a goody-goody. Always praising My name or sacrificing in My honor. I couldn't stand it. Besides, your father said . . . oh." The orb drooped.

I put an arm around the most shoulderlike part of the divine light. "Perhaps You should take some time off, Lord God Sir," I suggested.

"Maybe you're right," boomed God. "I just feel like everything's rushing out of My control, that I'm not connecting with people any-

Job: "You Should See the Other Guy!"

more. I used to be able to spot evil a mile off, but I'm losing My touch. Perhaps Creation needs a whole new direction, something less primeval, more ancient. Something the youth can relate to."

And with that the divine light turned and slowly disappeared. "I'll be back in an era or two," boomed His voice. I noticed that pinned to His back was a note that read TAKE MY NAME IN VAIN. Father had indeed been busy.

So the Biblical Age ended and was replaced by the Age of Myth, an era of fearful monsters and ironic demises. Sons slew their fathers and married their mothers, wives slew their husbands and were in turn slain by their daughters, uncles killed nieces, nephews murdered aunts, brothers married sisters, and so on and so on. Despite the wailing and gnashing of teeth that accompanied such moments, I was happy to be kept so busy. Transmuting souls into the Darkness calmed me and made me feel part of Creation. My unconventional upbringing had left me with low self-esteem and needy for the approval of others. Now I had the chance to get the approval of every living being that ever existed! By the Age of Myth even the most begrudging of the dead had to admit I was good at my job. Plus it kept me in great shape. One being's ultimate tragedy is another being's extreme calisthenics.

Before He had departed, God had subcontracted His divinity out to a host of minor gods. Interviews had been held in which prospective deities put forward their plans for their respective fields of expertise, and before long a whole new pantheon was created.

It was confusing at first. There were now gods of love, of war, of rivers, and of trees. There were gods of the hearth, of the threshold, of the alcove, and of the niche. There were even gods for things that had yet to exist. Velocipede, god of the bicycle, spent most of his time causing horses to bolt and carts to overturn in a vain attempt to prompt the development of his chosen phenomena. What's more, many of the gods had demanded a contractual rider that allowed them to create new beings, and God, being in such a rush to quit the earth, had agreed. I thought these new creations were lacking somewhat. Minotaurs and Centaurs, Sphinxes and Mermaids . . . they were little more than jumbled-up versions of already existing animals. I wasn't the only one to feel aggrieved. Disappointment among humans at these new chimerical beasts saw the formation of a reactionary group who yearned for the simplicity of the first Creation and sought to rectify the problem by wiping these new creatures off the face of the planet. This group called themselves "Heroes."

Minotaur: Derivative.

To the Heroes, any beast of mixed progeny was fit only for the slaughter. Such radical originalist creationists as Hercules, Perseus, and Theseus were soon laying down trails of sugar cubes with which to lure Centaurs into ambushes, while Minotaurs were tricked into entering china shops, where their human interest in tableware conflicted with their bullish urge for demolition, leaving the animal confused and easy to slay.

The budding monster conservationist movement was appalled. But no matter how hard they tried to humanize these new, unfamiliar creatures, there was something about Harpies, the hideous foul-smelling birds with women's faces, razor-sharp teeth, and earsplitting shrieks that made them distinctly unsympathetic to the general populace. Soon the monster population had been all but decimated, and the Heroes began to broaden their horizons.

The duck-billed platypus's strange combination of ducklike snout, webbed feet, beaverlike tail, and egg-laying capabilities was considered exceedingly unnatural, and it soon found itself besieged by legions of underemployed Heroes.

*"Grievous the Shouts of the Many Men Killed, /
by the Snapping Beak of the Beast Duck-Billed."—Ovid*

Attacks on giraffes, whom the Heroes thought were half-leopard and half-camel, and on leopards, which were said to be half-panther and half-lion, soon followed. When it was whispered that many of the Heroes themselves were demigods, the Age of Heroes ended in a wave of bloody internal purges.

I could hardly claim to be upset by the unceasing slaughter. The Darkness happily accepted all regardless of race, creed, or plausibility, but the new gods were forever interfering in my business, and that I could not abide. At the Battle of Troy the gods were diving in and out of the action like lifeguards at a whirlpool, saving each of their favorite warriors and whisking them to safety. The goddess Athena was always interrupting me, claiming that this soldier or that soldier was her personal favorite and could I make an exception and not send him into the Darkness. The *Book of Endings* swiftly became filled with strikethroughs and erasures.

I didn't like this. Each morning I would carefully mark out the soon-to-be-dead by region and then work out how long each area would take me. The meddling of the gods threw my calculations off completely. By now I considered myself something of a perfectionist. I reckoned that if a job had to be done, it was better that it be done quickly, and efficiently, than in a haphazard manner. Neither was I biased in my work. Be you prince or pauper, porpoise or penguin, I treated everyone much the same. I saw no difference between the brief lives of worms, or the long spans of turtles, the death of babies and the dying of nonagenarians. But now, on the battlefields of the Mediterranean, I could tell that those who weren't the gods' favorites were starting to get suspicious of my impartiality. After all, the buck stopped with me.

"Where's Achilles?" a dead soul would say.

"Standing over there," I'd say.

"Are you sure he didn't die?"

"Quite sure."

"But he was in the same chariot as me, you know?"

"Yes."

"And the chariot did go over the edge of a cliff."

"Yes."

"Then how did he survive?" he'd ask, pointing to the mangled wreckage of the chariot and his own dismembered body.

"Luck?" I'd venture, and the eyes of the dead soul would narrow suspiciously as the Darkness consumed him.

Furthermore, the gods were always competing with one another. They would often wait for me next to the souls of dead warriors whom they had drowned in a storm or had stabbed in battle and insist that they be given the credit for the kill.

"Mark it down for me, Death," I recall Aphrodite telling me as I hurried through a village decimated by an earthquake. "That'll show that tart Hera. What's the score at present?"

"Well, ma'am," I said, for I always thought it wise to stay on the good side of any divine presence, "that places you at eighty-four thousand and ninety-six."

"And Hera?"

"Still ahead of you, ma'am. One hundred and sixty-four thousand."

"Damn. Any big disasters planned for the future?"

I dipped into the *Book*.

"Well, there is a volcanic eruption at Vesuvius scheduled for next month."

"How many?"

"Over two thousand."

"Any chance I can help out? You know, divinely freeze them to the spot, or turn them all into statues or something?"

"Why would you do that?"

"For failing to sacrifice to me?"

"Have they forgotten to sacrifice to you?" I asked.

"Oh no. No, not at all. They're very good with their sacrifices at Pompeii. Always on time, always very plump cattle."

"So why do you want to help kill them?"

"Two thousand could really put me back in the game, Death. Don't you understand?"

That's the problem of having a pantheon of all-powerful beings;

everyone wants to show that they're more all-powerful than the other.

"I think the lava and fumes will do just fine, thanks," I said.

"How about if my wrath just causes the volcano to erupt?"

"I'm afraid you used your wrath last week on that landslide in Thebes."

"Oh, but that wasn't really my wrath, more my irritation. And, besides, it only killed twenty or thirty."

"Twenty or thirty members of the Theban royal family, who were, you may recall, beloved of Poseidon."

"Oh yes. He'll be sinking my ships again, I'm sure. Still, is there no way I can be worked into the Vesuvius eruption?"

When a goddess bats her eyelashes at you, it is an unsettling experience. I buried my head in the *Book*.

"Well, I suppose I could write off a few as having suffered just vengeance after having cursed your name, but I must inform you that the majority of the deaths are already allocated to Apollo."

"What!" squawked Aphrodite. "How so?"

"Well, some of their young defaced his temple the other day. They said they didn't believe in him."

"Good for them!" said Aphrodite. "Sometimes I don't believe him either."

"In him," I corrected. "They said they didn't believe *in* him."

"Oh," said Aphrodite. "Well, okay then."

Not believing in a god was a very serious affair, especially with faith now being spread so thinly across the massive pantheon. Without faith in their existence, gods slowly shrank and disappeared.

The same was true for God Himself, but He had circumvented this problem by inhabiting everything in Creation. If you believed in the rock in front of you, a percentage of that belief went to God. This usually ranged from 15 percent to 50 percent depending on the size of the object, with the rest of the belief going toward substantiating the object's own existence. (Even this fail-safe plan had its problems. When the eighteenth-century philosopher Bishop Berkeley suggested that there were no "real" objects at all but only ideas, faith in the world of the senses wavered. The very God Berkeley had devoted his life to serving almost winked out of existence as people stopped believing in trees, rocks, and the rest of Creation. Fortunately for God, Berkeley's theorem was refuted in 1753 when an idea fell on his head.)

Bishop Berkeley: Destroyer of Gods, Wearer of Hats.

To make matters worse, the number of gods was growing at an unbelievable rate. We all knew why this was. Olympus, where the new pantheon had their headquarters, had come to be known as "Mount" Olympus, so regularly was it shaken with the thunderous passions of the deities. The countryside surrounding it had become a quagmire of heavenly fluids, and vast, dirty underwear could be seen snagged in trees across half the earth. It was only the sudden onset of an ice age that prevented the entire planet from having to be dry-cleaned.

Heart of
Darkness

⊰⊹⊱

I **was fond** of glaciers, slow but amiable giants that bull-
dozed all the monocular and snake-haired skulls of the Age of Myth
beneath them. I used to like watching them as they flowed into the sea
to calve, the infant icebergs squealing and squawking with delight as
they drifted away from the shore, while the mother glaciers broke out
in bergschrunds and shed meltwater from every moulin in their fringe.

Ice, Ice Babies.

After the initial attack of hypothermia, the ensuing bouts of
deadly frostbite, and the subsequent starvation of millions of people,

my workload slackened. Humankind was forced to regress and re-group, and I was intrigued to watch the adaptations and innovations this new situation prompted. In my opinion, the most notable ad-vance that the Ice Age fostered came with the rise of the Evil Villain.

Famous nowadays for tying damsels to train tracks, Evil Villains were not always so prevalent, or ingenious. Indeed, up until the Ice Age the early practitioners of Evil Villainy had been hampered in their calling by a lack of fast-moving locomotive devices with which to crush their victims in a suitably spectacular and horrifying man-ner. The rise of the glaciers, however, offered Evil Villains a tempo-rary solution. Captive damsels were tied tightly to the snow line, and inch by inch, the giant tongues of ice slowly ran them over. Admit-tedly there were teething problems. The devilish process usually took from six months to two years, depending on the weather and the width of the damsel, and the Evil Villain was forced to keep his victim fed, watered, and warm throughout, if the full, shocking na-ture of his plan were to succeed. Many Evil Villains suffered hernias from having to sustain their diabolical cackling for months on end, and the lengthy intervening period between capture and slaughter meant rescues and escapes were common. I was assured, however, by the handful of people who were killed in such a manner that their ends had been "somewhat dastardly."

Trains: Represented a Significant
Technological Advance over Glaciers.

As all things must, even the glaciers had to die. I remember watching them retreating back to the poles, shrinking under the sun's gaze, until in a lonely cwm, corrie, or cirque, they exhaled their final icy breaths and thawed into puddles, whereupon I popped out their dripping souls and sent them on their way. The earth returned to a more temperate clime, Evil Villains set to work creating the internal combustion engine, and the Age of Civilization finally began.

It was the Sumerians who kicked things off. Imagine, if you can, an entire race of people grimly obsessed with the weather and you get some inkling of ancient Mesopotamia. Such meteorological obsessions seemed to stem from the fact that nascent society had located itself on a monotonous landscape of mudflats and marshland, the tedium of whose prospects was matched only by the certainty of its inundation. "Is it raining?" was the fashionable conversational entrée for more than fifteen hundred years (when it was eventually supplanted by the typical forthrightness of the Roman, "What do you do?" which retains the position to this day).

Despite being perpetually damp or drowned, the Sumerians managed to invent the stylus, a remarkable innovation that transformed not only learning but also warfare. For centuries anything that left a mark had traditionally been classed as a weapon, and for some time the pen wasn't just mightier than the sword, it *was* the sword. When the Sumerians discovered that such instruments could be used not just for slaughter but for scholarship, it radically reshaped their culture (although the rehabilitation of the typewriter, which they had invented as a particularly gruesome bludgeoning weapon, would not take place for many thousands of years).

I noticed that the Sumerians were one of the first groups of humans to establish a firm belief in an afterlife. You would have thought that, considering the unremitting misery of their lives on Earth, they'd be sick and tired of Life in general, especially an afterlife. But

*Ancient Sumerian Warriors Depicted with
Large Battle Typewriter (left), and Small
War-Bottle of Correction Fluid (right)*

they were gluttons for punishment, and with an imagination satu-
rated by the dampness of their unfortunate situation, the Sumerians
imagined a hereafter in which they would eat dust and clay in a dark
room, forevermore. The idea of a happy afterlife, like the idea of a
happy Life, was simply beyond their conception.

And the gods they had! A bunch of second-rate minor elementals
without a sliver of personality between them. There were gods of
streams and rivers, of rivulets and creeks, of drizzle and humidity, all
of whom were literally lining up to drown the Sumerians. At least
these gods didn't ask me for any favors and were moderately scrutable,
unlike Him. For instance, when King Sargon was overthrown by the
barbarians, everyone knew that the god Enlil had punished the land
because Naram-Sin, a king of Sargon's line, had sacked Nippur, plun-
dered the Ekur, and humiliated Lugal-Zage-Si, such that when the
Gutians invaded Akkad, Ur-Nammu was forced to seize power from
Utukhegal. It was plain for all to see.

As far as I was concerned, complex motives were unimportant as
long as any major massacres were noted in the *Book of Endings* with

plenty of time for me to prepare. Yes, I thought I had it all figured out in Sumeria, all under control. Little did I know that in those moist lands my existence would be changed forever.

I remember the day well. How could I forget? The usual prognostications, fearful sacrifices, and portents of divine satisfaction had been swiftly followed by the customary great flood, and the temple priests, who had relocated themselves to high ground just in time, were questioning the quality of their prophetic entrails. The storm was still raging as I glided about the pale, bloated bodies that scattered the flooded plain like confetti. It was slow work as schools of Fish Supremacists crowded around the bodies in order to heckle the dead.

(Fish Supremacists thought that anything that was not a cold-blooded aquatic vertebrate with two sets of paired fins and a body covered in scales was an inferior being. They had become a political movement around the time of the Great Transition, when some fish decided to leave the water for the land. There had been much talk of "quitters" and "degenerates" among the still-fish population, and the annual floods were seen as a settling of scores with the earthbound.)

Fish of Intolerance.

It was while extricating the soul of a well-known fisherman from a gang of rowdy carp that I heard a scream from above. I had, of course, heard many screams in my existence, and one grows used to their character, but this was different. Some screams are emphatic, challenging, precursors to a deadly action. Others are resigned, tired, bored, a by-rote shake of the fist at the characteristic remorselessness of the Universe. But this scream was delicate, graceful, a bloodcurdling shriek of pure unadulterated beauty ringing clear through the thunder and rain. It seemed to be emanating from the peak of the Great Ziggurat of Ur.

I looked in the *Book* but there were no fatal plunges scheduled from the Great Ziggurat of Ur until the following week, when the temple priests would be hurled from the summit in order that *their* entrails be studied. Nevertheless, this scream commanded my attention so much that I had no choice but to explore its source.

The Great Ziggurat of Ur: Twinned with Angkor Wat?

Arriving at the top, I saw that the screamer was a woman. She was dangling upside down from the peak of the Ziggurat, her robes and hair fluttering in the wind, her left sandal fortuitously snagged on a spur in the rock.

"This is peculiar," I remember thinking. "How is she going to survive this?" As I walked from side to side contemplating the strangeness of the situation, something even more peculiar happened; I noticed her eyes were following me.

During the Biblical Age I had decided to make myself invisible to the living. The reason for this wasn't misanthropy, far from it; rather, it was because my reputation had grown to such an extent that whenever I appeared in front of a group, the very sight of me caused panicked stampedes. Of course, I had only been drawn to the group to collect the souls of those crushed in the mad dash away from me. This made my head hurt when I thought about it, so to make things simpler I had grown imperceptible to all things. Except, it seemed, this woman.

I ducked into a stairwell, but still her eyes followed me. I ran from one end of the Ziggurat's terrace to the other, but still she watched me. I started leaping in the air, making large star-jumps, to make sure her eyes were not following my course by chance, but this only started her giggling.

"What *are* you doing?" she said.

"Um . . ." I hesitated.

"Ur, actually," she replied, eyeing me carefully. She spoke very calmly despite her precipitous position. "I'm Maud."

"You can see me?" I asked, checking over my shoulder to ensure there was no one standing behind me.

"No." She sighed, flicking her hair nonchalantly out of her eyes. "But I do find the only state in which I can bear to talk to myself is while hanging upside down from the Great Ziggurat."

She flashed a smile at me. Even upside down she seemed to be an unusually pretty human.

"Now look," she said quite abruptly, "why not just unhook my little sandal from this tedious brick and let me smash my body to pieces on the stones below?"

I didn't know what to say. Of course, many things had taken their lives before. In fact, suicide was a way of life for many creatures. I knew hundreds of unhappy radishes who had uprooted themselves in despair at their allotment in life. But never had I been directly asked for assistance in ending things. Life was usually fragile enough not to require my help.

"I don't think I can do that."

"I'd really much rather be dead, you know."

"But it's against the regulations," I said. I flicked through the *Book*. "You're not due to die for another twenty-three years."

"You are Death though, aren't you?"

"Well, yes."

"Then what are you doing here?"

I wasn't quite sure of that myself. In fact, I wasn't sure of anything when I looked into those deep brown eyes of hers.

"Look," I said, pulling myself together, "yes, I am Death, but I don't interfere. You've got to do that yourself."

"Well, that doesn't sound much like Death to me," she said. "And you're a little shorter than I expected, although it's hard to tell with you being upside down. Maybe, in fact, you're taller than I expected. You know, my soothsayer said I'd meet a tall, dark stranger one day . . ."

I should have walked away. It was not as if I was lacking for work. Yet I couldn't tear myself away from this woman, poised between life and me.

". . . but I said, 'Enheduanna'—Enheduanna's my soothsayer's name—I said, 'Enheduanna, we're in the middle of Mesopotamia, of course he's going to be dark, and as for tall, you think tall is anything over four feet.' "

What was she talking about? What was I doing listening to her? Why did I not walk away? Looking back on it, I realized my fate was sealed from the moment she said her next words: "Pretty please?"

And so, feeling as if my body was being controlled by some mischievous power (I checked with Father later and he said he had nothing to do with it), I walked over to her and, looking both ways in case anyone was watching, delicately flicked her sandal over the edge. I watched as she plummeted to her doom.

"Thank youuuu . . . ," she cried. There was the sound of a small thump. I hurried down the Ziggurat.

"Thanks again," she said, as I bent over to scoop her soul out of her bloodied and broken body. It was more radiant than any other I'd ever seen before. "That is a relief, I can tell you."

"Why did you want to die so much?" I asked.

"Oh, you know—boy comes of age, boy meets girl's family, girl's family draws up marriage pact with boy, boy complains girl's dowry is too small, girl's family says it is more than enough, boy says girl will die an old maid, girl's father throws in an extra camel, boy says that'll do nicely, father tells girl to cheer up and sprinkle herself with aromatic cedar oil, boy meets girl."

It was an age-old tale. But one thing still troubled me.

"How could you see me?"

"Well, you were just standing there."

"But people aren't meant to see me."

"Why ever not?"

I tried to explain the panics I had caused, and she nodded her head in sympathy. I had a strange urge to keep talking, but already the Darkness was starting to encircle her. I slapped it back.

"Would you care . . . ," I asked her shining, lustrous soul, as a strange wave of nervousness rushed over me, "to go for a walk?"

"I would be delighted!" she replied, smiling, and took my arm.

So it was that for the next few hours we gamboled happily through the flooded palace grounds, paddling through the diseased floodwaters, ignoring the cries of dozens of souls still stuck in their bodies. She told me that she had been the only daughter of the Grand Vizier of Ur, and that she had been a very independent child, somewhat fascinated with dying. She said she had pulled the legs off hundreds of insects in her youth and asked if I could recall any of them. I pretended that I could.

Maud didn't seem to mind the corpses that littered our way. In fact, she was fascinated by the grimaces of the deceased. I pointed out the first signs of decomposition in bodies and showed her how to pull the soul out of a small dead child, which she did with surprising ease, popping it out, brushing it down, and sending it off into the Darkness with a pat on its behind. As the storm passed and the sun set, we climbed the Great Ziggurat once more and looked at the blood-red sky together.

"What happens after this?" she asked.

"I'm not sure, Maud," I said. I had never been so open and unguarded in my thoughts on the afterlife before. "I think it depends on what you believe in."

"So if you believe in an afterlife populated with flamingos, you'll end up in it?"

"Quite possibly, although only if you've been very bad."

"How so?"

"Well, flamingos are very antisocial. Nobody would want to spend all eternity with flamingos."

"What if you really, really liked flamingos?" she asked, resting her chin on her hand. "What if your idea of Paradise was being surrounded by thousands of antisocial flamingos?"

"Well, in that case, I imagine you could have your flamingos," I said. "But don't expect them to thank you for it."

Flamingos: Ungrateful, Bad-Tempered, Pink.

She laughed, and I laughed too. It had been a long time since I had had any company. My last companion had been Phillip, an amiable raccoon, whose soul followed me around for years trying to consume the spirits of dead frogs. Maud turned toward me.

"What if I wanted to see you again?" she said. She didn't seem to be joking.

"Well, the one thing you can be sure of," I told her, "is that I'll always be around."

"I might well hold you to that, Mr. Death," she said, smiling.

The only time she grew morose was when she saw that her father, the Grand Vizier, had survived the flood. He was engaged in an argument with Maud's fiancé over a drowned camel.

"Oh, look at them," said Maud with contempt. "They care more about that bloody camel than me."

I was so intent on making Maud happy that I picked up a stone and threw it at the Grand Vizier as hard as I could. It knocked his hat clean off, and he and the fiancé ran away in a panic. How she laughed. I was about to repeat the gesture when she grabbed my arm and told me no, I shouldn't, I'd get in trouble.

She was right. Already I could hear the moaning of all the souls that still needed to be packed off into the void. But at that moment I didn't care. I had discovered the most fascinating creature in existence—even more fascinating than the unconscious newt—and one who seemed to understand me too.

*The Unconscious Newt Lives Its Entire Life
in a Comatose State, Waking Only to Mate,
Go Back to Sleep, and Die.*

She had to go, of course. It was almost sunset when we said our good-byes. I wasn't quite sure how to end things so we ended up shaking hands—a grim formality clung to the process. But at the last minute, as the Darkness slowly enveloped her, she ran toward me and hugged me. I was so shocked that I shut my eyes. When I opened them again, Maud was gone. I noticed the Darkness looking at me in a peculiar way.

"What?" I demanded. It shrugged. I took out the *Book* and scribbled her name in the margin and tried to go about my business. But no matter how hard I tried, I could not put her out of my mind. She lived on in my memory tenaciously, hanging upside down from the Great Ziggurat.

Once all the drowned souls had been dealt with, I thought I would try reaching into the Darkness to see if any trace of Maud remained. But the blackness was total, the emptiness unfathomable, the absence absolute. For the first time in my existence I felt angered by it. Why couldn't it have kept just a trace of her? Of her dark brown eyes? Of her sparkling laugh? Why did the Darkness always have to overwhelm and subsume everything?

Oh yes. It was with Maud that all my misfortunes began.

II

Odd Gods

⊰✢⊱

The rest of the epoch passed with alarming speed. The Tin Age rushed into the Copper Age, forging the dazzling Bronze Age. The over-the-hill Sumerians and the diminutive Akkadians merged to become the all-powerful Babylonians. Continents shifted, mountains grew, and fashions in dying came and went—to be killed by an arrow was particularly à la mode, by a blunt instrument oh-so-passé—but the souls I was collecting remained essentially the same: aggrieved, curious, bewildered.

You would think that I would have tired of the dead by now as a clerk tires of his invoices, or a poet of his rhymes. But despite spending eons in the company of the nevermore I was not bored. In fact, I felt quite the opposite. Whereas in the past I had rushed to foist the souls into the Darkness with only a modicum of small talk, I had by now become so proficient at my job that I could easily afford to press the dead on aspects of their past lives. An infinitesimal change had occurred within me, a tiny recalibration of the scales, a quarter turn of the screw. I found myself wanting to know the most bizarre minutiae of the deads' lives—what had been their favorite colors? What had been their favorite foods? What had they liked to do on hot summer days? Did they prefer puppies or kittens?

I must ask the reader to bear in mind that I wasn't taking any liberties I didn't think I deserved. After all, I had a right to relaxation and conversation as much as any other being. But what was it that drove me into this habitual interest with Life? What led me to embrace Life in such a reckless manner? It was not dissatisfaction or boredom. No, rather it was my natural surfeit of gloom, the settled and abiding darkness within me that drew me intrinsically to the light of Life, like a candle snuffer is drawn toward a candle flame. It was not long before I developed an insatiable appetite for the joys of the once-alive.

I reflected that this emboldened sociability had started after my meeting with Maud. I could still see her plummeting so gracefully from the Great Ziggurat. I felt a spring in my step whenever I thought of her body smashing into the ground, bones splintered and ears bleeding, vital organs ruptured, bile filling her lungs, surrounded by a billowing petticoat of blood. Then again, it was hard not to be sociable in the company of the Egyptians. Finally, here was a culture that knew how to die well.

The Egyptians were so obsessed with me it almost became embarrassing. From the moment they were born, it seemed as if they were preparing themselves to die, which, given the high infant mortality rate, was probably just as well. Instead of playing doctor and nurse, Egyptian children played grave digger and embalmer. Instead of building toy forts, they built toy tombs. The most popular answer to questionnaires asking teenagers what they would like to be when they grew up was "Dead," shortly followed by "Pharaoh," with "Scourge of the Jews" and "Professional Charioteer" tying for third place.

And how they met me in style! By asp bites and poisoning, with slit throats and brains pulled out of noses. It was all so refined. The pharaohs, in particular, were a hoot. They'd turn up dead along with their dead servants, dead horses, dead cats, and hundreds of different dead birds and insects. Usually I insisted that souls went into the Darkness unaccompanied, but I confess to feeling not a little flattered by the construction of the pyramids. It was nice to be appreciated, nice to feel wanted, especially after the miserable Sumerians.

So I let the Egyptians take it with them. I'd pluck out the pharaoh's soul and those of his entourage and then let them range about their tombs for a few hours, galloping on the souls of their dead horses, and ordering the souls of dead servants to feed them the souls of dead grapes. It was quite something to see.

And I admit, I shamelessly played up to my role. I knew how the Egyptians loved their animals so I began dressing in different costumes. If I knew they liked birds, I'd put on a falcon mask when I popped out their soul; if they liked dogs, I'd wear a jackal mask, and so on. I called it my *Mort Couture* period.

Me on the Nile.

Yes, I thought, the Egyptians really understood me, and themselves. But of course there were misunderstandings. I remember the soul of Tutankhamen laughing and laughing at one of my jokes until the ethereal tears ran from his incorporeal eyes.

"I will always remember you when I become a god," he said.

"When you become a what?" I responded.

"A god, Death," he said. "As I was in life, so shall I be in death."

I just nodded my head and let the Darkness take him. I couldn't bear to tell the poor kid the truth.

Of course, not everyone was pleased with the special treatment I gave the pharaohs. Many of the slaves who died during the construction of the pyramids felt particularly aggrieved. They always had chips on their shoulders when I came to spirit them away.

"Are you sure you wouldn't rather be taking the soul of a pharaoh?" a few would sneer as I shucked out their souls. "Why no animal masks for us?" It was very awkward.

Of course, the slaves had good reason to be angry, since so many of them had been tricked into slavery. They had been told that if they enrolled to build the pharaohs' tombs, and got six of their friends to do likewise, they would in turn have a pyramid built for them. In Ancient Egypt, obsessed with dying as it was, a pyramid was the height of desirability. Well, as long as the number of slaves kept growing, everyone worked happily, but inevitably the number of new slaves signing on simply dried up, and only a few pyramids ended up being built before the ruse was discovered.

A slave revolt ensued. The slave leaders decreed that rather than just one pharaoh being buried per pyramid, thousands of workers should be entombed therein. These inverted pyramids, carefully balanced on their tips, represented the pinnacle (or pedestal) of the slave rights movement in Ancient Egypt. They were, however, highly susceptible to strong winds, and the vast majority of them were sent whirling into the desert like spinning tops, never to be seen again.

The Great Inverted Pyramid of Giza (right).

-❦-

As the number of civilizations grew, so did the number of gods, and scuffles began to break out in the desert between rival bands of believers. For the most part the gods themselves didn't have anything to prove. It was their followers who were the problem.

I remember one time a god named Yahweh, one of the many minor manifestations of God who had been left to look after things in His absence, was dragged out into the desert by his followers to battle the god Baal. The problem was that the two gods were on friendly terms.

"Hello, Baal," rumbled Yahweh. "How's tricks?"

"Not bad thanks, Yahweh," roared Baal. "Same old, same old. Yamm sends his best."

"Still god of the sea, is he?"

"Yes, he's sharing it with Poseidon. Yamm's doing waves at the moment while Poseidon's busy with the creatures of the deep. I believe there was some argument about who controlled long-shore drift, but I think that's settled now."

"I'm glad to hear it," rumbled Yahweh. "Look, I am sorry about all this, Baal, but my boys are so damned devout."

"Oh, I understand," roared Baal. "You let them build a couple of temples to you and suddenly they think they own you."

While the gods chatted, their worshippers were brokering rules for a contest between the two supreme beings. Baal's priests had pushed for a pentathlon, but this was swiftly ruled out by Yahweh, who was nursing an old harvest-festival injury. After a while, the prophet Elijah, who was leading the supporters of Yahweh, approached his god.

"If you're the greatest god, the one true god," said Elijah, "then you must crush the false god Baal into the dust."

"But he's my friend," rumbled Yahweh. "Besides, if I'm the one true god, what's he doing standing right there?"

Baal gave a friendly wave at Elijah.

"This isn't funny, you know," snapped Elijah. "Would you prefer we didn't believe in you?"

"Oh, stop being such a stick-in-the-mud," Yahweh rumbled, and turned back to Baal to resume his conversation. "You know, Baal, wouldn't it be fine if we could somehow get rid of worshippers?"

"Well," roared Baal, "I hear it said that soon they'll have belief machines that pray much faster than humans, and with more feeling, too. Plus they'll be much smaller, so you can just carry them around in your pocket—Hey! You're disappearing!"

Yahweh had indeed started to shrink.

"Stop that!" rumbled Yahweh, spinning around to Elijah, who stood there smiling smugly.

"I've told them not to have faith in you until you crush Baal in your mighty hand, O Great One."

"But you're talking to him!" cried Baal, desperately trying to stretch Yahweh back to his full size.

"That doesn't mean that I have to believe in him," said Elijah.

I must admit I felt quite sorry for the gods, regardless of which mythology they came from. To begin with, they had wowed humans with tricks and miracles and sopped up the spiritual adoration. Slowly but surely, however, the believers came to realize that the real power resided with them. As I've mentioned before, gods theoretically can't die, but they need to be believed in, otherwise they just blink out of existence. Wary of this, many of the more cunning gods had a devout hermit or two tucked away in desert caves, just in case their entire belief system suddenly went apostate.

So it was that Yahweh and Baal were soon bullied into facing off against each other. It wasn't pretty. The air rang with obscenities and incense from both sets of supporters as they threw rocks at one another and then hid behind the hems of their gods' garments. Taking a deep breath, Baal turned to Yahweh's believers and roared, "I am Baal, son of Dagon and Ashtoreth, bull-horned king of gods, destroyer of Mot! Feel my wrath, unbelievers!" He bared his teeth and

Hermits: Spiritual Backup.

flames shot from his eyes. He winked at Yahweh who gave him a sur-reptitious thumbs-up.

"Well, set fire to these logs then," cried out Elijah. On one side of the battleground lay a pile of logs in a pool of water.

Baal looked upset. "But they've been soaked in water!" he roared.

"He's right, you know, Elijah," rumbled Yahweh. "They're completely drenched."

"That's the point," said Elijah sharply.

"Oh, very well," roared Baal, and sitting his giant form down, picked up two sticks and began to rub them together. His followers began to look at one another.

"Not like that," yelled Elijah. "Use your so-called divine powers, false god!"

Baal looked at Elijah as if he could just devour him then and there.

"I did mention the logs were *wet*, didn't I?" he roared, before stepping toward the woodpile and staring at it very hard. There was a divine grunt, and a tiny wisp of steam wafted up from the top of the logs.

"Oh, well done!" rumbled Yahweh. "That was good, wasn't it?"

"No, it wasn't," said Elijah. "That was probably just evaporation caused by the sun."

"Oh, give him a break," rumbled Yahweh, as Baal sat down on the ground with his head in his hands. "What do you want from us?"

"Look," said Elijah, "all we need to know is which one of you is the greater god."

Yahweh and Baal looked at each other. You could see what they were thinking: "Bloody humans. Never content with what they have." I had always found that the saying that all gods were jealous was not true. Many gods rarely minded who their followers worshipped as long as there was enough belief to go around. Nevertheless, there was a certain divine code that had to be followed in situations such as this. Sighing, the two gods rumbled and roared in unison, "I am."

A murmur broke through the crowd, and I could see the gods beginning to flicker a little as belief in them wavered.

"Oh, this is ridiculous!" roared Baal. "Why do you have to choose between one of us? Why can't you see that we're both special in our own different ways? Why can't you appreciate us for what we are, rather than what you want us to be? Why can't we just rule over our people as before? Those who like horns can worship me, and those who like beards can worship him. Why not?"

"I'm sorry," said Elijah, "that's not going to cut it anymore."

"But there's enough room for both of us in the heavens," rumbled Yahweh.

"No can do," said Elijah. "We're cutting our costs and downsizing to monotheism. Everyone's doing it. All those sacrifices add up, you know?"

"Well, if you insist that one of us must perish, let us go about this in the ancient manner," rumbled Yahweh. "The way that was foretold in the scriptures, that was marked by the mystical stones, that was seen painted in the sky by the desert prophets millennia ago." With some flair, Yahweh pulled a coin out from behind Elijah's ear and declared, "Heads or aqueducts?" before flicking it into the air.

"Aqueducts," roared Baal. The coin fell to the ground. Elijah stepped forward. "It's heads, I'm afraid."

"Oh, fiddlesticks," roared Baal as Yahweh's followers cheered, and whooped, and hoisted Elijah onto their shoulders. Yahweh was quite forgotten about. The chief priest of Baal dropped dead from disappointment, and I quickly went to work on his soul. Meanwhile the other Baalites began to drift away, tearing off their talismans and scouring themselves with thorns. Already peddlers were running among them, selling garments emblazoned with the legend I BELIEVED IN BAAL AND ALL I GOT WAS THIS LOUSY HAIR SHIRT. As for Baal, he was shrinking by the second.

"I hear there are some positions opening up in Inuit mythology," rumbled Yahweh consolingly. "Drop my name if it helps."

"But it's freezing in the Aleutians," said Baal, who was by now the size of a normal human being. "I'm not manifested for it."

I didn't give Baal much of a chance in the Arctic. The denizens of the North Pole were incredibly self-absorbed. They thought the world revolved around them. A Baal cult wouldn't last a decade.

I watched in sadness with Yahweh as Baal continued to shrink. By now he was the size of a large mouse.

"Doesn't *anyone* believe in me anymore?" he squeaked.

Suddenly, a voice popped up from the desert floor. "I still believe in you," it said. A small boy walked forward. He was carrying some of the bejeweled icons left by the defeated Baal worshippers. Baal looked at him with tears in his now tiny eyes.

"Well . . . that's very kind of you, sonny," he piped.

"When I saw you best Osiris in that earthquake contest last year," enthused the boy, "with your Pin-Baal Flying Headlock, I knew you were the best."

"Well, thank you, thank you. It was a good show, wasn't it?" Baal had by now stopped shrinking. He was the size of a grasshopper.

"You see, Baal?" rumbled Yahweh. "Don't get disappointed. Even He didn't have any worshippers at one point."

"Yes, I suppose you're right," cheeped Baal, blowing his nose noisily and looking at his new, much-reduced size. "Maybe I should go to South America. I've always fancied being a beetle god."

"Yes!" shouted the little boy. "A big black beetle with giant pincers and a taste for guts!" Picking up the great god Baal in the palm of his hand, they walked off together, Baal nodding attentively as the little boy spewed out ideas on human sacrifices and colorful headdresses. I noticed that spindly insect legs were beginning to grow out of the sides of Baal's body, and he was already attempting to make a rudimentary clicking noise.

Naturally I had cause to see the little boy again some seventy years later, by which time he had become high priest of the new cult of Baal, which claimed some thirty thousand followers along the foothills of the Andes. The boy now had a beard that reached down to his feet, and a tattoo of a beetle covered his face, chest, and stomach. His faith in Baal had never wavered. Baal was by now back to his old size, if not his old shape. He clacked his pincers loudly over the boy's dead body.

"He was a good boy," roared Baal when he saw me approach.

"Oh? Well then, just out of curiosity," I asked, "why did you bite his head off?"

"He wanted me to," roared Baal. "He said it would instill fear and awe in the others."

"Has it?"

"Oh yes. They're thinking of making it an annual tradition."

I removed the little boy's soul from the old man's body. It immediately turned to Baal.

"Did the blood spurt everywhere like we hoped?"

"Oh yes!" roared Baal.

"Excellent. Now, try to remember to be a little crueler. You can't be kind and gentle all the time, otherwise they'll lose respect for you."

"Right-o," roared Baal, snapping his mandibles happily. "And thank you, little one."

"It was an honor," said the priest as he began to disappear into the Darkness. "Oh, one more thing. I left some sacrifices on the altar. It's your favorite. Virgins."

"You think of everything," roared Baal.

The dilemma of the gods prompted me to think about my own situation. What would happen to me once everything was dead? It seemed improbably far off, even when you considered that I existed outside time, but it was an unsettling thought nonetheless. Would I spend my days vainly scrabbling around the earth, searching carcasses for the odd missed soul? Would I twiddle my thumbs and wait indefinitely for Life to begin again? Or would I in turn be absorbed into the Darkness, folding in upon myself until, with a slight pop, I disappeared into my own ether?

You would have thought that such a vision of utter annihilation would make me happy, but curiously it did not. I found the fact that there would be no one to remember me after I was gone strangely unsettling. Even the thought that I would be sent back to Hell was not as pleasing to me as it had once seemed. I imagined what my own torture might look like, and pictured myself surrounded by the living, unable to extract souls no matter how hard I tried, confronted on all sides by gloating existence and virulent being. It wasn't so terrifying. In fact, it was strangely thrilling, and after a while I grew confused as to whether I was imagining my Hell or my Heaven.

With the rise of monotheism in the western parts of Earth, over two thousand Egyptian and Greek gods were left unemployed, surviving solely on the belief of a handful of eccentrics, occultists, and rebellious teenagers trying to irritate their parents. Some gods offered their services for private functions, and among the wealthy and faithful it became de rigueur to have a god or two attending your dinner parties or bar mitzvahs. The majority, however, emigrated. Many found gainful employment in India, whose large population had always been willing to believe in anything as long as it diverted their minds from the abject misery of their day-to-day lives. Being blue and having lots of arms was generally recognized as a fail-safe way of succeeding there.

Fail-Safe Steps to Divine Popularity: Trunk, Tusks, Tutu.

India had always proved troublesome for me due to the widespread belief in reincarnation. "I want to be a bee," I remember one soul demanding of me after another mass trampling at the Kumbha Mela. "A little honeybee, buzz, buzz, buzzing all around and collecting honey, and if someone tries to stop me, I sting!"

I tried to explain that returns were outside my jurisdiction, but before I could, another one of the dead chimed in, "I want to be a strawberry. Juicy, firm, red! So delicious. The perfect fruit! Make me a strawberry, please!"

And so it went in India—within seconds there would be a cacophony of souls all pleading me to bring them back as their favorite thing. I later found out that most of these souls found themselves being reincarnated into beings that didn't believe in reincarnation at all, which tended to make my bookkeeping easier.

It was a matter of curious timing that, just as my hands were full with the first wave of Hindus, I saw Maud again. She was much changed—taller, darker skinned, not hanging upside down—but I recognized her in an instant. She was one of a tribe of fearsome Amazons who were slowly torturing a rival tribesman. I did not speak, but watched her from a distance, drinking in her every movement. To begin with, Maud caught the tribesman's left hand in her grip, and planting her foot upon her victim's chest, tore the shoulder from its socket. Then she and the others went to work rending his flesh, and slowly but surely his ribs were stripped clean by the Amazons' fingernails. The women began tossing his limbs about with blood-soaked hands, and the screams from the tribesman grew louder and louder until Maud chopped off his head and affixed it to a spear. A knowing smile played across her lips.

I hurried forward to the tribesman's mangled body to uncap his soul, and I felt her eyes on me throughout. As I set the soul free, I suddenly felt her hand touch mine. An onlooker, if one could have seen me, might have thought it no more than an accidental caress, but I knew what it was. I looked up from the dead body, and Maud was staring directly at me.

"Oh, the torture continues, does it?" interjected the soul of the dead tribesman.

"What?" I said, turning to look at him. The spell was broken, but Maud's touch had left me vibrating with excitement.

"I mean, it's not enough to have been tortured in life, I now have to watch this filth when I'm dead?" His soul rolled its lustrous eyes at me.

"What filth?" I asked defensively.

"You know exactly what I mean. All those lovey-dovey eyes between you and her."

"I can assure you that I never so much as . . ."

"Yeah, yeah," snorted the tribesman. "I may come from a stone-age jungle tribe that doesn't have a word for tomorrow, but I wasn't born the day before today."

I blushed. He was right. I turned to see if Maud had overheard, but she and her Amazonian colleagues had smeared one another in the tribesman's viscera and melted back into the forest.

Soon, however, Maud's tribe began to die one by one, poisoned by their food. Some of the Amazons blamed the gods, but since I found Maud waiting by the dead bodies on each occasion, I had a sneaking suspicion she was the one responsible.

"Thanks for the dead," I would bashfully say as I went to work.

"Oh, it wasn't me," she'd reply, fluttering her eyelids in a pretense at innocence.

"I just wanted to see you again," she admitted the next time. "Amazons are so boring. They're always going on about women's op- pression and men being awful, and they insist on chopping off their own breasts, which I don't think really helps their cause. I wanted to talk to you."

Amazons: Boring.

"You'll see me eventually," I said, tapping the *Book*. "Everyone does."

"I know," she said, blushing. "But can't you stay for a moment? Leave her." She gestured at the soul of the poisoned Amazon who glistened in my hands.

"Don't you lay a finger on her," snapped the soul, "unless you want to be eating your meals through a thin, hollow paper tube. Which reminds me, don't eat her soup."

So I left the soul there, and Maud and I walked through the jungle together, ducking under creepers and clambering over fallen trees, she alive, me Death. I cannot recall our conversation now, so light-headed was I, but it ranged across space and time, taking in the dying fashions of the day, and the new and up-and-coming viruses.

"When was the last time you took a day off?" said Maud, her eyes dark in the jungle light.

"Well," I said, "never. Something has always been dying, you know. That's what defines the earth, the fact that everything is always dying."

"And living," said Maud. "Don't forget, we're all living, too. Maybe you should try living one of these days."

I laughed, thinking it a joke, but she seemed serious, and so I imagined how strange it must be to have a soul, to be a part of the union of the living. How odd it must be to live within time and be beholden to a body. How curious to have a finite duration and a vulnerability to sharp objects. But this was mere fantasy. I sighed. Yes, I could console myself with the fact that I was immortal. But I didn't have a Life.

Eventually Maud was caught trying to poison the chief of her tribe and was buried up to her neck in sand to be eaten alive by ants. I had little doubt that she had allowed herself to be caught; this time she didn't want any mistakes. Seeing her name in the *Book* one morning, I cleared out my schedule to watch.

The sun beat down on Maud's face, which had been liberally covered in honey, and thousands of red ants crawled all over her, into her nose, under her eyelids, into her ears. She had never looked so full of Life.

"Oh!" she screamed, "arrrgh!" before winking at me and hissing, "It tickles something awful, though!"

Who was this woman who had no fear of dying? Who seized me with both hands? Who longed to be with me? The remaining

Amazons looked at one another confused. Her head was coated in ants by now, but Maud was giggling uncontrollably, causing the ants to fall from her face.

"Keep still or it'll never be over," I hissed.

"Oh, don't worry about me," spluttered Maud as her face swelled horribly with bites. "I'll be along in a minute."

After she died, we spent the rest of the day walking through the forest hand in hand as before. She showed me how all the plants of the forest were filled with life-giving nectars, and I showed her how a piranha could strip a man to the bone in less than a minute. I was enraptured by her company, intoxicated by her presence. All was going well when suddenly I heard a thunderclap and a deafening voice.

"Death!"

I swung around. Maud gave a little squeak and hid behind me in the edges of the Darkness. It was Gabriel.

"Hello, Gabriel," I said. I hadn't seen him since the void, before the Beginning of Time, but he looked the same, in that never-changing way that angels have.

"I knew you weren't a sheep!" roared Gabriel. His eyes flashed left and right. "Where is she?"

"Where's who?" I replied, trying to exude as much innocence and light as a being of unfathomable blackness could.

"The woman who was meant to be killed by ants. She was due in Heaven three hours ago."

"How did you know she was missing?" I asked. I was curious. I hadn't imagined they kept track of souls to this degree.

Gabriel eyed me suspiciously. "When the records don't balance," he sniped, "the alarms go off."

"Alarms?"

"Then we overturn the barracks, check the barbed wire, and set the angelic bloodhounds to trace the missing soul."

"I thought Heaven was meant to be a pleasant place?" I asked. "You know, clouds and harps."

"Pah!" spat Gabriel. "That's how it used to be done, but the system was soft. Michael was soft. Always worried about his hair. I've made a lot of changes since he . . . disappeared."

"Why?" I asked. "Surely Heaven doesn't need to be changed?"

"It needed a new direction," said Gabriel. "God's not going to live forever, you know."

"Really? Why not?" I asked. He ignored me.

"Something useful should be done with all that eternal salvation. It shouldn't be frittered away singing alleluias and combing one's wings. Something constructive should be done."

"Like what?" I asked. I was genuinely curious.

"Like roads!" cried Gabriel, his eyes glazing over. "And factories, and power plants! Heaven should not be stagnant, it should progress, it should move forward with the times. It's not like Hell, where the same old tortures can be dragged out again and again; thumbscrews never go out of fashion. But salvation needs to move with the times. Perceptions of Paradise don't sit still. Ecstasy must be rationalized."

"When did you go to Hell?" I asked. It was rare for Hell to get angelic visitors, and even rarer to allow one to escape.

"I instigated a cultural exchange," said Gabriel, puffing himself up. "The first one of its kind. I taught them the virtues of goodness, charity, and light, and they opened my mind to technology, computers, and microwave ovens. Your father's been busy since you left. He showed me the wonders of mechanical industry and enforced labor. He's been creating things you could only dream of."

Actually I couldn't dream. It was one of the many things the living had spoken of that intrigued me. It seemed to allow them to travel anywhere, they said, to do anything, to act out their wildest fantasies without any consequence whatsoever. It sounded wonderful.

"Well," I said, shaking such thoughts from my mind, "if you don't mind, I'm very busy . . ."

I made as if to leave, careful to keep Maud hidden in the Darkness, but Gabriel rushed in front of me.

"Don't try to distract me, Death; I can see through the arch-deceiver in you. Where is she?"

Gabriel: Archangel, Messenger, Killjoy.

"I'll tell you what, Gabriel. I'll retrace my steps and see if she slipped out of the void along the way, how's that?"

"You do that," said Gabriel, his beauteous face now close against mine. "I knew from the moment I met you that you were a fake. One of the other side. I don't know how you got the job, but I've been watching you. You may be able to get away with the odd raccoon or two, but not with a human soul. We need them to dig the irrigation ditches. You can never have too many."

"Irrigation ditches? . . . Are you sure you're going about this Heaven business in the right way?" I asked.

"Shut it, you spawn of Satan," snapped Gabriel. I noticed some angelic spittle on his lips. "I know everything about you, Death. Everything!"

"Then how many fingers am I holding up behind my back?" I countered. Maud let out a snarf.

"What?" said Gabriel. "Now?"

"Yes."

"Right at this very second?" said Gabriel. He had put on an air of absurd calm and was beginning to wander back and forth, attempting to peer behind my back.

"Or don't you know?"

"Of course I know. I'm all-knowing."

"I thought only God was all-knowing."

"I am blessed with His power. I can see through all things." He put his fingers to his head. Suddenly he stopped.

"Three!" he shouted. His eyes opened. A smile broke onto his face. I lifted up my hand. Only the middle finger was up. Gabriel turned red in the face.

"She'd better be back by twelve or it's Hell for the both of you!" he cried, and with a flap of his wings he launched himself into space.

Despite my bravado I was somewhat flustered. The moment with Maud had been ruined. We both knew she had to go. A funny thing happened, though. Just as I was spreading the Darkness around her she reached up and kissed me on the cheek, and suddenly vast waves of longing filled my body. I looked down and saw her disappearing, a smile on her face, and tried to drag her back out. But it was hopeless. She was gone.

I stood there motionless, but it felt as if great seas were crashing within my body. I felt unsteady on my feet. What was the meaning of this? I thought. But at the back of my mind I began to think that I knew.

I had heard it said by many of the souls I conveyed into the Darkness that at some point in their lives they had been struck down by an illness that seemed to be endemic in all living things. It was a form of nausea that led to extreme irrationality and a loss of composure. It was an infection both mental and physical, both emotional and chemical. When the souls spoke of it, it was in tones both hated and adored, as if this sickness held them even then in the twilight of their existence, compelling their attention even beyond the confines of Life. It was a plague and a pleasure, a virus and a virtue, a statement and an act.

The souls, they called it "love."

Maudness

꒰•I•꒱

It **was sometime** in the fifth century B.C., and Maud was hanging from the edge of a cliff by a withered tree root.

"I'm going to li-ive," she trilled as she heaved herself upward, hand over bloodied hand. The root trembled under her weight, but it did not break.

"Just . . . one . . . more . . . inch. . . ."

She looked up at me expectantly.

I wasn't quite sure how, but Maud seemed to be appearing on Earth more and more often. Every few years, it seemed, I would find her throwing herself from high things, or placing herself beneath heavy things, or eating poisonous things, or saying rude things to violent angry things, anything, it seemed, to try to get my attention. Sometimes she was a queen, sometimes a peasant. Sometimes she was a blonde, sometimes she was a brunette. Her name changed constantly, but she was always the same, irreducible Maud. She had human companions, of course, but I was the only one who stuck with her to the very end, and beyond. When Maud tried to dash out her own brains on a rock, and only knocked herself unconscious, it was I who was there to deliver the illicit coup de grâce, pounding her skull in until her face was a bloody, broken shell. When Maud failed to ingest enough poison to kill herself, it was I who smeared more on her lips, held fast her gnashing jaws, and forced her to swallow. When her partners failed to honor their end of a suicide pact, creeping away terrified as she repeatedly stabbed herself in the chest with a dagger, it was I who consoled her.

"You know something, Death?" she'd often say. "You just can't depend on the living."

In this life she was a Vestal Virgin and had gleefully let the perpetual fire in the Temple of Vesta go out. As a punishment she had been thrown off this cliff, only to be plucked from my embrace by a pernicious tree root.

"I think," she grunted as she pulled herself up the cliff face, "that I will live to be very, very old." Once again her eyes flicked up to meet mine. She was such a tease. I leaned down and tenderly loosened her fingers one by one.

"You mean to kill me?" she cried seductively. "Help! Help! You swine! You pig! You . . ." She started giggling and, raising a hand to her mouth, lost her grip. A look of mock horror and real excitement played across her face, and then she was gone, plummeting once more to her doom, bouncing off the rocky outcrops, her bones splintering, her skin ripping, her laugh ringing out ecstatically all the way down. Call it foreplay.

We spent the rest of the day haunting the priests who had tried to kill her.

"Call that a sacrifice!" she shouted at them from deep within the Darkness.

"Almighty Vesta!" cried the priests. "We did not mean to anger you."

"You have angered me!" she thundered. "Now you must die."

The priests swallowed hard.

"How shall we die, O Great Vesta?"

"Um . . .," said Maud, before intoning deeply, "by eating the excrement of animals."

I had to clamp my hand over her mouth to prevent the giggles from being heard.

"What?" said the priests.

"You heard me," said Maud, barely able to contain her giggles. "It's animal shit for you. Until you die."

The priests looked at one another.

"But . . .," said the head priest, "but that's disgusting!"

"Do not question the will of the gods."

"But . . ."

"Not another word now."

The priests shifted around uncomfortably, and a few of them started halfheartedly scanning the ground, while Maud and I, hardly able to suppress our laughter, ran away hand in hand.

Why was it that at these, our happiest moments, a lament sounded deep within me? Was it a premonition of what was to come, or was it, as I thought then, merely a side effect of this strange emotion of love?

I had initially thought love to be just another agitation of the human mind, one of the myriad neurochemical activities that seemed to prompt people's passing. Nevertheless, I grew curious about it in a way that I had not with similar human emotions such as faith and hope, anger and fear. Perhaps it was the sheer number of times that love was listed as a contributing cause in the *Book of Endings*. People would kill for more of it, waste away from a want of it, or sacrifice themselves due to a surfeit of it. Love seemed intrinsically linked to all human ends; there was so much of it about, it was no wonder that I worried I had caught a dose of it.

I remember asking Father what love was.

"Sex," he replied.

"That's it?" I asked.

"Well," he said, scratching his horns, "sex and long walks."

I asked Mother the same question. She blushed. "Well, when two people like each other very much . . ."

"Yes," I said eagerly. This sounded more promising.

"They have sex."

When I bumped into Urizel, my old angel friend, who was still guarding the muddy remnants of Eden, I asked him the same question. He pulled out a guidebook entitled *The Only Planet Guide*, and after flicking through a few pages declared, "Love is, on the one hand, a mechanism for surveying and thereby rendering problematic particular relationships between bodies, and on the other the creation of a reflexive consciousness of self-identity involving manipulation of symbolic representations of the self."

"You mean . . .," I asked, as Urizel flicked to the glossary section at the back.

"Sex, apparently."

What Is This "Love"?

I remember I had even asked God about it, back when He had still been around.

"Why do humans 'love,' Lord God Sir?"

"Aside from the sex?" He boomed.

"Yes."

"And the long walks?"

"Yes."

"Well, there are as many reasons for love as there are stars in the sky." God gestured as if to look at the sun. "Is that the time? I really must be off."

There was a pause, but the divine light remained.

"God?" I asked.

The light didn't answer.

"God? I can still see You. You're still here."

"Damn this omnipresence!" He boomed.

But if love was simply about sex, why did I feel it was about so much more?

Maud's increasingly frequent visits provided welcome breaks amid the frantic Classical period. It was an era of great innovation among humans, which always meant plenty of work for me.

In England, the Druids had finally perfected the art of human sacrifice, tenderizing their subjects with a combination of ritual torture and atonal folk singing, and seasoning them with just the right amount of parsley, sage, rosemary, and thyme. Indeed, the Druids greatly popularized sacrificing and were credited with taking it off the altar and into the home.

Druids: Loved to Barbecue.

Elsewhere, legal reforms swept society, such as those instigated by the Greek lawgiver Draco, who devised the "one strike and you're out" judicial system, calling for execution as the punishment for all crimes. Upon seeing the reoffending statistics plummet, Draco came to the conclusion that since all crimes were committed by the living, the only crime-free society would be one consisting solely of the dead. It was an idea way ahead of its time and would have succeeded if only his advisers had not suggested that he lead the way into this peaceful crime-free future. The collective sigh of relief upon his death sank ships as far away as Crete.

Meanwhile an economic revolution was taking place under the guidance of Croesus, the king of Lydia, who had invented coinage and thus made property much easier to steal. I remember overhearing the argument as he tried to persuade his minions to implement the radical changes.

"But this isn't the same as a cow," exclaimed the Master of Barter looking at one of Croesus's gold coins. "Where are its udders?"

"No, it's not *actually* a cow," explained Croesus. "It's worth the same as a cow. This way you don't have to run away with a whole cow when you're raiding the Scythians."

"How can it be worth the same as a cow if it doesn't have any udders?"

"Well, it's like this . . ."

"It doesn't taste like a cow either," grimaced the Master of Barter, biting into the coin. He winced. "It tastes much more painful than a cow."

"No, look . . .," said Croesus, but the Master of Barter was on a roll.

"And where's its tail? No one's going to think this is a cow if it doesn't have a tail."

"Guards!" cried Croesus, whose patience did not extend as far as his credit. The Master of Barter was swiftly garroted, the first of many fiscal tightenings to occur in Lydia that year.

Not far away, artistic developments were being furthered by the insatiably bloodthirsty Assyrian Empire (which had been voted "Best Empire of the Year" for 103 years in a row by subscribers to the *Assyrian Supplicant*, a hung, drawn, and quarterly). Their greatest ruler,

Ashurnasirpal II, had become obsessed with the relationship between the artwork and the viewer in his chosen medium of expression— impaling. Working months at a time, in campaigns ranging far into Asia, he displayed a remarkable aptitude for compositional effects that reduced the distance between spectacle and spectator until one was hard to differentiate from the other.

His finest piece, *Untitled # 65422 (Impaling)*, showed a remarkable sharpness of line and sag of body. It was praised for its figurative suggestiveness and remarkable lack of ambiguity by the Kassites, the Elamites, and the Cimmerians, whose long-preferred oeuvre of "not bleeding" and "avoiding conflict" Ashurnasirpal overthrew during his masterful "red" period.

Dominated by Verticality, Ashurnasirpal's
Unique Visual Rhetoric Was Interformative,
Transfictive, and Very, Very Painful.

Nevertheless, it was the Greeks who best personified this new age of scientific invention and theoretical research. Nowhere was this more the case than at Plato's Academy. Plato was the author of a plethora of popular tracts. *On the Soul, On Sensation, On Respiration, On Top of Old Smokey,* and *On and On with Plato* had all been bestsellers in both slate and papyrus editions. With the profits he had set up his Academy, a safe haven for the philosophically inclined, whom the general populace thought louche, hairy, and prone to saying awkward things at dinner parties. Indeed, Plato's belief that it was only through the method of dialectic that pure reason could operate was openly criticized as being "girlie" by the rival monologist school of Isocrates, who propounded the dictum that the only intelligent conversation one could have was with oneself.

The Academy was home to cutting-edge research in every field. Loud explosions could be heard emanating from the school, as the mathematician Archimedes attempted to calculate his law of buoyancy in a lead-lined bathtub buried deep beneath the ground. Similarly the animal psychologist, Aristophanes, accidentally discovered the world's first joke while inquiring into the hitherto mysterious motivations of pathway-traversing fowl. The results, read out in a paper to the academicians, caused such convulsions (later diagnosed as "laughter" by Hippocrates) that Aristophanes was believed to be a witch and was set on fire.

The philosophers may have thought hard, but they also played hard, and the Academy soon developed a reputation as a wine-soaked party college. Astronomy classes sought to pinpoint those stars that only revealed themselves when the viewer was drunk. Geometry classes attempted to understand the sudden increase in the earth's revolutions after an amphora of wine had been imbibed, while Ethics classes considered the least offensive places in which to vomit (this was also covered in Retcheric).

The debauched lifestyle of the philosophers enraged prudish Athenian society, and when Philip of Opus, the Academy's music instructor, composed a groundbreaking new dirge entitled "Fuck the Polis," battle lines were drawn.

Pericles, himself a great political innovator and the democratically elected dictator for life of Athens, decreed that he would tear down the Academy and construct a giant new building on the site—

Philip of Opus: Philosopha with Attitude.

the Acropolis—which would be open only to idiots and nonthinkers. He even had the Academy's top sage and mixer of drinks, Socrates, imprisoned and sentenced to death for refusing to empty his mind of all thoughts.

As it was, Pericles needn't have bothered. The Academy was ultimately destroyed by a vast explosion, the result of Archimedes' attempts to square the circle, and Socrates died soon after, while attempting to incorporate hemlock into a new drink that he named the "Politan."

When I met Socrates, he was remarkably calm. I asked him how he could be so serene even when facing me, and he replied that he had studied his life and was happy with it.

"The unexamined life," he said, as the Darkness consumed him, "is not worth living."

I didn't have time to ask him about the unexamined Death.

By then almost all the mythical creatures had disappeared, and those that remained were having a hard time adapting to this new, more rational world. The last Sphinx had fled Egypt on a boat to Greece, posing as both the ship's cat and first mate. When it arrived, it immediately became swept up in the philosophical fashion of the country. Combining the incessant questioning that defined the Socratic Method with a healthy carnivorous appetite, the Sphinx came up with a deadly riddle—"What has one voice but walks on four legs in the morning, two legs at midday, and three legs in the evening?"— that it would spring on unsuspecting Greeks as they went about their daily business. Failure to answer correctly, or within the allotted time period, or if there was any pause or hesitation at all, would result in the Sphinx biting the answerer's head clean off.

A frightened populace implored the remaining members of Plato's Academy to come up with a solution to the Sphinx's riddle. Hippocrates, the father of medicine; Herophilus, the father of anatomy; and Galen, the father of experimental physiology, began by removing two limbs from a cow at midday, and then attempting to reattach one of them again in the evening. The results were grisly, and the various solutions to the riddle rarely survived. Work soon shifted to ponies, and then deer, and eventually a collection of hobbled and mutilated animals were paraded in front of the Sphinx. None passed muster, although all were eaten.

Eventually, as the Sphinx's riddle claimed more and more lives, a desperate appeal was sent to Oedipus, the fabled eccentric, who had married his own mother so that he would never have to clean up his bedroom ever again (although it did mean he had to be in bed by seven o'clock). After some thought, a tantrum, and a little surreptitious help from his wife, Oedipus told the Sphinx that the answer was "man" ("an octopus with a limp" would also have been acceptable).

The Sphinx, however, was not satisfied.

"When is a door not a door?" it snapped.

"When it's ajar," replied Oedipus quickly.

"What's brown and sounds like a bell?"

"Dung."

"What's black and white and red all over?"

"A zebra with sunburn."

Oedipus: "Why Don't You Tell Me About Your Mother."

"Why is six afraid of seven?"

"Because seven eight nine."

In desperation the Sphinx finally asked, "What have I got in my pocket?" which was not exactly a riddle according to the ancient rules.

But Oedipus was unfazed.

"You don't have any pockets," he said, and the Sphinx, realizing its era was over, threw itself from its rocky perch to its doom.

I asked it afterward, "Why all the questions?"

"What questions?" it replied.

"All the questions you've been asking?"

"I was asking questions?"

"Weren't you?"

"Was I?"

"Did you just say something?"

"Did I just *slay* something?"

This went on for some time.

Incident at
Golgotha

⛧

I relate all the previous incidents to you to show you that, after an anxious start, I was quite content with my job. I was surrounded by interesting fatalities, a high mortality rate, and the perennial affection of my beloved Maud. So you can see that it was not unhappiness that made me act the way I eventually did; it was quite the opposite. As I watched tribes rise and fall, empires expand and shrivel, species be born and grow extinct, as I listened to countless last words gasped through innumerable contorted mouths I found myself becoming increasingly engrossed in the plot of Life. I saw how thrilling a Beginning and a Middle could be when combined with my usual province, the End. Increasingly I found myself wanting to be swept up in the whirligig of time, to jump and bound on the mortal coil, to leap aboard the crazy merry-go-round. No, it was not unhappiness that undid me, but delight.

I first noticed something was wrong when the date in the *Book* changed, for no apparent reason, to A.D. 1. I flicked to the index— no easy thing in a never-ending volume—and saw that there was a "Help" sigil. No sooner had I drawn the sign in the air with my finger than a fat little cherub winged into view from some far-off part of Paradise and fluttered to the ground in front of me. He looked out of breath and unenthusiastic. I showed him the *Book* and he said it was a "revision in the epoch," a "new eon update," a "Y-zero problem," or some such technical jargon, and that it probably wouldn't affect me in my day-to-day Death. He made me sign a chit and then disappeared. I would soon find out that he was quite wrong—it would affect me very much.

I quickly became distracted from this calendrical peculiarity by the even more peculiar opinions of King Herod of Judea. Herod was entering his dotage and had replaced the sagacity and wisdom of his early years with a paranoid depression centered on the threat posed to his reign by babies.

It was while viewing his own children and their increasing facility at walking and talking that Herod came to the terrifying conclusion that these blubbering bags of mucus, who could barely sit upright and putrefied the air with their effluence, were increasingly coming to resemble actual human beings. Herod's mind spun wild with the consequences. Soon, he ventured, these physical duplicates would not only start to look like real human beings but might take on human jobs, shop at human markets, grow human beards, and go on to be completely indistinguishable from adult human beings.

Whether Herod's madness stemmed from the tortures he had suffered at the hands of his own father—whose sadistic nurturing techniques had seen him labeled "the Antipater"—or whether it was just due to his crown being on too tight cannot be known for certain. But the more Herod walked the streets of Judea, the more his suspicions were confirmed. He saw children everywhere growing larger, heard fathers and mothers claiming that their children "would be the death of them," and saw those same children eventually burying their parents, their faces contorted in adultlike grief. Faced with such evidence, Herod came to the shocking conclusion that if children carried on in this manner they would soon take over the entire world. Gathering his advisers around him, Herod realized that there was only one way to prevent this from happening—kill all the babies in the world.

The Massacre of the Innocents was rather tedious for me, because the souls of babies aren't the greatest conversationalists. At that time I wanted to hear stories of Life, of love, of experience. Instead I got thousands of tributes to breasts, with the only variation being the preference for right or left.

The Horror! The Horror!

So, to set the scene for my downfall: the Romans were up, the Greeks were down, the Jews were in and out of captivity, the Chinese were building walls, and the Aborigines were eating so many colored mushrooms it was doubtful they were even on this planet at all. It was a warm day in the Middle East and I was touring Earth picking up my usual quota of beggars, lepers, princes, merchants, leeks, kestrels, and kumquats when I found myself drawn to the site of a crucifixion. I knew from experience that there's no point loitering around these sites waiting for someone to die because the crucified could linger for days. Indeed, there was one occasion when a crucified man lingered for so long he actually got better and went home.

Nevertheless, on that afternoon one of the crucified didn't look as though He was going to be hanging around for too long at all. He was very pale and had that traditional crucified look on His face— covered in blood, grumpy—but the funny thing was that when I looked in the *Book,* there was no sign of Him. Three people had been crucified that day, yet the *Book* only accounted for the deaths of two of them.

I did a double take. And then a triple one. I could not quite believe what I was seeing. In the millennia of casualties that had come before this, the *Book of Endings* had never made a mistake. It just didn't happen. Admittedly a few folk have had extremely close brushes with me, but I pride myself on knowing a thing or two about when people are going to die. There's a certain look they get that pretty much signals it's my time to shine. Even those who are about to get hit by a bus without knowing it have that look on their faces. It's a reflex look the body gives when it senses Life's end hurtling toward it. It's similar to the kind of look people get when someone hands them a new work project at five o' clock in the afternoon on a Friday. I call it the five o' clock shadow of Death. What I'm trying to say is that I *knew* this guy on the cross was toast, but the *Book* didn't.

Well, this crucified man starts having His side poked by a Roman centurion, and all sorts of blood and water are gushing out, and you could see His guts and He's not moving or saying a word, so I decide—*Book* or no *Book*—I'd better take a look for His soul. But when I checked, it wasn't there. I looked all over, in His spleen, gall bladder, kidneys, appendix, but this guy was as empty as the Darkness.

I looked around the foot of the cross in case it had dropped out, and even retraced His steps just to make sure it hadn't escaped along the way, but not a thing. Now listen. I'm no soft touch. I've dealt with beggars and babies, the weak and the infirm. People have pleaded with me, offered me all manner of bribes—gold, jewels, erotic pottery—to get them off the hook. I've heard it all before, but I don't make exceptions. Admittedly with Maud I bent a few rules, but I never let her live. There was an unspoken agreement between us that that was impossible, and although I had been growing increasingly remorseful at sending her into the Darkness, I never dreamed of *not* doing it. At least not then.

So I stood and scratched my head for a bit as the man's family and friends took Him down from the cross. First He doesn't appear in the *Book*. Then He hasn't got a soul. It was unbelievable. Where had He come from? What was He doing here? Millions of years had gone by and every soul—even the pesky dinosaur souls—had eventually been accounted for. And now some soulless John Doe was about to screw the whole thing up. I looked at Him ruefully as His head was being covered in a shroud and, just for a second, I could have sworn He winked at me! But no, I thought, I must have been seeing things. I looked again and the body seemed still now. Bodies without souls don't wink, I told myself. Then again, bodies should be in the *Book*. I had to get to the bottom of this.

Golgotha, A.D. 33: The (Cruci)fix Was In.

I started off with the usual suspects: the witch doctors, the soothsayers, the desert prophets, the hoodoo bone-men. Occasionally they'd accidentally say the right words in the right order and a certain soul would become sticky, or slippery, and I'd be fumbling with it all over the place. Creation, you have to remember, was somewhat imperfect; update had been added to update, patch added to patch. It wasn't too hard to hack into it with some pretty basic magic.

I cracked a few skulls but turned up nothing on the soulless man and was forced to call off my search as the number of uncollected souls began to build up. As I hurried to attend to a huge cholera outbreak in China, I was briefly waylaid by a random suicide in Jerusalem by the name of Judas. He was one of those remorseful types who wouldn't stop talking about some terrible sin he had committed.

"What sin was that?" I asked absentmindedly.

"I kissed Him," said Judas's soul, before promptly bursting into tears.

"Oh, come on now," I said. "We're not in the Bronze Age anymore."

I had heard his story before. It happened to a lot of first-century men. They sat around and watched the gladiatorial combats, had a little too much wine, shouted a little too loudly, started playfighting, and then, when they didn't know what else to do, began kissing each other.

I tried to tell Judas that these were Classical times, and that lots of men kissed other men, but this didn't seem to calm him down.

"I betrayed Him!" he moaned. This was getting complicated.

"You slept with someone else?"

"I betrayed Him with a kiss," groaned Judas.

"Now, look," I said. "I may be a supernatural force beyond your comprehension, but from what I've seen of humankind, a kiss doesn't mean anything. These days it doesn't even count as cheating. You were just . . . trying out other options."

Judas sniffed and ran a hand under his nose. "But there are no other options. He was the one true Lord!"

Whoever Judas's boyfriend was, He had really done a number on him.

"You were a fisherman weren't you, Judas?" He certainly smelled like it. "What's that old saying: 'There's plenty more fish in the sea'?"

"But He was the Almighty."

Admittedly I may not have known a lot about love, but I knew a sap when I saw one. If only I had paid more attention to him, I could have saved myself a lot of trouble. But I was in a rush, and he was dead, so I heaved his soul into the Darkness without a second thought.

The case of the missing soul weighed heavily on me the next day. Since it wasn't logged in the *Book of Endings*, I couldn't get into any trouble, but I had no doubt that Gabriel would hear about it sooner or later. I had a strange feeling. It felt like someone was walking over my grave, even though this was impossible on a number of metaphorical levels. I was so perturbed by the lost soul that I even popped in to see Father, just to make sure there hadn't been some prearranged sale that he'd been hiding from me.

Following his flirtation with radical socialism in Heaven, Father had rejected the foibles of his youth and embraced capitalism. He had taken to buying souls as investments, to sell to other demons for torture, and his recent founding of the Soul Exchange allowed him to set the price of souls according to their sins. Venial sinners were cheap, since their torture was usually limited to blunt, manual, rust-free instruments, while mortal sinners carried a premium, demon buyers much preferring the wide scope such malefactors allowed in terms of general all-round nastiness. During times of virtue—when miracles and good weather led people to believe all was well with the world—sinful souls skyrocketed in value. In times of war or political elections, there was always a sin surplus, and the sinner would be quite unable to sell his soul for love, money, or even halfway decent guitar-playing skills.

As the years went by, the sin trade grew more complex. You could now buy malefactor-backed insecurities, or trade on the eternal transgression markets. Futures could be bought in the yet-to-be-damned, and slightly tainted souls were packaged together into heavily doomed bonds. Such was the rampant speculation that a "Sin Bubble" was created, a huge monstrous sphere of evil that ended up crushing Hell's investors against the Soul Exchange's spiky walls, leading to rapid deflation.

On the Floor of the Soul Exchange,
Insider Trading Was Rife.

Many changes had been wrought in my absence from Hell. The gates now opened automatically, and the vast fields of the damned that I remembered had been subdivided into uncountable personal hells. There was a Hell of Stones, in which pickaxed demons smashed stones into gravel. The Hell of Gravel lay next to it, in which gravel was smashed into pebbles. While in the Hell of Pebbles, which lay next to that, pebbles were ruthlessly mocked by larger stones— pebbles being notoriously insecure about their size.

There were tiny hells for the claustrophobic, huge hells for the agoraphobic, and a spacious antechamber reserved for Oscar Wilde, in which the great wit was scheduled to be seated at a mammoth dinner table populated by everyone who had ever chosen him as a hypothetical dining companion. In the distance I vaguely caught sight of a Unicorn being chased across a rainbow by a horde of prepubescent girls who were pulling at his mane and tail and squealing at him to let them ride him. "I think I'm going to be sick!" I heard him cry. "Fuck off, you little turds. Leave me alone!"

I arrived at the Palace of Pandemonium and was directed to my father's office. He was sitting behind a vast obsidian desk and immediately asked me whether I was there about the sub-damned soul debacle.

"Father?" I said. "It's me. Death."

I could almost hear the vast, fiery Rolodex of his brain twirl, and then he remembered.

"Oh," he said. He picked up a large cigar. "What are you doing here?"

I told him that I had come upon a body without a soul and wondered if he was in any way responsible. He mused over this news with a frown.

"Humans without souls? This is very worrying. Very worrying indeed. The damage this could do to the market is incalculable, and our synthetic souls are nowhere near ready yet."

"Have you come across anything that could explain this?" I asked.

He stood up and paced the room deep in thought, before leaning back on a filing cabinet that snorted and reared beneath him. Something seemed to be troubling him. He said that he had recently been tempting people in the desert, where it's much easier to buy a soul at a knock-down price. He boasted that he could regularly pick up a soul for little more than some water and a sunhat. He paused again, playing with his flames.

"But there was one man . . ."—an unfamiliar look of discomfort played across Father's brow. According to Father, this one man had claimed to be the Son of God. This was hardly an original proposition at the time. Hundreds of people were popping up every day claiming to be Nephews of God, Second Cousins of God, Old School Friends of God, People Who God Owed Money To, and so on. Such fantasists were grist to Father's infernal mill. He said he liked to tease them by asking them to do miracles—turning rocks into water, throwing themselves onto the top of tall buildings—all the usual temptations. To begin with, this man seemed to be following the pattern of other so-called Messiahs. He was coming up with all sorts of excuses as to why He couldn't use His "powers." Usually these ran the gamut of medical reasons ("I've got a headache") or mystical reasons ("because it's a big secret") to spur-of-the-moment explanations ("your orange sun saps my strength").

"Usually I barely have to try," said Father, shrugging his giant shoulders. "It's like shooting fish in a barrel. But with this one it was different."

"How was it different?" I asked.

"Well, He turned down every offer I made for His soul, even my good ones. I offered Him wealth, and power, and always having the exact change on you, but He wouldn't budge at all. He said that I'd never get His soul out and started giggling. And when I asked if I could just take a look at it, He got all defensive and ran off."

"What was His name?" I asked.

"I don't know," said Father. "Whenever I put the contract for His soul in front of Him, He kept drawing crosses on it as if it was all a big joke. And all the while . . ." His voice died off.

"What is it, Father? Tell me."

"Well," said Father. "All the while I was tempting Him, He just kept winking at me."

Could Father's winker be the same as my winker? Thoughts raced through my mind, and I left Father in an unusually anxious state. I was heading for the gates when I felt a hand on my shoulder.

"Master Death?"

"Hello, Reginald."

He looked terrible. His feathered wings were even filthier than before, the bags under his eyes more pronounced.

"It's . . . it's really very, very good to see you again," he said slowly. "How are you?"

"Actually, I'm a little busy right now, Reginald."

"Of course you are, Master Death, of course you are. I was just wondering if you could see your way toward helping me finally get out of here. You don't know what I've been going through." I saw Uncle Puruel stick his head out of Reginald's ear, wave to me, and then crawl back inside. Reginald didn't flinch, although his eyes grew watery.

"Look, Reginald, once I've dealt with this, I'll see what I can do."

"Oh thank you, Master Death, thank you. Do you know how long it might—"

"Good-bye, Reginald," I said.

Things were growing very strange indeed. Could the obstreperous being that Father had met in the desert be the same as my soulless body? Upon returning to Earth, I decided to go and visit the corpse to see whether I could pick up any clues. However, I was somewhat shocked upon my arrival to find that the cave in which my soulless body had been buried was empty. This wasn't particularly unusual. Many people did strange things with bodies after the soul had left, but I didn't normally concern myself with that. What worried me was that I might now never be able to solve the mystery. I was leaving the cave, feeling disconsolate, when I heard a hiss come from a nearby bush. This was odd, as bushes are usually quite polite. I walked over to it and who should suddenly spring to His feet but the soulless man Himself!

"Surprise!" He beamed.

He was very much alive. In fact, He seemed completely healed, barring the holes in His hands through which He kept peering at me in a rather disconcerting manner.

"How can You see me?" I asked.

"Well," He beamed, "I look at you and there you are."

"Where's Your soul?"

"Wouldn't you like to know!" He beamed at me. "I guess you didn't do your job very well, did you?"

"What are You?" I asked. "Some kind of god? A zombie?" He didn't look like a god. Gods are vain. They like to have manicures and haircuts, and this guy was a mess. Similarly, He was much chattier than your average zombie. "If You are, You know the rules; You've got to be in the *Book* or on Olympus."

"Oh, but I am in the *Book*," beamed the man. "Just not yours."

Winker.

He was beginning to irritate me.

"Well, look, why don't You come over here, let me take Your soul, and we can forget all about this."

"You'll have to catch me first!" He beamed, and started running away, looking over His shoulder at me and squeaking with excitement. And so it was that I found myself chasing a bearded madman halfway across Jerusalem. The strange thing was that no matter how fast I was, He was always a bit faster, ducking, diving, and parrying my grasp.

"Blessed be My feet!" He beamed as He vaulted a table of vegetables in the market. "Blessed be My athletic prowess!"

I don't feel fatigue. It's one of the benefits of being a supernatural creature, along with good cheekbones, yet there was something incredibly exhausting about this pursuit. No matter how fast I moved, He was always just one step ahead of me, taunting me. Eventually I lost track of Him in a bazaar.

The whole thing didn't make any sense. If people stopped having souls and their bodies took to resurrecting themselves, then Life would become just a meaningless charade. With no restrictions, no finitude, Life's precious fragility—the exquisite mortal balancing act that engenders all the wonders of existence—would be overturned.

The dying leaves, the growing plants, the fluffy puppies—all were delightful *because* of their tenuous survival. Yes, I suddenly realized, I liked Life just the way it was. Really liked it. And now some born-again joker without a soul was threatening it? Didn't He realize what He was doing? No soul? It was ridiculous! After all, if no one ever really died, what would become of me?

The following week I was busy taking the soul out of a small lizard who had been trampled in a crowd, when I heard a familiar voice. Looking up, I saw the crowd that had done the trampling had converged around none other than the soulless man. He was standing on the side of a mountain, beside four rather pale-looking men, who kept giving one another nervous sideways glances.

"Cower, mortals!" beamed the soulless man to the multitude. "On your knees! On your bellies! Get on the ground and crawl to Me!" There was some consternation among the listeners, and the four pale men conferred in hurried whispers. One of them quickly stepped forward and addressed the crowd.

"What His Lordship means is 'Blessed are the meek, for they shall inherit the earth.'" The crowd let out a sigh of relief. The soulless man raised His arms to the throng.

"Hideous mortals! You are fit to eat nothing but My feces and drink nothing but My urine!" There was even greater dismay in the crowd, and the four pale men, sweating profusely, huddled around together once more.

One of them was eventually pushed forward. "Wh . . . what His Lordship means is, 'Blessed are you that hunger, for you shall be satisfied.'" There was a low murmur of disbelief from the crowd.

"Or perhaps you'd prefer to take a bite out of Me?" continued the soulless man, ranging wildly in front of the crowd, offering out His arms. "Go on, take a bite. Get your free blood of Christ! Get your free body of Christ!"

One of the pale men fainted. The crowd burst into uproar. One of the pale men desperately tried to calm them down.

"That's all for this week. Thanks for coming. We'll be telling you what His Lordship *really* meant by that last . . . bizarre . . . statement next week. Do please try and come. I'm sure you're all dying to know. Holy Grails are available from Luke, shrouds from Matthew—they're lovely, Italian-made, get 'em while they're damp—and once John recovers, he'll be selling nails from the cross. Perfect for hanging pictures. Thank you, you've been a wonderful audience. Good night!"

The Sermon on the Mount, or the Rant in the Levant?

The crowd slowly began to disperse, leaving me standing there, amazed and a trifle scared at what I had just heard. Just then the soulless man who had called Himself Christ caught sight of me, leapt in the air, clicked His heels, and skipped away.

This time, though, He would not get far. I cornered Him in an alleyway in Jerusalem and walked toward Him slowly, giving Him the whole talk of how I was inevitable and how He could not escape, when suddenly He shut his eyes, put His hands together, and smugly murmured, "Beam Me up, Daddy."

And with that He shot into the sky and was gone in an instant. A horde of the newly devout began wailing around me in ecstasy. I stood there for a moment, shocked, and then it all clicked. The immortality, the arbitrary nature, the capitalized letters at the start of pronouns—God was back.

Paradise

I had never been to Heaven before, and many of the signposts along the way had been defaced or bent the wrong way, so it took me longer to get there than I had originally anticipated. All the while I was seething inwardly. Yes, I knew that God was the great Creator; yes, I knew that without God none of this would exist—including myself—but why on Earth was He meddling in this way with Life, the Life that I understood and cared for? It wasn't as if God had been all that interested over the last few eons. And now He thought He could just send one of His manifestations round to screw everything up!

When I finally arrived in Heaven, I was surprised to find it ringed around with a wall covered in spray-painted, Kabbalistic graffiti. Why did Heaven need a wall? To stop people getting in, or to prevent them getting out? The reforms Gabriel had boasted of centuries ago seemed to be well under way.

I eventually found the gates. Just looking at them reminded me of my childhood. Admittedly they weren't made out of the bones and organs of a thousand tormented creatures, nor did they scream when they opened, but they had hinges and bars and that was good enough for me. Standing in front of the gates was a large angel wearing pince-nez and poring over a book that looked very similar to the *Book of*

Endings. A badge clipped to his white robe read HI, I'M . . . PETER. Behind him sat an older female angel. She was knitting furiously.

"Next," he said without much enthusiasm.

"I'm here to see God," I said.

"Oh, you are, are you?" said Peter, a condescending smile playing on his lips.

"Yes," I said.

"Who is it?" screeched the female angel.

"Apparently he wants to see God, Mother."

Peter's mother took one look at me and sneered. "Leave him alone," she screeched at me. "Peter, come and cut my toenails."

Peter gave a visible shudder.

"Look," I said, "I'm Death. I really need to speak to Him."

"Death, eh?" said Peter. "A little out of your neck of the woods, aren't we?"

"There's been a problem, one of yours, I think."

"I doubt that very much," said Peter. "Problems aren't really what we're all about. Up here there are nothing but solutions and explanations. We leave problems to your father's lot. What was the name of this problem?"

"I'm not too sure. He had a beard and sandals."

"Well, I'm sure that's not going to be hard to find, is it now?" said Peter sarcastically. "I mean, that only happens to be *the* look of the era."

"Yes, I see your point. He did mention the name 'Christ,' though. Ring any bells?"

"Jesus Christ!" blurted Peter.

"I didn't get a chance to find out His first name."

"Are you sure?"

"Very sure."

"Oh dear, oh dear," said Peter. "He must have escaped again. Hold on, I'll show you in."

Avoiding the withering looks of his mother, Peter swung the gates open.

"Take note," said Peter with forced gravitas, "the celestial spheres, the sound of the Universe in motion." An electric door chime sounded as we stepped inside.

"Behold," he continued, "the Elysian Fields." Some rather tatty and overgrown grassland lay ahead of us. It was covered in litter.

"Hark, the heavenly jubilee and loud hosannas." An out-of-tune trombone played somewhere in the distance.

"It's not very good, is it?" I said.

Peter looked at me irritably. "We're going through a transitional period," he said, and led me on.

My first impression of Heaven was that it was like a rather run-down casino, but without any gambling; just tinkling noises, watered-down drinks, stained carpets, and a lack of clocks. The clouds on which it was perched seemed threadbare, and shabby, like they hadn't been changed in a while, and everywhere you could see that numerous theological loopholes had been patched up with clashing doctrine.

Heaven, in the Brochure.

We strode onward, Peter leading the way, through an area in which giant filing cabinets, miles high and miles wide, were attended to by distinctively gray angels.

"I didn't think there'd be clerks working up here."

"This section is Clerk Heaven. There are millions of people on Earth who would think it wonderful to be a clerk," sniffed Peter over his shoulder.

I heard a scream, followed by a cry of exultation.

"What was that?"

"That's Flagellant Heaven," said Peter. "They're whipped regularly and for all eternity."

"You mean there's whipping in Paradise?" I said.

"There are thousands of people on Earth who would think it wonderful to be whipped," said Peter. He sounded less convincing this time.

"But isn't that sinful?" I asked.

"No actually, quite the opposite. As long as you're not enjoying it *too* much."

"So they're not enjoying being in Heaven?" I said. I was finding all this rather hard to take in. At least in Hell you knew where you stood, which was usually neck deep in shit.

"Well," Peter paused. "I imagine there are a handful of people on Earth who would think it wonderful to be here and not enjoy it." He smiled weakly.

In the distance I saw a vast pyramid of angels balancing on the end of a pin.

"It's a favorite hobby up here," explained Peter. "I believe the record is some six hundred thousand." There was a sudden cacophony, a lot of frantic arm waggling, and what sounded like thirty-two thousand feather pillows falling on top of one another.

We continued on our way. I noticed that behind almost every cloud bank lay large ragged holes cut in the clouds. Circles of angels two or three hundred deep gathered around them. They all seemed to be peering at something far below. Despite Peter's best attempts to guide me away from them, I pushed through one of the crowds and saw that the holes gave rather good views of the damned in Hell. The angels were thrusting one another aside to get a better view.

"What's going on?"

"Well, okay, this is a sticky one," admitted Peter. "Part of the happiness of the blessed consists in contemplating the torments of the damned. It heightens their awareness of their own bliss, you see?"

"Doesn't this detract from their happiness?" I asked, watching people jockey for better positions. "I mean, they have to pity them, right?"

"Oh no," said Peter shaking his head. "The sense of their own escape far overcomes the sense of another's ruin. Justly inflicted pain is rare on Earth."

I looked at the saved and saw them grinning at one another, swamped with satisfaction. It was strange, but the more I looked at them, the more the angels in Heaven bore a striking resemblance to the devils in Hell. Some of them had even slicked back the feathers on their wings to resemble scales, while others had actually affixed fake horns, which flashed red, to their heads. They wore their harps slung low and spoke with a distinctive hellish accent. A couple even flicked their cigarettes at Peter as we passed. He pretended not to notice.

On we strode through Heaven's wide expanse. We passed a giant blackboard, on which were marked an array of arrows and circles, shaded triangles, and interlinked geometric shapes. Many parts had been rubbed out, and in the midst of it all somebody had scrawled JESUS WAS HERE.

"What's that?" I asked.

"That," said Peter, "is the Grand Scheme of Things."

"It looks rather messy," I said, trying to make sense of it.

"So are Things," said Peter coldly.

The clouds became thicker and began to reach up to our waists. Suddenly I heard a yelp, and sweeping the clouds away, I saw that I had stood on a baby angel with little feathery wings. I brushed more

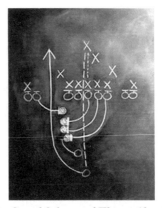

The Grand Scheme of Things (detail).

clouds away and saw that the floor of Heaven was littered with them. The baby angel I'd stood on began to cry, and Peter swiftly picked it up and began rocking it back and forth in his arms.

"Coochie-coochie-coo," he said to it, before turning to me. "We've got to make it quiet, otherwise . . . too late!"

From all around us the sound of weeping and sobbing slowly emerged. At first there were only a handful, but more and more joined the choir, until thousands of squeals and wails began to pulverize our senses. It was an unstoppable waterfall of caterwaul. I had heard much bawling in my existence, but the sheer intensity of this was horribly new.

"What are all these babies doing here?" I shouted to Peter as we broke into a run. He flung the baby he had been coddling into a cloudbank.

"We call this the Field of Screams. You know how high infant mortality is," yelled Peter over the thundering waves of crying. "At least fifty percent of the total population of the dead are babies at the moment, and since they died before committing a transgression, we get stuck with them. Gabriel has been talking about making gurgling a sin, but I don't think it'll get through Parliament."

Eventually the crying died away and we came to a vast building.

"Regard," said Peter hurriedly, as we swept inside, "the magnificence of the Parliament of Heaven." Inside, gray corridors led on to gray rooms. The ceilings were exceedingly low. But from somewhere inside the building emanated an unmistakable dazzling light. Peter ushered me into a small antechamber and said we had to wait. I was not the only one there to talk to God, it seemed. I recognized Job talking to what seemed like a heavenly advocate.

"Why am I still covered in sores?" he whined. "I mean, what kind of Paradise is this?"

Across from him sat Diogenes complaining to another advocate that he had lived in a barrel throughout his life, and that it seemed somewhat unfair to have to do so in Heaven, too.

"I mean, a life of self-sufficiency and poverty meant something on Earth, but isn't it rather beside the point up here?"

Eventually a heavenly page beckoned us inside. The main chamber was much larger than I had expected. Lining either side of the room were rows of benches on which hundreds of angels sat or stood, shouting and singing frantically at one another. It was mayhem. Feathers flew in the air, and I had to duck on numerous occasions as angels swooped overhead, dropping reams of parchment behind them. At the far end of this maelstrom stood a throne on which hovered the unmistakable blinding white light of God. Gabriel stood to His left, signing pieces of parchment frantically and shouting orders to the cherubs that swarmed around Him. God looked displeased. Jesus slouched in His chair to the right hand of God with His fingers in His ears. An argument had obviously just taken place.

I would later appreciate that God's biggest problem was that He inhabited everything. Therefore, when He argued with something, He was really arguing with Himself. Jesus took full advantage of this.

"You shouldn't have done that, Jesus," boomed God.

"No, *You* shouldn't have done that, Daddy," beamed Jesus.

"Call Me God when We're in company."

"Are You speaking to Yourself again?"

"No, I'm speaking to You. Job was very upset when You suggested he learn to like his boils."

Jesus started slapping His own face. "Stop hitting Yourself!" He beamed at God.

Jesus and God: Sometimes They Sulked for Hours.

"Ghost! Ghost!" boomed God.

From out of the corner of the room came a thin white emanation that looked rather like a torn bedsheet.

"Yes, Lord."

"Will You kindly take My son to His room?" boomed God.

"But He never listens to Me," bewailed the Holy Ghost.

"Of course not," beamed Jesus, "You're Him."

"No, I'm *not*," bewailed the Holy Ghost, and then, noticing an inquiring expression emanating from the blinding white light who was all things, swallowed embarrassedly.

Peter took this moment to cough and introduce me. "My Lord, Death is here to see You."

The vast blinding emanation seemed to turn toward me.

"Why, hello, Death. Long time no see. As you can see, I just couldn't stay away. The creeping things called out to Me. Anyway, what brings you here?"

"Well, Lord God Sir, it's Him." I pointed to where Jesus had been, but He had disappeared from His chair. I looked around and saw Him hiding behind God's light sticking His tongue out at me.

"Him," boomed God. "He's My great new direction for Heaven, if only He'd learn to control Himself a little. I know, I know, I am too indulgent. But He is My only child after all. What's He been getting up to?"

"He's been pretending to be human, Lord God Sir," I said.

"Ah, yes," boomed God. "I let Him take human form every now and then. He gets so bored here in Heaven. You know how it is with children. Anyway, I'm sure whatever He did can be cleared up in a jiffy."

"I don't think so, Lord God Sir. He was telling people they should *eat* Him. I think He might have started an epoch-changing religion. Look at the *Book*." I showed Him the date change, and the emanation of light seemed to rub what might have been its chin.

"Hmmmm," God boomed, and looked toward Jesus, who was by now making parchment airplanes and throwing them at me.

"He was acting like some kind of candyman-cannibal god, God. I mean, getting people to eat you? Come on. It's crazy. So, You see, O Lord, I really think You should step in and do something before the humans get too worked up about it."

"Don't worry, Dad," beamed Jesus. "I'm sure they'll all forget about it soon. Man is but grass, You know."

"No, he's not," I blurted. "He's taller, less green, and doesn't photosynthesize. Grass is but grass." I turned to God. "How can You just sit there and let this happen?"

As soon as I said these words I regretted them. One should never underestimate a parent's love for his or her child (especially if that child happens also to be the parent).

"Do you not think that I knew this would happen, Death?" boomed God with slightly more irritation than I would have preferred. "Do you not know this was foreseen?"

"Of course I knew You knew God, it's just that—"

"Through His death"—the divine light gestured at Jesus—"all mankind shall be redeemed."

"But He didn't even die," I squeaked.

"Yes, I did," beamed Jesus. "You saw Me."

"You winked at me," I countered. "That's not dying, that's pretending. And besides, if You were dead, why were You running around asking everyone in Jerusalem to poke their fingers into Your side?"

"My son's sacrifice," boomed God, who didn't seem to be listening to me anymore, "has saved mankind from original sin."

"But—"

"He paid for the sins of mankind through His blood, through His sacrifice." Jesus was just sitting there grinning; the argument between the two of them was forgotten.

"But—"

"Through the sacrifice of His blood," boomed God, "the torture of His body, He redeemed mankind through His sacrifice. Do you understand, Death? Do you understand the meaning of sacrifice?"

Something inside me snapped.

"What is it with You and sacrifices?" I shouted. "Sacrifice, sacrifice, sacrifice! Don't get me wrong, I love dead things, they're my whole Life, but You're obsessed. Why can't You do anything without something dying first? Do You get some kind of perverse pleasure out of that? Why do You want everything to die before it reaches Paradise? And why do You insist on showing Your power and majesty through earthquakes, disease, and flooding? Why are You always killing things? What is it, exactly, that You've got against Life?"

The angels in the main hall of the Parliament fell silent. I felt Peter inching away from my side. Jesus sat up in His throne, a look of smiling disbelief on His face. I felt a peculiar sensation in my belly.

"He's gone wrong," beamed Jesus.

"You have gone a bit strange," boomed God, eyeing me carefully. "What's all this talk about 'my whole Life'? You don't have a Life. That's your whole point, isn't it?"

I didn't know what to say. He was right. What was I talking about? Why should I care if things were sacrificed or not?

"And only the other day," continued God, "Gabriel was telling us about certain irregularities concerning your souls. What do you have to say to that?"

I didn't know what to say. The whole Parliament was now listening intently.

"Perhaps I can refresh your memory," said Gabriel, stepping forward, his voice like poisoned honey. "We've been auditing the souls you sent us, Death, and we've found quite a few discrepancies. Numerous examples of souls turning up late, or, on one or two unforgivable occasions, early."

A murmur rang through the angelic audience. Gabriel began to stalk back and forth in front of God. God was now viewing me with cold detachment. Jesus clapped His hands together in excitement and drew His knees up beneath His chin.

"Got an eye for the ladies have we, Death?" thundered Gabriel.

There was much angelic muttering.

"Do you scratch their backs if they scratch yours?"

There was uproar in the chamber. Salaciousness was obviously a prized commodity in Heaven.

"Oh, very droll, Gabriel!" boomed God. "You're so much better at this than Michael was."

"Or should I say *slap* their backs?" continued Gabriel, a grimace of satisfaction playing on his lips. He turned to face me. "Some have been wondering whether the human known as 'Dido, Queen of Carthage' threw herself onto her funeral pyre or whether she was pushed. You know how these little things mean a lot to us, don't you, Death? With one she's saved; the other, she's damned for all eternity."

Happy Days with Maud.

I lowered my gaze. I could still remember the arch of Maud's back beneath my hand, her arms thrown joyfully in the air, that go-hither look in her eyes as she was enveloped in the flames, her skin bubbling and bursting, her attendants running frantically around her. Oh Maud! How I wished you were with me now.

"If you admit that you gave her a little push, she'll be saved, you know," said Gabriel. "She'll be able to spend the rest of her days in Paradise. Of course, you will be condemning yourself to extinction, but of course, is that not what *sacrifice* is all about?"

Gabriel turned obsequiously to God and bowed. A smattering of applause sounded through the Parliament.

It was all so absurd. Why did it matter if she fell or if she was pushed? Didn't the forces that ruled the Universe have anything better to do than quibble over the final destination of some poor girl's soul?

"We found a handprint on the back of her soul, you know," said Gabriel, eyeing me carefully.

For the first time in my existence, I believe, I felt terror.

"But," said Gabriel, unable to draw a reaction from me, "it was indistinct. You didn't by any chance . . . help her on her way, did you?

Maybe she was taking too long, being too indecisive, and you gave her a little . . . boost?"

I shook my head in denial. It was all I could do. In front of me, God, Jesus, and the Holy Ghost huddled together until they seemed to merge into one being—a blindingly bright bedsheet with a beard. They separated and stared long and hard at me.

"You are dismissed for now," boomed God. "But don't go leaving Earth anytime soon. We'll be keeping an eye on you."

As I hurried away, out of the Parliament, I heard a voice shout, "Jesus reigns in Heaven, bitch!" It was followed by the sound of a somewhat muted slap, as of a high five being performed between a ghost and a man with holes in the palms of His hands.

I stepped outside onto the cloudbanks and felt something trickling down my forehead. It was thick with perspiration. I was stunned. I had never sweated before. Only living things sweated and I wasn't. . . .

Suddenly I felt incredibly claustrophobic. The entire Universe stretched before me and yet I felt hemmed in by a monstrous, arbitrary feeling. I wanted to get back to Earth, away from this infinite inhumanity. I wanted to be surrounded by Life again, the dirty, doomed Life that I knew so well, where no one was all-knowing, where you could only be in one place at a time, where when you were dead, you stayed dead.

I stared frantically at the fields of screaming babies, the peepholes into Hell, the flagellants' chambers, the thousands of angels balanced on the head of a pin.

I had to get out of there right away.

Addicted to Life

⊹⊱•⊰⊹

Back on Earth I was wracked with doubt. What meant this endless procession of nights and days wherein I moved as if I had some useful purpose? Why was I forced to eradicate the things that made me happy? But in that question lay the real problem. Why was I trying to be happy at all? Ah, Life! That cursed bright flower had already thrust its roots deep within my being.

How I wished that I had the possibilities offered by even the most meager of human lives. The thrill of walking the tightrope of existence, of being in time, being in peril, being in the wrong, being in over one's head, being in love. But being, it seemed, was not within my range.

The sight of a scarlet battlefield, which in the past had inspired in me a heightening of the senses, now seemed a dull and sterile prospect. Was it that I was bored? Once you have sent a billion importunate souls into the hereafter it would seem only natural to become jaded. But I knew what troubled me was something more than just otherworldly weariness. The act of freeing a soul from a particularly mangled corpse began to disgust me. I even began to look away when scooping out the soul. Coupled with the physical revulsion was the nausea of moral uncertainty I now felt. It had suddenly occurred to me that it might not be all that pleasant to die. After all, you didn't die when you were ready; there were no announcements, no invitations, nothing. One moment you were on Earth and the next you were gone. It was all very depressing.

Why was I always finishing things, never starting them? I longed for new beginnings, not old endings. It was hardly surprising that I should begin to wonder whether I should retire; or rather, whether I *could*.

What, though, were my prospects? I supposed I could return to Hell, but the gates were now automatic and needed no guarding, and the very thought of working for Father buying and torturing souls sickened me.

It was then, faced with the futility of my situation, that I began having mad, foolish thoughts. I started imagining Maud and myself sitting in a buttercup field, plucking up the kisses that grew upon our lips, with the sun streaming down and the buttercups singing to us in their strange buttercup language. We would put our heads down deep in the flowers and luxuriously follow the activities of the tiny insects crawling here and there in the forest of grass. And when the sun grew too hot, we would go into the woods where bluebells blanketed our every step. And we would be full in the completeness of our love, happy in the oneness of our being, and hopeful, one day, of seeing a little Death stumble into the world.

It was mad, but I just couldn't shake it. I was Death, Destroyer of Life, and all I wanted was a cottage by a stream, a pot of hot soup on the stove, and someone to love me. I was emptiness incarnate, but I wanted to fill the void that was my being. Almost against my will I found myself collecting living things. I kept the souls of dead puppies just inside the Darkness so that no one could see them, and whenever I had a spare moment I would play with them. Yes, it was mad. Yes, it was obscene. But my hands started to shake with excitement when I held and stroked their soft, plush hair. I kept telling myself that an understanding of Life was fundamental in understanding myself. But who was I kidding? I was hooked deep. The monkey was on my back, and I didn't even realize it. I was chasing the wizard and riding the dragon and thinking it was fine. It would take me many years to admit what I now know for sure.

I was addicted to Life.

I don't know whether I had become more sensitive, or whether I was being tested in some way, but a sudden surge in dying helped me momentarily focus on my work and push these troubled thoughts to the back of my mind. It was the Romans who were largely responsible for this boom in dying. Never before in the field of human conflict had so much blood been spilled from so many by so few. Not only were the Roman soldiers equipped with the latest Iron Age weapons—iron filings to blind the enemy, branding irons to scald the enemy, clothing irons to rapidly de-crease the enemy—but they were also extraordinary trainers of war animals. After bombarding an enemy for days with lettuces and other greens, the famed War Tortoises of the Ninth Legion would be unleashed, creatures famed for the exceedingly slow but unstoppable swathe they cut through enemy lines. Looking back on it, I marvel at the Romans' ingenuity, but at the time the sight of a soldier being slowly masticated gave me the shivers.

The Dread Roman War Tortoise: One Hundred Feet
Long, Sixty Feet High, Lapsed Vegetarian.

The Roman engineers were no less brilliant. They defeated the underground kingdom of Carthage—so long a thorn in Rome's side—by first raising it to the ground and then destroying it. What's more, the bloodthirstiness of the average Roman citizen was unequaled. Orgies mingled with executions, wine with poison. It was a bloodbath, a slaughter sauna, a Jacuzzi of gore.

The Roman leaders were extremely difficult to deal with. I remember the indecisiveness of Julius Caesar when he was faced with crossing the Rubicon. Thousands stood ready to be slaughtered, and I had steeled myself for the task, but Caesar was mystified as to how he could transport his pet chicken, pet fox, and pet bag of grain across the river in his little one-man boat without the fox eating the chicken or the chicken eating the grain. As it was, the fox died of dropsy, the chicken was sacrificed, and the bag of grain was eventually made praetor by the emperor Caligula shortly before being eaten by Consul Incitatus, the emperor's horse (the children's song "Old Caligula Had a Senate" was one of the most popular of the age).

If they weren't being indecisive, the Roman emperors were paranoid delusional.

"Who sent you?" asked Emperor Tiberius when I appeared to his soul.

"No one," I said, through gritted teeth. "I am Death."

"Was it Naevius Sutorius Macro? Or Tiberius Gemellus? Yes, yes, my own grandson, he sent you, didn't he?" He drew out his sword's soul from the soul of its scabbard and waggled it in front of my face. What was I doing here?

"Now look," I said, struggling to instill some understanding into the man, although finding it hard enough to convince myself. "I am the End of Days, the Destroyer of All Things!"

"Or was it Gaius Caligula?" continued Tiberius, pacing back and forth frantically. "Yes, he would do something like this."

"Do something like what?" I said. My patience was wearing thin. "You died peacefully in your sleep."

"I'm sure that's what you'll tell the people, isn't it?" crowed Tiberius. "Died in his sleep, happily ever after! Then how do you explain the position of that pillow?" He pointed at the pillow on which his body's head rested. "I was smothered to death."

"But it's *beneath* your head," I said, growing infuriated. "Your head is on top of the pillow, how could you have been smothered with it?"

But Tiberius's soul was not listening. "I should never have poisoned you, Germanicus! If only Drusus was here to see this infamy, he would avenge me. Why did I order Sejanus to poison him? Or maybe he never died. Maybe it was Drusus all along, who killed me in revenge for my ill treatment of Livia Julia, who betrayed me to . . ."

This went on for some time, although I finally tricked him into hiding in the Darkness by pretending the Praetorian Guard were about to burst into the room to torture his soul.

Speaking of the Darkness, I had noticed changes in it, too. It lagged behind me and had trouble digesting souls. Although it was still as black as night, there was somehow something less dark about it. Admittedly you couldn't see your hand in front of your face when you were wrapped within it. But you *could* now imagine that a hand might be in the general vicinity of your face. This was worrying.

But who am I trying to kid? I hadn't wrapped myself in the Darkness for years. It now seemed more of a ball and chain than the old friend who had comforted me during my first days on Earth. Each day that went by I felt less and less connected to it.

"You don't understand me," I'd say to the Darkness.

As ever, there was no reply.

"We've grown apart."

It looked at me blankly.

"Why don't we talk anymore?"

It said nothing.

"Okay, you're right, we never talked, but maybe we should."

It remained silent.

"No, no. It's not you; it's me."

Silence.

"But you haven't helped."

Silence.

"I just think, maybe it would be best if . . ."

Silence.

"I just need something . . ."

The Darkness moved toward me, to envelop me like it did in the old days, but I thrust it back.

"Something! Not nothing!" I shouted, and stormed off, leaving it splashed across the ground, whimpering silently.

The Darkness Had Changed.

It was during this period of uncertainty that I ran into Maud again. She was being starved to death in a Roman prison cell, having recently poisoned the emperor Claudius. Her body was emaciated and she waved to me weakly and whispered that she was actually feeling a lot better than she looked and expected to be let out very soon. It was that old game of ours, the game of Life, but I was reluctant to play along. I knew that I was being watched.

But how could I be unmoved when I saw that she had hidden a single cherry just for my arrival. She announced that she was going to eat it now unless someone—at this her eyes flickered to me— unless someone knocked it from her hands.

"Perhaps this cherry," she whispered, her mouth salivating uncontrollably, "will let me survive until I am reprieved?"

She looked at me expectantly—her beautiful jaundiced brown eyes with their slowly dilating pupils made me shudder with Joy. "Thank the gods," she repeated with an extreme effort, "that there is no one to knock this cherry out of my hand as I do not think I could survive another moment without it."

At this she weakly waggled the cherry by its stem, enticing me to act, to intervene, to enter Life for a second. Her cracked lips now lingered on the cherry's taut flesh. She looked at me again, puzzled this time.

As I stood there, torn between my love for her and caution for myself, I felt a wave of sadness sweep over me. Why couldn't I spend eternity with Maud? Was I doomed to go through the endless years without a single companion? I watched Maud fumble the cherry and fall backward, a massive hemorrhage now rocking her body back and forth in graceful epileptic spasms. She coughed up a bouquet of blood, and her eyelids flickered daintily. She was so very beautiful, and dead.

"Do you have any idea how hard it was not to eat that cherry? Wasn't I convincing?" she said, as I released her soul from her withered body. "Anyway, let's go and haunt the jailor for a while. The bastard ate his supper outside my cell every day just so I could smell it."

"Look, Maud, I'm sorry. I don't know if I can this time."

"Why ever not?"

"It's just that . . ."

"You look strange," she said, peering at me. "Have you put on weight?"

"I can't spend any more time with you," I replied, avoiding her gaze. I gave the signal, and the Darkness reluctantly began to creep forward. Maud looked shocked.

"Is it someone else?" she said. "Is it someone else who dies better than me?" Tears formed in her eyes.

"No," I hissed, "not at all. Look, you've just got to go to the other side. I think I'm being watched."

"Well," said Maud, wiping her eyes, "if that's the case, I don't want to cause you any trouble."

"Maud . . ."

"No. No. I don't want to and I won't. I'll see you around," she said. And with that she leapt into the Darkness before I could stop her. I peered into it after her but of course I could see nothing. Nothing, the once-beloved nothing, which had kept me safe and cold in its emptiness, now filled me with utter loneliness. I could no longer relate to this hollowness, this fruitless abyss from whence none returned. And as I contemplated my alienation from the null, from out of the socket of one of my eyes rolled a globular ball of clear salty liquid that rested quivering on my cheek before splashing to the ground.

What was happening to me?

The Lost
Weekend

꾀•ı•꾀

The decline and fall of the Roman Empire should have
been the best of times for any self-respecting herald of the void, but
despite the volcanic eruptions, earthquakes, slave revolts, and gladiatorial combats, I felt a malaise spreading through my system.

One awful day, as I was transporting the last of many thousands of
souls slaughtered during yet another violent subjugation, I heard
someone whisper from behind me in a voice as soft as the rustle of
leaves, "Love . . . your . . . work."

I spun around, but no one was there; only a few torn flags fluttered in the wind. I went back over my steps to make sure that I
hadn't missed anything—the Darkness had been showing increasing
signs of dyspepsia—but the battlefield was picked clean. As usual,
none had survived.

Then, just a few years later, as I scooped up hundreds of souls devastated by a plague and catapulted them unthinkingly into the great
beyond, I heard another voice murmur into my ear, "Splendid . . .
top-class . . . well done."

Again I turned around and again there was no one to be seen, just
the buzzing of flies and the cries of the birds of carrion.

And then again, quite soon after, while collecting the souls of a tribe decimated by starvation, I heard yet another voice, clearer than the others, say, "Black . . . it really suits you, you know."

It got worse from then on. As I traversed Earth's fields of devastation I heard more and more strange compliments winging to my ears on the wind. I received congratulations on a job well done, and sometimes even a smattering of applause when I wrested a particularly troublesome soul out of its body. Had the stress of recent events begun to warp my mind?

Things eventually came to a head when I was directed to a city whose inhabitants had been besieged by a rival army, grown weak from disease, and eventually wasted away. I looked upon the multitude of souls in need of collecting and felt strangely tired. This was a new feeling. As massacres go, I'd had much worse. When earthquakes had swallowed up whole civilizations in the past, I had not been overawed by the scale of the devastation. When tidal waves had swept entire countries to their doom, I had taken it in my stride. Yet now I felt a strange and intolerable weight pressing down on me as the low murmur of souls began their carping.

I remember blowing out my cheeks, rolling up my sleeves, and hitching the increasingly ill-tempered Darkness to me in preparation, when a conversation broke out in my head.

". . . always a pleasure to watch . . ."

". . . that time in Scythia, I can tell you . . ."

". . . we were impressed . . ."

". . . very impressed . . ."

". . . we'd be nothing without you . . ."

". . . nothing . . ."

". . . nothing . . ."

There was only one thing for it.

I ran.

I ran as fast as I could away from the city. Ran, despite the irresistible pull of the dead clawing me back toward them. I ran as if my very existence depended upon it, as if by staying I would be forced to confront something that was unendurable. Yet the voices followed me.

"What's he doing?"

"Running away . . ."

"From what?"

"Us, I think."

"Why?"

"Too good for us?"

"Who does he think he is?"

"Who does he think he is?" The question reverberated through my mind, stopping me in my tracks. How I wish I had known the answer. I cried out, "Show yourselves!" and from out of the air around me three figures began to emerge.

The first was a tall, mustachioed man riding a horse. He wore armor, dented and rusted by heavy use, and a horned helmet stuck with arrows. He was covered head to toe in blood and seemed vaguely familiar.

"Have we met before?" I asked.

"I should say!" chortled the man, and a thousand swords seemed to clash within his laughter.

"I'm War," he said, and extended a gore-soaked hand. "How do you do?" He had very good manners. I was obviously hallucinating.

"War?" I said. "I thought War was a condition of open, armed, often prolonged conflict carried on between nations, states, or parties. You're not a proper noun. You're not even a real person."

"Well that may be, old fellow," said War, twirling the tips of his mustache, "but considering you're the final cessation of vital functions in an organism, I think that's rather a case of the pot calling the kettle black, right?"

The hallucination had a point. If this was a figment of my imagination, it was a pretty sharp one. A second figure began to appear next to him, doubled over in a coughing fit, a cloud of flies buzzing around him, blurring his edges, lending him a soft-edged hue that could not quite disguise the figure's rotting flesh bulging through his ill-fitting chain mail. A sickly horse stood knock-kneed behind him.

"That's Pestilence," said War, slapping the figure on the back, and sending a shower of maggots over the both of us. "And that," said War, gesturing to another appearing figure, "that's Famine." A woman appeared on a black horse wearing voluminous robes that hung lightly off her stick-thin frame. A skeletal arm kept rubbing her nose, and she kept turning round in her saddle, asking, "Does my bottom look big in this? It does, doesn't it? Oh, I'm a whale!"

I chatted with the three of them. It was actually quite nice to have some company, and the Horsemen of the Apocalypse, as they referred to themselves, were keen to tell me how much I had influenced them when they were just three young entities named Skirmish, Allergy, and Going to Bed Without Any Supper.

The Horses of the Apocalypse: (from top left) *Precious, Waterbiscuit, Blackie, and Mr. Jenkins.*

It was strangely enjoyable to talk to beings who shared in my hopeless situation, and I was just about to ask them if they ever felt that there was more to their existence than mindless slaughter when a voice from out of nowhere cried, "Fellas! Fellas! Wait for me!"

A fourth figure was now appearing, a creature that was bright pink and covered in an inflamed rash. His skin was fiery red, his hair was dry and frizzy, his lips horribly chapped. He rode a sickly pale horse that smelled strangely of coconut oil.

"Who's he?" I asked.

"Sunburn," replied War, shaking his head.

"Sunburn?"

Pestilence shrugged his shoulders. "We thought we'd lost him. We've been trying to get rid of him for years."

"Oh yes, yes, very nice," said Sunburn, picking over the dead that surrounded us. "Come look at this, War. I wager a good number died from old Sunburn. They should have stayed in the shade!" He raised a fist to the sky. "Look on my works, ye mighty, and despair! Cover up all you like!"

"Listen, Sunburn," said War, "none of them died from you. Who dies from sunburn?"

"Lots of people," said Sunburn, defensively. "What about Saint Eustace?"

"He was roasted to death," said War.

"Same thing," said Sunburn.

"No, it's not," said Famine. "He was locked in a brass bull and cooked."

"Famine's right," said Pestilence, flies swarming from his mouth.

"Is not the sun made of flame?" spluttered Sunburn. "And was not Eustace roasted by flames? Was not his skin wracked with a hot prickly rash, blisters, and tenderness so that his sheets felt as if they were scratching him all through the night, and that prompted him to hide in the shade for the rest of the week wearing a large straw hat and applying lotion to his limbs?"

"No," said the three.

Sunburn turned his peeling pink back on us and began to sulk.

"When many people die from the same cause, a little of us is created," explained War. "But with Sunburn, we think it was millions of minor inconveniences."

"I'm a killer, I tell you," muttered Sunburn. "A stone-cold killer."

"Well," said War, "only Death can tell you for sure." He turned to me. "Has anyone ever died from sunburn?"

The Horsemen looked at me expectantly. Sunburn swallowed.

"Well, it's hard to say," I said, stalling for time. I didn't want to be the cause of any strife. "The *Book* only gives primary causes. Secondary causes are harder to judge." Sunburn looked relieved, and I quickly changed the topic of conversation.

Saint Eustace Dies from Uncertain Causes.

"So, Death," said Famine, cheerily, "do you fancy joining us on a global pandemic?"

"We could save you some time if you hung around with us," said Pestilence.

"Two birds with one stone," said War.

"And nice weather guaranteed," said Sunburn.

I could see the Darkness was avoiding Sunburn as much as it could, shrinking away from his throbbing red body, but I didn't care. The Darkness would just have to put up with it. Yes, perhaps I should

have paid heed to it. Perhaps I should have said no. But this seemed
to be the chance I needed to get back to my old self, to rekindle my
love of dying and finally put paid to my unnatural dependence on
Life. So I agreed to go with them. When, later on, the doctors told
me that I had not tried hard enough to reject Life, I pointed to my
days with the Horsemen as proof that I tried to break free from the
cycle of addiction. It was my last-ditch effort, it was a shock treatment. I thought it would save me. As it turned out, it was the worst
thing I could have possibly done.

They killed and killed and killed some more and I followed
in their wake. I was drunk on disaster, and there was a kind of intoxicated camaraderie between us all. Thousands died every day, in every
way, in hideous, horrifying agony. The innocent and the guilty suffered
alike. Screams, the like of which I'd never heard before, rang out in my
ears. Fire and destruction ran wild across the continents, subsuming
whole mountains in tidal waves of gore. I shoveled souls into the
Darkness hundreds at a time with barely a word spoken. A febrile en-
ergy had gripped me, and I felt free of my previous uncertainties. If I
concentrated solely on moving souls into the Darkness, I barely
thought of Life at all. The Horsemen and I turned the earth into a
charnel house, until the ocean foam was tinged with blood, the earth
beneath our feet stained scarlet, and all this under bright sunny skies.

Amid the carnage and atrocities, the Horsemen would often play
practical jokes on one another. Eventually they plucked up the
courage to try them on me. I'd wake up in the morning to find myself
impaled with arrows, or beset with oozing pustules. Terrible stomach
cramps would double me over at the most inopportune times, and I
was constantly breaking out in liver spots. To get even I set the Darkness on them when they least expected it, half-extinguishing them,
pulling them back from the brink of the void only when they had almost melted from existence. This calmed them down a bit. War told

me that he had gone so far into the void that he had seen his own personal Hell, a land of peace and friendship populated by devils who negotiated disputes in a calm and orderly fashion, never raised their voices, and gladly turned the other cheek. He shuddered at the memory. Luxuriating in all this bonhomie, for the first time in a long time, I felt as if I belonged.

I can see now that I was in denial. I was trying to cover up my doubts with a veil of callous brutality. But that is all it was—a veil. As the Horsemen romped across Earth for another century, that veil slowly began to slip. I was carrying out my work faster and faster and with a flamboyance that inspired awe in my fellow travelers, but the nausea was starting to return. Cold sweats wracked my body, and Pestilence swore that he wasn't to blame. I tried to hide my tremors and continue my work with the same flair I'd been showing of late—juggling souls until they were dizzy, then kicking them callously into the Darkness—but I was losing focus. Life was once again growing inside me, reaching out through my thoughts, turning my once beloved work into a horrible, hateful, and monstrous thing.

To make matters worse, everywhere I turned, I was reminded of Jesus. People were being eaten by lions in His name, being crucified for saying they believed in Him, hurling themselves toward me all because of Him. What madness had He inspired to get the living to give up their most valuable commodity? I seethed inwardly. Why had He been allowed to have a Life and not me? What made Him so special? Why should He have known what it was like to run through the streets, to scab His knees, to fly a kite, even to fall in love, so the rumor went? It was nepotism, pure and simple.

Not even the invention of gunpowder could perk me up. In fact, it did the opposite. Propelled by guns, cannons, and bombs, Creation now came hurtling toward me at breakneck pace. I wanted to tell them all to slow down, to stop, to enjoy it! There was no need to fight. There was no need to kill one another. Life was a many-splendored thing that could satisfy all. The fact was that I longed for the Life that they seemed so happy to throw away. But I couldn't stop them and I couldn't join them. I was in the middle of a whirlwind of fatality.

By the twelfth century A.D., I found, to my horror, that human souls had become completely unpalatable to me. I could no longer grin and bear it. My hands now began to shake as I tried to ease a soul out of its body, and when I saw it sitting there, glistening and gleaming with the evanescence of the eternal, I would often gag. The Horsemen began to exchange looks among themselves when they saw me with trembling hands stooping over the bodies, fumbling, unable and unwilling to squeeze their souls out.

One day, as I fumbled frantically with the soul of an orphan in front of the Horsemen, War put an arm around my shoulder and took me for a walk.

"What's going on, old chap?" he said.

"Oh, nothing, nothing," I said unconvincingly. The sweat dripped off my forehead.

"You can tell me, old boy," said War. "We're all in this together, you know?"

I decided to be straight with him.

"What are we doing here?" I asked. "What's it all about?"

War rubbed his barbed-wire stubble.

"Killing everybody in the world, I imagine."

"What's the point of that?"

"Well, it'd be awfully crowded around here if we didn't."

"But don't you ever want to stop killing and live a little?" I asked. "Aren't you curious about Life in all its infinite variety?"

"Not really," said War. "*Strife*, yes. Life, not so much."

"But what about the birds and the bees and the coconut trees? The lambs in the field, the cows in the pasture, the kittens, the puppies. What about the puppies?"

War was staring at me.

"And the amoebas. What about them? The mitochondria? The box jellyfish? The screech monkey? The blue whale? The closed-bottle

Puppies: What About Them?

gentian? The long-spurred violet? The potato? The tomato? The goshawk? The newt?"

"What about them?" said War. He was backing away from me slowly.

"O to be a pilchard—small, silvery and slender, spawned and schooled and then surfaced, salted and swallowed! O to be a persimmon, astringent and tart, a strikingly colored pheasant, a reeve, a reed, a ray . . ."

I felt a pressure pushing down on me, crushing me. And now I could feel the dead surrounding me. They pressed up to me. Swarmed over me. A million effervescent souls of pure being clambering on top of me—laughing at me, shouting at me, screeching at me. And something was beating in my chest. Beating so hard. Something wanted to get out of my chest. Through my mouth! But what was it? What was trying to escape? More souls now came flocking toward me. Hundreds. Thousands. The Darkness was quivering, helpless, shrinking, becoming little more than a stain, a tarnish, a tinge. I was being subsumed, subsumed under a mountain of Life.

I put my head down, shut my eyes, and for the second time in recent years, I ran.

My Day
with Maud

When I opened my eyes again, I was standing on a
beach. The Horsemen were nowhere to be seen—I was quite alone.
Small white clouds scudded through the sky. Three children raced
across the sands to bathe. White birds swooped down from above. A
group of monks in long robes walked in single file down to the sea.
The waves thundered, the children shouted, the birds sang out, and
the monks lifted up their robes and began paddling gleefully in the
shallows. I felt again that great unexplained pounding rising within
me, like a jackhammer of affection. I turned my gaze to the ground,
partly to control this peculiar sensation, but also because the view was
so beautiful I felt I might hurt it by looking at it for too long.

Somehow I knew exactly what needed to be done. Years ago I had
set out hopefully on my earthly mission. I had embraced mindless
slaughter, hideous executions, bloody murders, and insane mayhem. I
had waded knee-deep in gore, welcomed every deadly innovation,
and applauded each new killing device. Now I could barely restrain
my contempt for them. I had come to loathe my own morbid nature.

For the first time in years, the Darkness was nowhere to be seen. I
was relieved. There are times when you have to let go of your child-
ish pursuits. The facts were plain: I was sick of existing in a vacuum,

outside of time, without companionship. I wanted to live. No. I wanted to live with Maud. I looked in the *Book of Endings*—her ends were always eye-catching—and found that her latest incarnation was set to die that very decade. I didn't question the fortuitousness of this timing. I didn't wonder whether I was being set up. All I knew was that I had to see her.

I found her dangling precariously above a swamp. Her wimple had caught on a tree branch, a tree branch that was slowly bending toward its breaking point. The horse from which she had been plucked watched peacefully fifty yards away. I felt as if I was standing on a precipice above a bottomless abyss. For the first time this prospect terrified me.

"Coo-ee!" cried Maud as she gave me a wave, the wimple's strap cutting deep into her chin. "Here we are again. Although I'm thinking that this time I really might escape. If I could just grab hold of that branch." She motioned pitifully to a tree branch well out of her reach and flashed me another smile. My whole body was shaking.

"You know, Maud," I said, my voice breaking, "I think you might be right."

I reached over and pushed the tree branch within her grasp. She looked at me quizzically.

"What are you doing?"

"Grab hold of the branch, Maud," I said.

"But I'm scheduled to go, aren't I?" she questioned.

"I don't care," I said. "Take the branch."

"If you're teasing me . . .," she said, eyeing me cautiously as she grasped hold of it. At that moment the strap on her wimple broke and dropped into the swamp below. The branch snapped back toward me, and Maud swung into my arms. We held each other in silence. I stroked her hair. Yes, I thought, this is right. This is the right thing to do.

"Things are about to change around here," I told her.

Maud looked at me with her big brown eyes. "How exciting!" she said.

-᚜᛭᚜-

And so it was that on October 5, 1582, I, Death, began saving lives. *The Book of Endings* told me where and when every being in the world was scheduled to die; I now set out to thwart their ends. I raced across battlefields, pushing soldiers out of the way of cannonballs, replacing swords with sticks, defusing bombs, waylaying armadas. Like a black spirit of goodwill and benevolence, I snatched poison out of cups, performed the Heimlich maneuver on the choking, freed burning witches, prevented bar brawls, and performed mouth-to-mouth resuscitation on man and beast alike.

I brokered a truce between the quarreling red and gray squirrels, taught sharks the joys of abstinence, watered parched flowers, and persuaded lemmings that they were still young and had so much to give.

Lemmings: "If All Your Friends Jumped Off a Cliff,
Would You?"

I raced across the world in a giddy hysteria, preventing meteorites from crushing villages and lightning from striking priests, and even stopping a Flemish pig from floating into space due to a gravitational abnormality in the vicinity of Ghent.

For ten whole days no one died, and Maud never left my side. She talked to me and encouraged me, she fascinated me and fueled me, and with her I felt that my decision, though sure to bring the weight of Heaven and Hell down upon my head, was the correct one. I wanted everything to live, and to love living. I wanted everything to know how special Life was, how it should not be wasted but embraced and cherished. That was how sick I was.

After ten days I felt my message was getting through. It felt like a new epoch was beginning, one in which violence had been replaced by friendliness, anger exchanged for tranquility, in which Life was no longer a bauble to be misused, but something to be cherished.

At the end of that fateful tenth day, Maud and I found a charming hollow behind a little wood. A brook babbled through it and we sat there, letting the leaves blanket us, munching contentedly on the bread and butter we had been given by a grateful farmer whom I had saved from being pecked to death by his scheming chickens. I had never eaten before. I had never had a need to. But at the end of that glorious day I was ravenous. And what an experience it was! Placing things in your mouth! Chewing! Swallowing! Burping! Such unknown sensations thrilled my body. Life drew me ever closer with its soft, sunshiny smiles.

I had saved a black kitten and a golden puppy from being forced to fight each other in the savage Elizabethan betting halls of London, and Maud and I played with them until the night came and they slept. No one had died. Life was everywhere content. Maud snuggled close to me "to keep warm." To keep warm! Imagine! Oh, the humanity!

Glorious, marvelous, wonderful, incredible, extraordinary day! As my companions slumbered I promised myself that I was going to be Earth's great protector, not its destroyer, and that Maud and I would live happily ever after forever. None would die, all would live. Including me.

And now, for the first time in my existence my eyelids felt heavy. As night crawled over the sky, I inhaled deeply. A yawn! Maud snuggled closer. The kitten and the puppy slept with their paws outstretched. The trees rustled in the breeze.

Interlude

⊰•∴•⊱

I remember waking to the sound of rushing water. Something warm was dripping down my chin. I lifted my hand to feel my face. It was butter. I had a pat of butter the size of a musket ball stuck to my cheek. It was melting slowly into my mouth.

My nose was filled with the sweet scent of flowers and my eyes were stuck shut with sleep. I opened them and looked around and saw that I was sitting on the bank of a river with my back against a willow tree. There was no one else around. I knew that something was missing, but I couldn't place what.

The sun was shining. A small fluffy kitten slept in my lap. I looked at my clothes. They were covered in crumbs. I smacked my lips with contentment, which sent a rich succulent taste through my mouth. Ah, butter.

Beside me on the grass lay a golden puppy. It stretched out its legs and rolled its feet, shaking itself awake. It looked at me expectantly. Its tail wagged. I recall smiling at it lazily. I knew that something was missing and that I should be doing something else, but I couldn't remember what. What's more, I didn't care. A large black book lay splayed open next to me. Most of its pages had been ripped out. I saw that a small flotilla of paper boats was bobbing up and down in a pool farther downstream. My eyes began to close again. I shifted myself to get even more comfortable when the puppy barked.

I shushed it.

It barked again, and I heard it scamper away from me. I did not open my eyes. Let it bark. Let it run. Let it live.

I stroked the kitten in my lap.

I heard the puppy bark again, then whimper, then go silent.

I opened my eyes.

I was no longer alone.

Three dark figures stood before me silhouetted against the sunlight.

"There he is," said the one on the left.

"Is that really him?" said the one in the middle.

"It must be," said the one on the left.

The one on the right stayed silent. He had something in his arms. I shaded my eyes from the sun, but I couldn't make out their features.

"Who are you?" I asked.

"You don't know?" said the one on the left.

"No."

"He doesn't know who we are," said the one in the middle. "He's lost his marbles."

The one on the right still stood silent. Something was wriggling in his arms.

"What do you want?" I asked.

"We're here to help you," said the one on the left. "We're your friends."

"I'm sorry, but there's been a mistake. I've never seen you before in my life. Please go away. You're blocking my light."

"Blocking his light!" cried the one in the middle.

"Look," said the one on the left, "you must know why we're here."

The interlopers were beginning to irritate me. I forced myself to sit up.

"I have no idea who you are or what you're doing here," I said. I was feeling sleepy again. "So why don't you just run along."

The kitten stirred in my lap, and I stroked it. I suddenly remembered the puppy. I sat up and looked around, but could not see him.

"Puppy!" I remember calling. "Puppy, where are you?"

The three figures seemed to be shaking their heads at me.

"Have you seen my puppy?"

By now my eyes were adjusting to the light. The figure on the left was carrying a sword and wearing a helmet. The one in the middle was so thin she almost disappeared into the sunlight behind her. And the one on the right, the quiet one, seemed to be surrounded by flies. And he was holding something. He was holding something that was no longer wriggling.

Something golden.

"Puppy?"

It landed at my feet. It was almost unrecognizable. Its fur hung limply off its now emaciated frame. Its eyes were festering with maggots. And it had an arrow through its head.

"Puppy!" I cried. My eyes were filling with tears. "Puppy!"

"Oh dear," said the one in the middle. "He's not meant to get like that. Better not tell him about the woman."

"How could you?" I howled. "How could you!"

The three figures stood silently watching me. But I was feeling hot with rage. Burning with anger. I felt as though I was about to burst out of my body in a flaming frenzy of wrath. I staggered to my feet, but the world began to spin. It was so hot. So unbearably hot. My skin itched and crackled. My vision blurred. The world began to spin.

"Fellas!" I heard someone cry. "Fellas, you almost lost me again!"

Everything went bright.

III

The Clinic

❧❧❦

I awoke in an unfamiliar room. The walls were black. I felt all warm and fuzzy inside until I remembered what had happened to the puppy. And then a sickness entered me, and a familiar cold fell around me.

I saw that the kitten was sleeping next to me. I picked it up and it purred. It was warm, and I rubbed my cheek against its soft fur.

"Ahem."

There was a man sitting in the shadows across from my bed.

"How are you feeling?" he said.

"I feel fine," I replied. Everything felt slightly unreal.

"Hmm," he murmured, displeased. "Well, don't worry, it'll get worse."

"What?"

"It'll get worse. We'll soon have you feeling terrible again."

"But I don't want to feel terrible."

"Yes, you do. And you will."

I looked around. There was a desk and a chair and a closet and a window.

"Who are you?"

"I'm a doctor."

"Where am I?"

"You're in a special facility, the oldest in existence, for the treatment of psychological disorders."

"Psychological disorders? But I assure you I feel fine." I rubbed my face against the kitten face again. It comforted me.

"That is the problem."

"What do you mean?"

"We will need to monitor you carefully, and we will probably need to give you some toxification drugs."

I started whistling.

"And a banshee will be here in a few minutes to wail at you."

I smiled.

"Do you understand? You're a very lively person. This needs to change."

The kitten had woken up and was batting at my leg with its paws.

"You're fine for now, but I think you'll start to feel some more extreme things soon. Moments of euphoria, inexplicable instances of elation."

He was right. I felt happy. Despite my strange surroundings I felt very, very happy.

"What have you been doing in the last few days?"

"Oh," I said, and tried to recollect. "I've been playing with my kitten and with my puppy. I've been going for long walks, breathing in the air, waving at all the little birds."

"And what did you do before that?"

"I was with someone. Someone who I liked very, very much. But I can't remember who . . ."

"No. I mean before all this happiness. What do you remember?"

I thought back. All I could remember was blackness, emptiness, nothing.

"Nothing," I said.

"That's very good. Hold that image. What would you like to be doing now?"

I thought, and slowly the answer swelled within me, building in size, growing and growing until it was a gargantuan wave about to break with indescribable force.

"I want to skip and live and be happy." I gasped. "I want to see and speak and climb trees and never come down. I want to paint my existence on the map. Straight onto the map. In glitter paint." I took a deep breath. "And I want to fly kites. Fly kites high into the rainbows. Ride unicorns wildly through the . . ."

I paused. Something was scratching at the back of my mind. But the feeling was submerged as the swell rose again. I jumped up on the bed.

"Control yourself, Death," cried the doctor, but I was too busy bouncing up and down to heed his calls.

"I want a room of feathers, and bright balls, and soft, squeezy objects that never hurt if you drop them on your foot. I want whimsical stories and joyful operettas, I want lightness, and happiness, and love. I want . . . I want . . . I want . . . Maud?"

Suddenly it all came flooding back.

"Where is Maud?" I asked frantically. "What have you done with Maud? Where is her body? Where is her soul?"

"Nurse!" the doctor called, and a burly Black Wraith materialized in front of me and knocked me onto the bed and held me there. I cried out for Maud. Desperately, hungrily, insatiably. I thought of Puppy, and then Maud. O Maud! Not again. You were meant to live this time. *We* were meant to live this time! Suddenly bluebirds sprung up in front of my vision. I tried to grab them but I couldn't quite reach them. They perched on my body and twittered away, singing such sweet, sweet songs. I never felt the needle.

All the doctors at the clinic were white-coated, faceless beings who carried stethoscopes around their necks despite having no ears in which to wear them. They were indistinguishable from one another and seemingly interchangeable. All carried a certain disinterested air about them that filled one with an immense sense of dissatisfaction. This, I gathered, was part of the healing process.

Dr. Faustus, Founder of the Clinic, Had Been Disbarred for Malpractice, Malfeasance, and Malevolence.

At my second interview, the doctor assigned to me told me that my record showed that I was thoroughly selfish, undisciplined, and immature and that he would not tolerate any misbehavior on my part at all during my stay. My kitten had been taken away from me. He said that I was there to become enthusiastic about dying again. The pangs of misery I had previously felt about Maud had been replaced by a quite unjustifiable optimism. It seemed to me that no sooner would I leave the clinic than we could begin things again, just as they had been before. Sitting in the doctor's study, I was perversely happy with the thought of a new start.

"You've been spending a lot of time in the company of humans, haven't you?" he said, flicking through my file.

"Yes," I replied. "That's my job."

"But have you or have you not been fraternizing with humans on an extracurricular basis?"

"Occasionally."

"If you're not honest with us, Death, we can't help you."

"Perhaps I don't want to be helped."

"Oh, I think you want to be helped, even if you don't know it.

How often have you been carousing with humans, talking with them, spending excessive amounts of time with them?"

"Once or twice a century."

"Be honest now."

"Four or five times a century."

"Death . . ."

"A decade."

"Death . . ."

"A day."

"You do know humans are highly toxic?"

"What do you mean?"

"Life," said the doctor coldly. "Humans are positively teeming with it."

"Well, yes, that's why I like spending time with them," I said. "What's wrong with a little Life now and then?"

"A social life often precedes a biological life."

I didn't understand, and the doctor didn't bother to explain but beckoned me to lie down on the table in the room. He put on his stethoscope, clipping it where his ears should have been, and began listening to my chest.

"Now, I want you to think about Life," he said, his head still close to my chest. And so I did. I thought of fresh air; and green trees; and bounding, leaping creatures; and above all someone to share it with. Maud, Maud, Maud. Suddenly the creature in my chest returned. The creature that wanted to escape.

"Oh dear, oh dear," the doctor said to himself. "This is not good at all."

"What?" I asked, shaken from my reverie.

"You've developed a severe physical dependency on Life. It's progressed further than I've ever seen. You're very lucky to still be Death."

"But that's preposterous," I spluttered when suddenly the doctor, in one swift motion, thrust both his hands into my chest. There was some wrenching and twisting, a squelching sound, and a strange feeling of butterflies fluttering in my stomach. The doctor grunted and strained, and eventually, there was a loud pop, and he fell backward. His hands were clutching a still-beating heart.

"I bet you didn't know you'd grown this, did you?" His empty face leered triumphantly.

I stared at the heart. It was beating in and out. Blood spurted from its severed arteries. So that's where the thumping noise had been coming from. That's what had been trying to escape into my mouth.

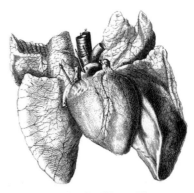

Heart: In the Wrong Place.

"First you'll grow a heart, then a nervous system, and, if you're not careful, flesh and blood too."

He peered at my forehead.

"It already looks like you've developed sweat glands. Is that what you want, Death? To be able to sweat?"

I reached out to the heart, but as soon as my fingers touched it, it went into a spasm and stopped beating.

I allowed myself to be taken to a small black room in which lay a mountain of soft toys. There were teddy bears, and elephants, and dolphins, and baby humans, all made from the softest, plushest fur. The doctor told me that I wasn't allowed to leave the room until all the animals had been torn apart. The door slammed shut and I was left alone. The hours passed. I did not rip the toys apart. Instead I arranged them in order of size, gender, and likelihood of compatibility. When the doctor came to check on me, he shook his head in disappointment, and when he later discovered that the number of stuffed animals in the room had in fact *increased,* I was locked in my room under close observation.

The clinic sat on a lonely promontory located in the shadow of the mountain of Purgatory. I was told that it had been specifically designed to appear in a different way to each patient, as an aid to his or her rehabilitation. For instance, if the personification of Happiness arrived at the clinic suffering from a melancholy ailment, he might see himself attending a beautiful marble building bathed in sunlight and warmth, in an attempt to lift his spirits. For me, however, the clinic was quite different.

To my eyes, the clinic's main building was black and wretched and caved in on itself like a collapsed lung. The grounds seemed to have been carefully devastated to promote thoughts of maximum wickedness. There were stony ravines and dense bushes of thorns, two small churning lakes of fire that belched out molten rock, several wide pastures of rusty nails, and a swamp full of loathsome creatures with needle-sharp teeth into which I was encouraged to push things. It was hoped that this would inspire within me the longing for pain and suffering that I had lost.

It was Eddie who first showed me around the grounds. I ran into him as I was being pursued by a swarm of carnivorous bats as part of my treatment (to Happiness they would have looked like a flock of gentle doves). He grabbed hold of my arm and we ran into a forest of electrical pylons, where my shock therapy usually occurred. We stood back and watched as the bats flew shrieking into the high voltage lines and burst into pretty orange flames.

Eddie had been at the clinic, on and off, for most of his existence, he told me. He had been there so long, in fact, that he was now able to see all the different ways in which the clinic appeared to the other patients.

"Don't like *your* clinic much," he told me. "Bit gloomy for old Eddie."

Eddie had originally been named Bad Flute Playing, but had swiftly found out that the role he had been given in Creation was a completely unviable proposition. He had changed his name to Eddie because he thought it sounded better. Eddie was doomed.

"I mean, why, Death? Why would there need to be a personification of Bad Flute Playing? Look at you. Someone's always dying; it makes sense to have a Death. But Bad Flute Playing? It's hardly one of the great archetypes of experience now, is it? Sure, I've plugged up a few blowholes in my time, loosened some embrasures, weakened some diaphragms. It's actually quite difficult to make someone sound bad on a bone pipe or a tin whistle—they practically play themselves—but increasingly I began to ask myself what the point was. There's only so much tuneless puffing you can take pleasure in before you start looking for a challenge."

It was said that shortly before Eddie was dragged to the clinic, he had been directly responsible for the formation of Genghis Khan's historic 550-piece recorder orchestra, whose ethereally precise and immaculately played music had mesmerized Khan and waylaid him from subjugating the Russian steppes, in direct contravention of the Great Scheme of Things. When the powers-that-be found out, Eddie was packed off to the clinic. Without his assistance, Khan soon tired of the orchestra and proceeded to crush every member to death, alongside their instruments.

"You should have heard those Mongols," said Eddie dreamily. "It takes a real barbarian to bring out the sensuousness that lurks within a flute."

There was no hope for Eddie, no hope at all. He had come to love the sound of a well-played flute. He could not bring himself to know dissonance, tunelessness, or atonality ever again.

The clinic was filled with people like me and Eddie—embodiments gone wrong, personifications with minds of their own. Every-

Genghis Khan: Recorder Record-Breaker Breaker.

one in the clinic had strayed in some way from their intended role. Life had inveigled its way into our beings with its infinite variety and shiny bright colors. It had found out the empty hollows of our existence and flooded them with the thrill of being. We had become overpersonified, growing personalities where there should have been none, and had begun to see our simple roles as increasingly pointless and reductive. Immersed in the gamut of Life, we could no longer be beholden to just one simple action. We had started as personifications, but we wanted to be *persons*.

Eddie and I used to spend many hours discussing what we would like to do on our return to Earth. I told him about my wish to live with Maud, and he told me how he wanted to create a society based purely on the diatonic scale.

We weren't the only ones doing this. Some patients sat on the benches deep in concentration, trying to remember their proper roles in Creation. But the slight, sly smiles that would slowly break out on their faces signaled they had gone back to dreaming of the exact opposite.

The entity in the next room to me was Ritual. He had been sent here after it had been discovered that he had been encouraging modernization and innovation and persuading people to abandon their age-old practices.

"How can people affirm their membership in the collective if you keep changing what they're doing?" I heard a doctor ask him.

"Maybe," squeaked Ritual, "they shouldn't be part of the collective." He let out a high-pitched laugh. "Maybe they should try something new instead of the same old boring things day after day after day?"

"But you can't get a cathartic emotional discharge if it's new. New is no good."

"Maybe people should stop having filthy emotional discharges and think with their brains once in a while," cried Ritual. "It's always incense and chicken blood and national anthems and 'you-did-this-to-my-forefathers-so-I'm-going-to-do-this-to-your-grandchildren.' It's always doing the things your ancestors did. As if they were so big and clever. Ritual! Pah! It's just a way of saying you don't want to learn from your mistakes."

His voice was rising. Throughout the clinic, patients suddenly broke with their prescribed daily routines and ran wildly through the building. In the operating theater, doctors put aside tried and tested surgical techniques and decided to improvise.

"People like doing the same things over and over again because then they don't have to think," cried Ritual. "It's brainless! Be new! Change! Develop! Mature!"

The Black Wraiths swept in to subdue him.

Another of the inhabitants of the clinic, and one of the oldest, was Lachesis. She had once been one of the original three Fates, whose job it had been to spin, measure, and cut the thread of men's lives. It was the Fates who had been responsible for compiling the *Book of Endings*. Lachesis, however, had grown uncertain and indecisive. She had been found by her sisters in the cellar of the Castle of Destiny, surrounded by thousands of miles of thread that she had been making into cat's cradles. Her much publicized fall into the addiction of autonomy did not dissuade the other patients from asking her about their own fates.

"Well, it may or it mayn't happen, mightn't it?" she would say.

"But you're one of the Fates," the patients would cry. "You have to know."

"Who knows anything, dearie?" she would reply. "So much potential, so many ends, so many futures all possible but unknown. On the one hand . . ." And she would shuffle off, talking to herself.

"She's developed a taste for the infinite possibilities of Life," one of the doctors told me. "Her treatment is simple; we're going to try to wean her onto the I-Ching. That'll cut her choices down to sixty-four. Then we'll see if she can handle the major arcana of the Tarot deck, which will give her twenty-two different possibilities to choose from. From there we'll go to a pair of dice, and with any luck we'll work her down to the flipping of a coin. Once her horizons have been suitably diminished she'll be ready to decide the fate of men again."

"But isn't she better like this?" I asked. "At least now she has a full choice ahead of her instead of just blindly following one future. She's gained independence from her own fate."

"That's not what she's for," said the doctor, looking at me with a stern eye.

"But why can't we be something other than what we were made to be?" I said. "We didn't ask to be created after all."

"Look, Death, let me tell you a story," said the doctor. "A frog and a scorpion are standing on one side of a river, and the scorpion says, 'The only way I can get to the other side is if you carry me on your back.' Well, the frog looks suspicious and says, 'Why should I carry you? You'll just sting me.' But the scorpion says, 'Why would I sting you? If I sting you, we both drown.' So the scorpion gets on the frog's back and the frog starts swimming; halfway across the river, the frog feels a sharp pain in his back. With his dying breath he croaks, 'Why did you sting me? Now we're both going to drown.' And the scorpion replies, 'I'm a *scorpion*, it's in my nature.' It's in Lachesis's nature to be decisive; it's in your nature to deal with the dead. Somehow or other you've both forgotten this."

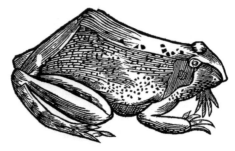

Frogs: Naturally Gullible.

"I don't remember that happening," I said.

"Remember what happening?" said the doctor.

"The scorpion killing the frog. It doesn't ring a bell."

"Well, I don't believe that it's . . ."

"And you'd think I would remember that, as it's quite unusual."

"No, it's a . . ."

"I mean, I've seen some pretty weird things, but a scorpion riding on a frog's back I have not."

"Death, listen to me . . ."

"I mean, could a frog even do that?"

"Death . . ."

"I love frogs, you know. I like their little ribbits and tiny hops and big bulging cheeks. I like the way they always look so content with themselves. You never see an anxious frog. Well, except when they're being stung by scorpions, I imagine. And another thing—"

"Nurse!" cried the doctor.

And so it went. I would show the slightest attraction to Life and suddenly I'd be surrounded by a horde of Black Wraiths who'd drag me back to my room, where Banshees would wail at me for hours on end and I would be forced to watch as jackbooted doctors stamped on my flower arrangements.

One of the clinic's most famed treatments was patient-on-patient therapy, in which inmates were paired off with each other in the hopes that some type of restorative reaction might occur. My first partner was Sympathy, who had been withdrawn from her role in Creation for obvious reasons.

"Oh boo hoo hoo!" she mocked. "Mr. Death can't go on killing things! Mr. Death doesn't want to get his hands dirty! Big fucking deal, sunshine. You think you've got problems? You don't know the meaning of problems! Look at me! I'm meant to be kind and concerned, I'm meant to feel your pain. But if the truth be told, I couldn't give a flying fuck! I'm sick of pretending to care about other people. What about me?"

"I know what you mean," I said. "There were times on Earth when I thought—"

"Who gives a shit, Death? Really. I mean, who gives a shit?"

"Well quite, I mean, that's what I thought as well, but—"

"You're not listening to me, Death, and I'm certainly not listening to you. You are the dullest being I have ever spoken to in my entire life. What did you used to do, bore people into the afterlife?"

"Now, look—"

"No! Don't say it! The sound of your voice makes me sick!" She stormed off, shaking her head in irritation. Eddie passed her on the way.

"Hi, Sympathy," said Eddie. "Still only feeling sorry for yourself?"

"Fuck off, you breathy freak," she spat, before stopping and looking him up and down with disgust. "I mean, Bad Flute Playing? What the fuck? You shouldn't even exist. You're a joke. A bad one. One that doesn't make people laugh. One that people wish had never been said. One that makes people uncomfortable just remembering it. That's the kind of joke you are."

Eddie shrugged his shoulders. He had been in the clinic long enough not to take offense at such outbursts. He told me there was a time when Meekness had gone on a rampage, and Eddie had only just avoided being crushed in his mammoth serrated jaws by disguising himself as a nearsighted mouse with emphysema. Meekness had been so stunned by this incredibly diffident vision that he had immediately shrunk back to his normal size, apologized to everyone, and gone back to Earth the next day.

One day, on our way back from a long walk in the forest of burning tires, Eddie and I came back to the main building to find a huge commotion taking place. There on the top of the building stood a figure I recognized as Misfortune. He was old and haggard and bent double, and his nightgown was ripped in the most awkward places. He wore a noose around his neck, the other end of which was tied to the clinic's flagpole, from which a black flag flew at half-mast.

"He's escaped again," said Eddie as he drew up beside me. "They usually don't let him near anyone else because, well, you can see."

Bits of masonry were falling off the building, slamming into the ground around us. A sudden fissure opened up in the ground and swallowed up one of the other patients. It began to rain. Knives.

"What's he doing here?" I asked. "He seems to be working fine."

"That's how unlucky he is," replied Eddie.

"I'm sick of bad luck," cried Misfortune. "Nothing ever goes right. Ever. It's not fair."

"Don't do anything foolish," the doctors chanted in unison.

"I'm not," cried Misfortune. "I'm doing the wisest thing I can possibly do."

"Let's talk about this," intoned the doctors as one. "It's not as bad as it seems."

But it was. Misfortune tightened the noose around his neck, stepped off the building, and fell. The rope snapped taut, the muscles in Misfortune's neck bulged, but at that precise moment the knot tying the rope to the flagpole came unbound. Misfortune continued to fall, though, and seemed set to end it all when twenty feet from the ground his billowing nightshirt caught an updraft of air and inflated. He floated down to the ground in complete safety.

"He tries it every few days, but he keeps surviving," said Eddie. "Last week he tried to slit his wrists but ended up cutting his nails."

I later heard that some of the doctors believed Misfortune had in fact contracted a virulent form of Good Luck; how else to explain his remarkable escapes? But anyone who saw his tear-stained face as he was led back to the high-security wing would have recognized this diagnosis to be well wide of the mark.

Visitations

⤙✦⤚

I **did not** respond well to the treatment. Everything just seemed so morbid now. How could I possibly be enthused about ending Life when it was the one thing I truly cared for? I didn't even bother going through the motions of recovery. I remained optimistic and happy. I secretly spat out the depressants I was given, and to the despair of my doctors, I began to jog.

"What are you doing, Death?" they'd cry.

"Keeping fit," I replied.

"But you don't need to," they'd complain. "You're not alive."

"It never hurts to be prepared," I'd say, and bound off.

One morning, as I ran through the grounds of the clinic, I heard a sound like a million screams hurtling toward me. It was Mother. I stopped in my tracks as her giant serpentine body slithered purposefully toward me. Father followed, his wings stirring up a hurricane.

"How . . . How . . . are you, son?" said Mother, trying to contain the molten tears gushing from her empty eyes.

"Fantastic," I said. "Couldn't feel better. Really, really happy."

"Oh, the embarrassment!" thundered Father.

"Hush now, dear," said Mother sadly. "It happens to lots of beings. Look at the Seven Deadly Sins."

The Seven Deadly Sins had begun as Mother's protégés, but had since become the clinic's most famous patients. It was rumored that they had suffered a collective breakdown at the hands of Saint Thomas Aquinas in a theological scuffle one night in a Paris monastery, when Aquinas had assaulted them with a barrage of homilies, disputations, and doctrinal strangleholds. The results were gruesome. Sloth had become manic-compulsive, Anger was now apologetic, Pride had let himself go, and Gluttony had become terribly thin. Avarice gave away all her clothes, and Lust now suffered from terrible headaches. Only one Deadly Sin seemed quite happy with his lot, unfortunately, and that was Envy. You could see them roiling down the corridors of the clinic together, exuding virtue. It was very sad.

The Seven Deadly Sins: In Deadlier, More Sinful Times.

"What made you do it, son?" asked Mother. "We thought you liked your job."

"I did, Mother," I replied. "I did, but something happened to me. I met someone."

"Who was it, son? Was it Boredom? Was it Change?"

"No, Mother, it was a girl."

"A what?" said my parents in unison.

"A girl, a human girl."

"A mortal!" roared Father. "But that's revolting!"

"Quiet, dear," snapped Mother. "It's not his fault. Is it, son?"

"I want to be with her, Mother," I said quietly. "I want to be with her, in time, in Life. I don't care if I have to die. I think I . . . love her."

Mother reared back on her tail in horror and let out a hideous roar that shook the buildings of the clinic. Flames exploded from Father's mouth, engulfing a passing doctor and blackening the already-burned Fields of Char. They were taking it rather well, I thought.

"What did we do to deserve this?" bellowed Father. "Didn't we always treat you with hatred and contempt? Didn't we always ignore you and dislike you? And now this!" He put an arm round my mother, whose body was wracked with inhuman sobs.

"Let's go," she howled to Father. "We'll be back, son, don't you worry. It's just . . . such a shock. We'll be back . . ." She waved goodbye without even looking at me, and with one flap of his wings, Father hoisted her and himself into the dark sky.

I sat down and decided to make a daisy chain.

"We've found someone much more your type," said Mother. Weeks had passed and my parents had returned to visit me. "You know, someone who's *not* mortal."

"You should have come to see me, son," said Father. He had calmed down somewhat. "I know lots of nymphs and demonettes who'd have done anything for you."

"Now, now, dear," said Mother. "Let's introduce them."

Mother disappeared in a puff of acrid smoke and returned moments later with a hideous black-faced hag smeared with blood. She was completely naked except for a garland of skulls and a girdle of severed hands.

"Death, meet Kali," said Mother, before whispering, "she's just your type."

It was true. I should have liked her. She was your typical goddess of destruction, a devourer, wild-eyed and maniacal with four arms to boot. But I felt no initial spark with her as I did with Maud. Mother

Kali: In the Era Before Handbags,
Four Arms Were a Godsend.

and Father left us alone and we sat awkwardly, avoiding each other's gaze.

"So you're Death," said Kali. "I think we met at a mass sacrifice once."

"Yes," I said. "I was the one in black."

"Yes," said Kali. She looked around at the miserable clinic and grunted her approval.

"Do you like blood?"

"In moderation," I said, trying to be hospitable. "I mean it can make things a bit slippery if there's too much of it . . ."

"I love blood," said Kali. "I love the taste of it." Her bleeding tongue protruded coquettishly.

"Of course," I said.

I offered to show Kali around the clinic's grounds. Her necklace of skulls clattered loudly as we walked.

"So what does the Great Kali like to do to pass the time?" I said.

"The Great Kali destroys souls, devours life, annihilates the living, murders the—"

"Yes, naturally," I said, "but when you're not devouring and annihilating, what do you like to do then?"

A quizzical expression played upon her face. "I rend," she said uncertainly. "And I rip."

"But you must like doing other things."

"I . . . I . . . I don't know," said Kali; she looked confused.

"There must be something?" I asked. I was perhaps being a little too aggressive, but I longed to hear if she indulged in Life too.

"Knitting? Cooking? Bird-watching?"

Kali's four arms hung limply by her side, and her fiery face was looking to the ground. A dribble of viscous, black snot dripped from her nose.

"N-no," she said, choking back a sob. "I rip and . . . I rend."

I suddenly felt exceedingly sorry for her. The poor girl had never done anything but what she had been told to do. What a tragic waste. I reached toward her to comfort her.

"Get your hands off me!" she cried, flames bursting forth from her head. "Men! You're all the same! Always trying to change us and make us something we're not! I hate you!"

And with those words she disappeared in a puff of sulfurous smoke. I heard a slow, sarcastic handclap.

"Oh, well done, son."

It was Father.

"A nice goddess like that, too. She was falling all over you. And now your mother's in tears again. You know you're the laughingstock of Hell? All the demons are getting on my back about it. It's not good for the family name. When are you going to grow up?"

"Oh, shut up!" I cried, and jogged off.

My parents' visit left me in a bad mood, and I was congratulated on my surliness by the doctors that evening. However, by the next morning I had already blanked it out of my mind and was relapsing back to my joyful new self. I was humming contentedly in the clinic's Spit Garden, ignoring the oozing brooks of phlegm that bubbled through the ground at my feet, and mulling over the hypothesis that bunnies are the most delightful creatures in the world, when an awe-inspiring blinding light appeared in front of me.

"Who is it?" I cried.

"How many awe-inspiring blinding lights do you know exactly?" boomed a rather irate divine voice.

"Oh. Hello, Lord God Sir."

"Yes, well," He boomed. "You caused Me a lot of trouble, you know? Stopping people from dying! What did you think you were trying to do? It caused Me no end of problems. I even had to ask the pope to help out, and you know how I hate asking favors from him. He now says he wants to wear that silly hat of his again."

"But what happened to the people I saved?"

"You don't understand, Death; those days never happened. We've removed them from the calendar. They are un-days, false memories, nothing more. We got rid of your days and started afresh."

"Won't that look a bit awkward to future generations? I mean, ten days missing in a year."

"That's why We got the pope to do it. He's always doing crazy stuff like that."

Gregory XIII: Thank You for the Days.

"Anyway," boomed God, looking me up and down, "how are you feeling?"

"Terrific," I replied.

"Hmmm," He boomed. "That's too bad. You haven't been having any dark thoughts of late, have you? Visions of catastrophe and disaster?"

"No. Sorry, Lord God Sir. I've mainly been thinking of the small furry things in Creation. You really did a good job on them, You know."

"Well," boomed God, "that's very kind of you, Death, very kind indeed. But really, you of all people shouldn't be thinking of such things."

"Why not?"

"Because it is unnatural!" cried a harsh voice. There was a flutter of wings and the angel Gabriel appeared by God's side.

"Gabriel has helped pick up the slack, limp and drooping, while you were away. He doesn't think you should have your old job back, do you, Gabriel?"

"I just don't think that we should have outsourced such an important role to someone who is, after all, the son of Satan," he sniffed. Gabriel had changed. His wings were sleek and greased and his robe seemed off-white. He was wearing black eyeliner.

"Between you and Me," boomed God in as conspiratorial a fashion as one can when one's voice shakes the heavens, "I think he's always rather wanted your job. Gabriel never liked the living much."

"But he's an angel!" I protested, suddenly feeling rather protective of my role as the dread destroyer of Life. "It doesn't make any sense."

"If an angel can become lord of Hell, then I can become Death," cried Gabriel.

"Yes, well, Satan is something of a . . . special case," boomed God, as if He was none too keen on discussing the details. But Gabriel was on a roll.

"I am Gabriel, the Angel of Death! Merciless, cruel, avenging. None escape Gabriel's dread grasp."

Despite God's blinding divine light, the clinic seemed to be growing increasingly dark. A black emanation was issuing forth from

Gabriel's body. I felt a chill settle within me, and then a shock of recognition.

"Is that *my* Darkness?" I asked.

It was just as I remembered it, uniquely formless, shapeless, amorphous, and it was reaching out toward me plaintively. I was surprised to find that I had actually missed the Darkness. I tried to touch it, but Gabriel pulled on a leash and jerked it back.

"It is *my* Darkness now," said Gabriel, slapping the Darkness down as it reared up in anger. It collapsed into a puddle and whimpered silently to itself. Gabriel leered at me. There was nothing behind his eyes.

"But God," I protested, "You can't have people 'falling to their Gabriel,' or being 'Put to Gabriel,' it sounds silly."

"I know, I know," boomed God out of the corner of His eminence. "But he's been pestering Me for eons for the job, and when you went wrong, what else could I do? Now maybe when you get worse again we can talk about having you back. Until then though, I'm afraid the matter is closed. Gabriel is the new Death. Oh, and another thing."

"Lord God Sir?"

"There was a soul that kept on being reincarnated due to an irregularity within the Department of Reincarnation. I don't know if you noticed. Name of Mab? Or Mabel? Or Madge?"

"Maud," I said quickly.

"Yes, well, whatever," boomed God. "It seems she kept on being reincarnated not through any religious belief, but through the sheer force of her will. There must have been something on Earth that held an irresistible pull for her. I can't imagine what it was. I mean, I know it's good and everything, but still . . . all very irregular. Anyway, We have corrected this error. She will be walking the earth no more."

I was stunned. A bunch of grapes appeared in my hand.

"Get bad soon," boomed God, and disappeared.

"No," I cried. "No! No! No!"

I collapsed to the ground. There was no hope. None whatsoever. Maud was gone and I would never see her again. I looked up.

Gabriel still stood there, smiling.

"You went too far, Death; I warned you. You shouldn't have spent all that time with that sheep. It was unnatural."

He leaned close toward me. His breath stank of milk and honey. "She screamed, you know, when I came for her."

"What?" I said.

"When I uncorked her soul by the river, she seemed to like it."

He smiled to himself.

"She said I was a much better Death than you."

I remained silent.

"She said she wanted a real Death to usher her into the void. Well, she got it from me! The whole Earth is going to get it from me. I got rid of Michael, now I can get rid of you."

I could hold it in no longer.

"Shut up! Shut up! Shut up!" I screamed in his face.

"You make me sick," shouted back Gabriel. "Life makes me sick. There's only one solution. Kill it! Kill it all!"

Gabriel laughed, an unpleasant, morbid laugh, the sort of laugh that would once have made me feel all cold and Death-like inside. With a flap of his wings he was gone. I looked at the grapes God had put in my hand. They had withered.

No Maud. No Life. No Death. What was I? What had I become? For the first time since my arrival in the clinic, I wished I was back at my old job. To think that Gabriel had sent my beloved Maud into the Darkness—the poor old Darkness, now shackled to an angel!— it was all too ghastly for words. What other desecrations would Gabriel wreak in my absence? It was daunting to imagine myself re-turning to Earth, returning to the playground of my love, but the idea of Gabriel taking my place was insufferable . . . unbearable . . . unendurable! It was wrong! He was not Death! Only I *could* be Death! Only I *was* Death! Only I . . .

I heard a sound. I turned around and saw two of the deadly sins, Pride and Envy, trying to hide behind a large spittoon in the garden.

"It wasn't our idea!" squealed Pride.

"Sorry, Death," said Envy. "The doctors called us in to try and get you back to your old self again. Did it work? Did you feel me at all?"

I lunged toward them. Pride ran away screaming (he still needed a lot of work), but Envy stood rooted to the spot. I grabbed him by the throat.

"Honestly, Death, I didn't want to. But they said if I didn't do it, I'd be stuck here for good."

I tightened my grip.

"The thing is, I'm never happier than when someone else does well. I just want to slap them on the back and say, 'Congratulations!' But I can't. I've got to get everybody to feel resentful, as if they didn't deserve it. 'Envy by name,' they say, 'Envy by nature.' And now here I am. Quite happy, too. I don't regret not being back on Earth one bit, even though my old pal Jealousy is still there. Good luck to him I say."

I lifted him up into the air. He began to talk more quickly.

"I mean, it's not as if I'm all that good as a sin in the first place. Some people go through their entire lives without feeling me. But I like to be felt. Getting felt is one of the most attractive things about the job. It's not like I'm like you, Death. I mean, I'm hardly common to all. I wish I was."

He was starting to turn green in the face.

"In fact, sometimes I've lain down at night and wished I was you, Death. You have it easy. Respect, admiration, a definite presence. You affect every single person individually! Not like me. Sometimes people don't know whether they're feeling me or Jealousy and that's very annoying because we both have quotas to fill, you know?"

His voice was now a strangled gasp.

"And sometimes I just wish Jealousy had an accident, you know? Nothing too bad. Just having his eyes sewn shut with wire or something. I mean I'm a sin, after all, one of the original seven, and he's more of an emotion, the little sod."

"That's very good, Envy," said a voice. It was one of the doctors. "You're coming along nicely. You too, Death. I think these patient-on-patient sessions are really helping."

I dropped Envy to the ground.

"You see, Death," said the doctor, "you can't deny yourself. No matter what you think. It's all still there, just waiting for you to return. There's a tunnel at the end of the light, and it's growing darker and darker."

I turned away from him and took in the devastation around me. The broken carapaces of the hideous many-legged insects crunched beneath my feet, the black sun above offered no heat, the vultures screamed as they landed on limed branches. Hopelessness, obliteration, and discordance were everywhere. A sharp breeze brought a cloud of choking fumes up from one of the lakes. It was growing harder to remain happy here, harder to remain hopeful. That was, after all, its point.

I must have cried in my sleep that night, for the following morning my pillow was cold and damp. I tried to hide it from the nurses, saying I had eaten it in a rage, but when they saw the salty tear tracks on my cheeks, they informed the doctor. He immediately sat me down and proceeded to rip out my newly grown tear ducts.

"How could you let yourself get into this state?" he grunted, slowly extracting the long, rubbery tubes from my eye sockets.

I didn't have an answer. All I could think of was how virulent life was, how insatiable its appetite, how tenacious its hold had become. And yet I hadn't felt bad being in its thrall. I hadn't felt bad at all. How strange to suffer from a disease that made one feel *better*. In such cases was the cure as much an ailment as the disease?

The last of the ducts came out with a snap, spattering me with saline, and the doctor checked for any further growths. It was there, sitting in a pool of spilled tears, that I realized what I must do. If I was ever to see Life again, I would have to return to being my old self. But if I returned to my old self, I would have to renounce all chances of living, all chances of Life. It would be a supreme sacrifice.

So I began to keep apart from the other patients. I had to remain aloof. Company brought out the best in me. I didn't like doing it, I had so many friends, but I had no choice. One day Sympathy grabbed me by the arm in the cafeteria.

"You can talk to me if you want, Death," she said. "If you've got to get something off your chest, I'll listen to you." She had improved, but I just put my head down and walked away, leading her to begin screaming, "Too good for me now, eh? Well, fuck you, Death, and your inability to transport people to the afterlife! You're a big girl's blouse, that's what you are, a big girl's blouse!"

I began to concentrate on my treatments. When placed in a room with a crying baby, I did not pick up the rattle and make goo-goo sounds but remained impassive. Upon seeing a kitten playing with a ball of string I suppressed my smiles, and when that kitten accidentally tied itself up, I stood by as it mewed pathetically.

Shock Therapy.

I forced myself to smile while watching torture and shrank away from the color pink. I showed no interest in the sound of a babbling brook, only pricking up my ears when that babbling grew into a full-blown flood. On the clinic's practice killing fields I moved like wildfire, uncorking dummy souls and flinging them into a synthetic Darkness. The doctors nodded their heads in approval. I began to seek out the shadows and bask in their emptiness. I felt the joy and spontaneity leaking from my existence. In group therapy sessions, when asked a question, on any subject, I would invariably state, "Death is the only answer," and would note the tick on my interlocutor's clipboard.

Weeks went by, months went by, but I didn't swerve from my task. Slowly the Joy was squeezed from my body like toothpaste from a tube. I was relentless, unstoppable, like a force of nature once more. No one dared approach me. My old friends whispered to each other as I swooped past them. I was eventually called into my doctor's office.

"You've done very well," he said, "very well indeed. Your test scores have all come back negative, you haven't had a new organ growth since the tear ducts, and you killed the hamster we left for you in your room."

"Its time had come," I said.

"Yes, yes it had. But we're still not convinced that you really *believe* it, Death. Some of us worry that you're just pretending to be better so you can go back to Earth. You can understand our concerns, can't you?"

I felt an anger swelling up inside me.

"I'm afraid we're going to have to delay your release until we're satisfied you're back to your good old, bad old self."

"What more do I need to do?" I asked. "Tell me."

"We'll have to think on that," said the doctor, absentmindedly picking up some other papers. "Remember, have a bad day."

I stormed outside into the horror and desolation. I was furious. I hurtled down to the Field of Impaling and kicked at the spikes that grew from the ground. I had played by their rules, I had done everything they wanted me to. I had renounced Life forever. And now this! Who knew what Gabriel was getting up to on Earth. Who knew what liberties he was taking with the living. My living. I heard the sound of light piping coming from behind me. I tensed. The last thing I wanted now was company.

"Death?" said a voice.

"Not now, Eddie!" I snapped.

"Death?" came the voice, more plaintively now. The anger burst inside me. I swung round and screamed at the top of my lungs (though they had actually been removed some time before), "NOT NOW!"

Eddie held in his hands a large cake with candles in it, but the sudden shock of my scream sent him staggering. He desperately tried to keep the cake balanced, but in doing so lost his footing and toppled backward onto a three-foot-tall spike. A sharp trill sounded, and then silence. The spike had gone straight through Eddie's back, and out through his stomach, skewering the cake, which his hands still clasped tight. The spike poked through the black icing on top, which spelled out the words, "To Death, Happy Travels! Your Dear Friend, Eddie."

I didn't quite understand what had happened at first. I thought he was joking, playing, pretending. And then it hit me—I had killed him. I dropped to my knees and held his head. I didn't know what to say or do.

Eddie spoke in wispy words that drifted away on the breeze. "Baked you a cake . . . for your release . . ." He coughed. Each word was painfully off-key.

"But I wasn't going to be released, Eddie," I cried. "They said I wasn't ready."

"Well," spluttered Eddie, "this . . . this ought to help."

I felt like crying, but Eddie, seeing the distress on my face, cautioned me. "C'mon now, Death. This is your big chance! Don't blow it . . . be firm!"

I could see a crowd of doctors and patients running toward us.

"The world doesn't need a Bad Flute Playing," gasped Eddie, "but it does . . . need . . . a Death."

The crowd was getting closer and closer.

"But Eddie . . ."

"You know what has to be done."

"No, Eddie, I can't."

"Yes, you can," warbled Eddie. "Do it."

"No . . ."

"Do it now!"

Eddie's head fell to one side. I took a deep breath and plunged my hand into his chest. And the strange thing was, it felt good. It was good to be back inside a body. It felt like Home. Eddie's soul popped out with no complaint and sat there staring at me with a wry smile on his face. And then in a whisper, which only I could hear, he said, "Time to go, Death, time to go."

It was then that I heard an unmistakable sound. It was the sound of nothingness approaching, of the void yawning, of never-ending emptiness unfolding. The light was growing dim and the doctors and patients now started to glance around. And then, from out of the black sun came the Darkness, swooping down, reaching out for me with its infinite tentacles. It enveloped me, and hugged me close. I unclasped the broken leash that still hung from it. It turned toward Eddie's soul and then hesitated and looked at me questioningly, but I beckoned it forward. In an instant Eddie's soul was gone, leaving behind it only a lingering A-flat.

The Darkness swarmed around me and I embraced it. We became one once more, and I realized there would be no more organs, no more hearts growing within me. Nothing would grow there ever again. The Darkness let out a contented howl of silence and I suddenly felt ravenous, hungry for souls. It was only then that I noticed the circle of doctors and patients standing around me.

There was a silence, and then slowly but surely, they began to clap. The clapping was sporadic at first, disbelieving, but slowly it began to grow in strength, grow more powerful, grow into a roar. Other patients joined in the circle, and they too were clapping. I heard Sympathy shout out "Death!" and soon it was picked up by the others, "Death! Death! Death! Death! Death!" I got to my feet; the cheers were raucous, the handclaps deafening. I tried my hardest to stifle a smile.

"I am . . . the End of All Things!" I roared.

They cheered.

My doctor stepped forward. "Well," he said, looking at Eddie's body and the impaled cake, "I guess the proof really is in the pudding!"

And everyone laughed except for me. And that was good too.

Homecoming

⋯✦⋯

I tried not to show it, but I was nervous about leaving the clinic. What if Life was too much for me when I returned to Earth? I was scared that upon seeing puppies and kittens, and clowns and custard pies, it would all begin again. I felt stronger, but I was scared of being dragged into Life again.

Mother came to escort me back to Earth. She said a lot had been happening since I had left, and she and Father were busier than ever. As we traveled through infinite space I kept my eyes on the clinic.

"Where do you want to start?" Mother asked. "There are all sorts of wars going on at the moment, and I believe the Spanish influenza is about to strike. You'll be ever so busy."

"Take me to a petting zoo," I said.

"What?"

"I want to go to a petting zoo."

"You're joking, aren't you, son?" said Mother. "That's a joke, isn't it?"

"No, I'm not; and no, it's not."

There was concern, dismay, and shock on Mother's face. The snakes on her head were standing upright hissing.

"I really don't think we should go to a petting zoo, dear," said Mother. "How about a nice dungeon to begin with? Or maybe a torture chamber?"

"You can go there if you like," I said, "but I'm going to a petting zoo."

"But, dear," spluttered Mother, "what about the clinic? Your treatments? All your hard work? How about we start off at a hospital ward? That'll be nice and easy."

"I'm going to a petting zoo, Mother," I said quite calmly. "You can come with me or not, either way is fine, but you shouldn't waste your time trying to stop me."

"Oh dear," said Mother. Her tail lashed back and forth. "This is all my fault."

But for once it wasn't. For once Mother's sinful nature was not leading me astray. I needed to do this for myself.

Our flight to Earth was nearly instantaneous. We didn't speak. Mother kept gnawing at her talons, and I let the Darkness swim around me happily. It must have been sometime in the early twentieth century when we returned, because trousers were in.

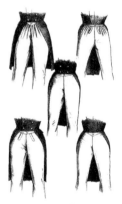

The Pants of Time.

We headed straight for a large municipal zoo, and then to the small offshoot next to it, the zoo without bars, where children ran among the animals, shouting, pointing, and touching. I felt the dull, solitary echo of a thud in my chest. The Joy was rising.

Mother stood back and covered her face with a claw. I noticed the children near her begin feeding the animals in strict contravention of the signs. And what animals there were! Cuddly, fluffy sheep, horses with long flowing manes, jolly piglets snorting, funny goats chewing, silly cows mooing, busy chickens clucking. I walked through it all, within touching distance of them all. The Joy was increasing, the thump in my chest now a deafening tattoo beating out the tune, "Life, Love, Life, Love." I searched inside my chest but could find no heart. The doctor had warned me of phantom organs.

It felt shockingly good to be back on Earth again. I felt stronger, more powerful, more blissful than ever before. I let my finger trace the outline of a sheep, and an electric thrill went through my arm. My urge for Life was strong. I turned around and I saw a sign that sent paroxysms of painful Joy through my body. It read simply, RABBITS.

I was drawn to the rabbit enclosure, and the Joy rose to even greater heights. It was laughing and singing and urging me to love. The Darkness had sensed something was wrong and had shrunk around me. It was clinging to my feet. I saw the bunnies wrinkling their noses at some lettuce leaves, and the Joy seemed to be singing, "Live! Love! Hug the Bunnies! Tickle Their Noses! Rub Their Fluffy Little Tails! I Am Meant For You. You Do Not Have To Be Death. You Can Live Like Things. Do What You Want To Do. Forever And Ever, A Man."

A white-bellied cottontail hopped slowly toward me. It had a small piece of lettuce tucked in its mouth. It raised its nose toward me and sniffed the air. I stopped moving. I closed my eyes and took a deep breath. All I could smell was sawdust and fur. The beautiful aroma of Everything, the sweet stench of Life. It made me shudder, it shook me. I could feel it, like dappled, bounding happiness all over me. And the Joy was now crooning, "Pick It Up, Pick It Up, Pick It Up."

I gasped.

"Pet It, Pet It, Pet It."

I extended my hand.

"Call It Barry The Bunny, Call It Barry The Bunny, Call It Barry The Bunny."

Soft. Sweet. Dear. Love. Fur. Whiskers. Heart. Smile. Life. Life. Life.

I suddenly heard a commotion happening behind me. I opened my eyes. The Joy loosened its grip. One of the boys who had been feeding the animals in the regular zoo had been attacked by the monkeys. They were clawing and biting him. I looked at Mother. She shrugged her shoulders. And from out of nowhere I felt the pull of the dead. An enormous, powerful sense of duty, crushing the Joy beneath it.

Crack Rabbit.

I left the bunny behind me and strode over to the cage. The enraged monkeys had torn off the little boy's head and had begun to throw it to one another. The screams from the startled onlookers faded into the background, became my clothes again, my skin, part of my nature. I reached into the boy's body and removed his bright lustrous soul, and the Darkness swallowed him up in an instant. There was no thumping in my chest anymore, just a calm, empty serenity.

I was back.

From out of the sky came the flapping of wings, and an angel fell clumsily to the ground. He had deep dark rings under his angelic blue eyes and was unshaven, his hair mussed, his halo flickering sporadically. It was a few moments before I recognized the angel as Gabriel. He barely recognized me.

"Where is he?"

"Where's who?"

"The boy decapitated by monkeys," said Gabriel, flicking frantically through a book. My book. The *Book of Endings*. Pages drifted to the floor. I saw that there were many annotations and attached memos and that in lieu of the Darkness, Gabriel had a large black garbage bag in one hand. It had a hole in the bottom. I only now began to hear the sound of souls complaining, a vast tumult of white noise that I had barely registered before. Gabriel had been lax.

"He's meant to be *here!*" shouted Gabriel frantically, pointing at the spot where the boy's body lay.

"I have dealt with him."

"No," shouted Gabriel. "No. I am Gabriel, Angel of Death."

"All come to Death, eventually," I intoned. It felt wonderfully bad.

"But you can't. You're sick!" said Gabriel.

"I am the cure to all sickness," I said. The old lines were all coming back.

The *Book* fell to the ground, spilling pages, and Gabriel dropped to his knees, desperately trying to patch it together again. I could now hear the sound of souls more distinctly.

". . . call yourself 'The End of Life,' do you, Gabriel . . ."

"Has infinity begun yet?"

"Come on. Hurry up. I died three hours ago . . ."

"I shall be making a complaint, you hear, a complaint . . ."

On the ground Gabriel was on all fours. He had given up trying to patch the *Book* back together and was now sobbing quietly. It was quite pitiful. I helped him to his feet.

"I never knew it would be so hard," he said, wiping his nose with the back of his hand. "I mean the sheep are always complaining if you don't get them immediately, and the puppies!" He looked to the sky. "God! How do you deal with the puppies!"

I sat him down and he began to cry on my shoulder. Shuddering sobs. Around us a whir of ambulances and police formed a background tableaux of disaster. The parts of the boy's body were being carried away, and the monkeys were being shot. Throughout the zoo, children were being emotionally scarred for life. It felt good. I popped out the monkeys' souls with one hand, absentmindedly. One tried to climb onto my back, but I flicked him nonchalantly into the Darkness.

Gabriel blew his nose on the hem of his garment. He looked at me, fluttering his big blue eyes. "Thank you, Death," he said.

"That's all right, Gabriel."

"I should have listened to you."

"All listen to me in the end," I said.

"It's just that . . ."

"Yes?"

"Sometimes . . . I get so lonely."

I felt Gabriel's hand on my knee.

"I think it's time you went home," I said to Gabriel, lifting up his hand and putting it back on his lap.

"Oh, I wish I was dead!" cried Gabriel.

"That can be arranged," I said.

Second Goings
and Comings

The sun set, the sky darkened, wounds festered, people drowned—all was bad with the world once more. I barely had time to ponder the strange turn of events in my existence before I was rushing to clear up the vast backlog of the dead left by Gabriel. Fortunately my jogging in the clinic had kept me in pretty good shape. I swept across Earth like a pale gale, like a pain hurricane, like a gloom typhoon, popping out souls here, ushering them into the Darkness there. I was unquenchable. The reception I received from the dead when they saw me was really quite touching.

"Good to have you back, Death," the souls would say. "Didn't think much of that last chap. Who was he again?"

Not many people had a good word for Gabriel. It seems some of the souls had straight up refused to come out of their bodies when they saw him.

"He just didn't look right," they'd tell me. "What with all that backcombed hair and eyeliner."

It was unfortunate that Gabriel had chosen to take my place just as some of the most caustic fin de siècle wits had died. They had not been gentle with him.

"A darling boy," said one, "but hardly the harbinger of finality one had been led to expect. I mean, the poor thing was leaking gravitas with every word he spoke."

"And those feather wings!" chimed in another. "It was like being swept up by a pillow. Can you imagine anything more ghastly! You could see the concentration on his face. He was trying so hard."

"He *was* trying," chimed in another. "Very trying."

So I was greeted with open arms. In fact, some souls almost leapt out of their bodies to welcome me. It only goes to show that one should not try to mess with people's notions of their own demise. Say what you want about progress and change, but when it comes to envisaging one's end, leering skulls and unfathomable blackness never go out of fashion.

It was one of the busiest eras yet, what with the world wars, the ethnic genocides, the aggressive physics, the hostile chemistry, Spanish influenza, elevator shafts, threshing machines, cheap cigarettes, and the increasing availability of fireworks.

Some Still Preferred to Die the Old-fashioned Way.

Soon all the traumas of the past were pushed from my mind. Until, that is, I got the call.

I was in Chicago in the late 1930s, dealing with the grisly aftermath of a circus parade that had coincided with a big game hunters' convention, when a fat cherub appeared beside me, red in the face and out of breath. It said that I was wanted in Heaven immediately.

I hadn't heard anything from Heaven since I had shipped Gabriel back there. I had taken the stony silence as a sign of embarrassment. Now, as I flew back to its graffiti-laden walls, I began to wonder whether omnipotent beings disliked being shown up.

I found Peter strapping his mother into a girdle.

"Oh . . . Death . . . hello," he said, over his mother's grunts. He sounded anxious.

"Anything the matter, Peter?"

"Oh no. No. Not at all," he replied, studiously avoiding eye contact. "Nothing the matter. Nothing."

"What is it, Peter?" I asked. I was getting worried.

"Well, it's just that . . ." At that moment the elastic on his mother's girdle broke, sending Peter crashing down through a cloud and catapulting his mother clean over the walls of Heaven. It seemed I would have to find out for myself. I pushed open the gates.

Things had not changed very much in Heaven. It was still in need of renovation. The one big difference was that a vast stadium was under construction. Its seats seemed to stretch into infinity. What could it be for? I carried on past it, and in the distance I saw Jesus standing at the head of a group of angels, leading them in what looked like a mass crucifixion workout. The angels had large wooden crosses that they were dragging behind them in time with Jesus. They wore crowns and bracelets made of thorns, and whenever they went to wipe the sweat from their foreheads with them, they cut themselves hideously.

"And lift your eyes up," beamed Jesus in a chirpy, slightly out-of-breath voice, "and lower them again. Wince once and cry out—all together now—'Eli, eli, lamai sabactani!' And sag. Well done, everyone! It is finished." The angels collapsed, exhausted and bleeding.

I marched on toward the Parliament of Heaven. It was chaos as usual. Angels flew about the hall shouting, parchment and scrolls fluttered down from the ceiling, harps were being tuned, sandals slapped on the hard cirrus floor. At the head of it all was God. He was struggling to play paddleball. Jesus appeared beside Him, a towel hung over His shoulders. He picked up another paddleball racket and began playing expertly.

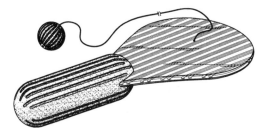

Paddleball: Sport of (King of) Kings.

"Now why did I ever create *this?*" boomed God as He swung wildly at the ball. I stood waiting until He caught sight of me. "Ah. Death. Feeling worse, are we?"

"Yes, thank You, Lord God Sir."

"Very unfortunate that thing with Gabriel. Obviously his halo was faulty and overheated his brain. That's what happens when you outsource production to the damned—very cheap, but shoddy workmanship. Anyway, We're having them all recalled." I looked around and indeed none of the angels I could see were wearing halos, although some had substituted plates that hovered uncertainly over their heads and every few minutes would crash to the floor below.

"Tell him, Dad," beamed Jesus.

"What?" boomed God. His divine light had become entangled in the paddle's elastic. "Oh yes, I'm glad you're here, Death. We've just been having a little discussion. We're going to phase you out."

"What?" I cried.

"Phase you out," boomed God, as He tried to untangle Himself. "Yes, Jesus has convinced Me that *you* should die."

I didn't know what to say. After all I had gone through, this was my reward?

"I'm informed that it's 'ironic,'" boomed God, "and Jesus thinks We haven't been ironic enough of late."

"Not since My crucifixion," beamed Jesus. "Crucifying God? You can't get much more ironic than that!"

"So you see," boomed God, "now *you* have to die, because that'll be very, very ironic."

"But not as ironic as *Me* being crucified," beamed Jesus.

"But Lord God Sir?" I said.

"Yes?"

"I've just finished cleaning up the mess Gabriel left."

"And a splendid job you've done, hasn't he, Jesus?"

Jesus beamed silently.

"But what will happen to all the dead souls if I die?"

"Jesus is going to take care of them," boomed God proudly. "He's been thinking of making a comeback in which everybody lives forever and all the dead are resurrected. We're going to call it 'The Second Coming.' Got a nice ring to it, hasn't it?"

"But that's stupid," I said.

"No, it's not," beamed Jesus. "Tell him it's not stupid, Dad!"

"But it is!" I said. "If everyone's going to be resurrected, why bother having them live in the first place? Why not just start them all off in Heaven?"

God and Jesus looked at each other.

"Because . . . ," boomed God uncertainly. "Because . . ."

"Because . . . We're inscrutable," beamed Jesus, and crossed His arms.

"Yes, yes, quite right," boomed God, "inscrutable, and ironic. So there you have it. Who knows what We'll do after that. Probably something equally crazy. Maybe We'll give everyone four legs. Anything to idle away a few hours, really. Killing time is simple, but killing eternity takes forever."

I stood there and let them speak.

"Anyway, by way of publicizing the Second Coming and the life of the world to come," boomed God, "We were thinking that Jesus should fight you. There should be a little back and forth, you should get Him in a headlock, say, and it should look like it's all over when Jesus will suddenly flip you over His head, leap onto the ropes and perform His . . . what's it called again, Jesus?"

"Do you mean My 'Battle Stations of the Cross'?" beamed Jesus.

"Yes, that's the one," boomed God, turning back to me. "This will destroy you completely."

"I'm going to take you down to downtown," beamed Jesus, "and show you around, you clown."

"Yes, thank You, Jesus," boomed God, turning back to me. "I do think I let Him stay on Earth just a little too long, don't you? Anyway, the match will be watched by every being in Creation, either in the stadium We're building—did you see it?—or, for those in Hell or Purgatory, on pray-per-view. Okay?"

"But I think I'm doing good work on Earth, necessary work."

"Yes, We're sure you are," boomed God. "But if everyone is going to live forever and ever, We hardly need you now, do We?"

"I can do other things," I said. "I don't just have to do dying. . . ."

"Yes, yes, We're sure you could," boomed God, "but We thought it would make people rather nervous if you were loitering around while they tried to enjoy eternity. You're hardly inconspicuous, you know."

"So that's it, is it?" I said. I suddenly felt strangely calm faced with my own extinction. I guess I had seen so many endings I had become completely inured to them, even my own. I looked at the Darkness fondly. Soon I would be sending myself into it forever. I consoled myself that there were worse ways to go. At least I still had my dignity.

"Tell him about the other thing," beamed Jesus.

"Oh yes. Jesus thinks that all of Creation would like it very much if you winked out of existence in, say, Round Two. He thinks Creation would like that a lot."

"Round Two, you're through!" beamed Jesus. "You're so old, I'm so new!"

"Yes, *thank You*, Jesus," boomed God. "So why don't you come back in seven days' time and We'll wink you out of existence." He and Jesus picked up Their paddleball rackets.

I was astounded.

"At least make it a fair fight?" I pleaded. "You owe me that much."

"We don't owe you anything," beamed Jesus. "On the contrary, since We created you, it is you who owes Us everything."

"If—"

"No ifs," beamed Jesus.

"But—"

"No buts," beamed Jesus.

There was the sound of a strangled boom. God had got Himself entangled in His racket's elastic again.

"Let me help You, Father," beamed Jesus.

"I can deal with it Myself, thank You very much, Jesus," boomed God frustratedly.

"Exactly," beamed Jesus.

I turned my back on the divine beings and sloped away from the Parliament. Nobody seemed to pay me much attention. I walked through the Gates of Heaven where Peter was now sitting, his hands wrapped in wool, as his mother knitted.

"So you've heard the news," said Peter, embarrassedly. "I am sorry."

"That's okay, Peter," I said.

"Good luck in the fight with Jesus."

"Thanks, but I don't think it'll be of much use."

"Oh yes. Yes, quite." Peter paused. He was struggling to formulate a question. "Any . . . idea in which round you might . . . disappear?"

"Round Two," I said. "I'm being phased out in Round Two."

"Thanks, Death, you're a real pal."

As I swooped back down to Earth I thought about my destiny. It seemed strange that after all the hard work I had done on Earth, after nearly losing myself forever to my addiction with Life, and after my painful rehabilitation at the clinic, that I was now being "phased out." Such an ugly phrase. It lacked a sense of finality, the clear cut that separated the living and the dead. If only I could be shot through the heart, have a grand piano drop on my head, be guillotined, I would not find it quite so bad. Instead I would slowly fade from sight, like a bad memory. I didn't think my own demise very ironic at all. But it did seem poetic, albeit like the kind of poetry that doesn't rhyme or make sense.

Despite the imminent arrival of the Second Coming, and the subsequent mass resurrection, I continued with my job. As it had at the beginning of my career, concentrating on the dead calmed me— the slip-sliding of the souls, the empty bodies, the quiet of the void acted as a balm to my worried thoughts. Of course, I couldn't help but tell some of the souls how lucky they were to die when they did, as soon no one would be dying at all. When the souls heard this, they felt rather pleased with themselves—after all, as once-in-a-lifetime experiences go, nothing really compares with dying—and became very friendly to me, saying how sorry they were that I was going. Some even said they'd put in a good word for me with God, but I told them not to worry. I was ready to die.

There was not an inch of the earth that I had not covered in my existence, but I thought now would be the time to visit those places that held a particular significance for me. I went back to where Eden had been and found Urizel was still there, vigilantly guarding it, even though Eden had been devastated and was now home to a smelting works. It had been so long since Urizel had been sent to guard it that I rather suspected Heaven had forgotten about him entirely, but Urizel did not seem unhappy.

"Never let it be said that Urizel doesn't know how to follow an order," he said to me, as he swept back wave after wave of health and safety inspectors who tried to pass through the factory gates. "None shall pass!" he screeched.

There had been many changes, I thought to myself, as I surveyed the world that had been my home for so many millions of years. Volcanoes that had once been the sites of sacrifices and suicides were now scattered with complacent tourists, who only rarely slipped and fell into the bubbling lava. Hospitals that had once been the great shipping stations into the Darkness now dangled the sick and dying just out of my reach, with a marionette's assortment of tubes and catheters. It seemed a shame to leave Earth just as Plutonium and Uranium had discovered their métier, and when bungee jumping and hang gliding would soon become popular activities. There were so many of you now, so many ways to go. At times it seemed as if I was being tempted to stay by the ever-growing varieties of your ends. How fitting, I thought, that my farewell should come amid such a cornucopia of slaughter.

My only regret was that the one person I would most like to have spent my last hours with was nowhere to be found. I visited the site of the Great Ziggurat of Ur, where Maud and I had originally met. The faint echo of her scream—that glorious first scream—seemed to be imprinted on the landscape, imbuing the rocks, the sand, the wind itself with her very essence.

I shook myself free from this reverie and opened the *Book of Endings* to see who was next. I was somewhat troubled to realize I had reached the last page. I stole a glimpse at the last name on the list. It was mine. A shiver went through me. I slammed the *Book* shut.

I was really going to die. I was really going to disappear forever. How terrifying to be able to measure out my existence in mere hours. There would be no more souls for me, no more thoughts, no more Darkness, even. There would be no more—

"Excuse me, are you Death?" said a small voice.

I looked down and saw a small raccoon standing on its back legs looking at me. Its head was slightly cocked.

"Er, yes." The shocking realization of my own death must have made me visible again.

"Hello," he said as he extended a paw for me to shake. "My name's Phil the Raccoon. I'm named after an ancestor of mine— Phillip the Raccoon. They say you two were friends. You let him chase after frog souls when he was dead. If he was anything like I am, I know he would have loved that."

"What do you want?" I said, slightly perplexed. I glanced quickly at the *Book of Endings*. I didn't want to spend too long looking at it. "You're not due until tomorrow afternoon."

"Really?" said the raccoon. "What do I die of?"

"I can't tell you that," I said, largely because I didn't want to look in the *Book* again.

"Distemper, I bet," said Phil the Raccoon. "Or maybe rabies. I've been feeling dry-mouthed all week. Then again, maybe that's because I've been looking all over the world for *you*. Word on the street has it that you're not going to be around here much longer. Me and some of the other woodland creatures held our regular Tuesday night séance the other night. Everybody in the spirit world's talking about Death being phased out."

"Yes, yes, it's true," I said. There was no need for it to be a secret.

"I also hear that there's some big money being put on you to take a fall in Round Two? And I mean *big* money. Know anything about it?"

"How do you know about that?"

"Come on, Death, don't be so naïve. There's no gambling in Heaven. Where do you think the angels place their bets? Right here on Earth is where, and Phil the Raccoon provides a full and discreet nocturnal bookmaking service for those of the saved who accidentally wander out of Heaven while everyone's asleep."

Raccoons. Always with their schemes. I had once met a raccoon who had attempted to assassinate Archduke Rudolph, the Crown Prince of Austria, in order to inflate the price of strudel, which he had sold short. As it was, he was caught by the royal bodyguards as he clambered into the archduke's bedroom, intent on savaging him in his sleep. The raccoon had been turned into a hat, which became all the rage in late-nineteenth-century Vienna. Strudel prices, however, had remained low.

Raccoons: Good Schemers, Excellent Headwear.

"Well, why do you want to know about the fight?" I asked.

"Call it a surfeit of Free Will," said Phil the Raccoon, "or maybe I'm just looking after my best interests. I had an angel in the other day who was putting everything he owned on you going down in Round Two—money, an old harp, a girdle, and the pearl handles he'd filched from some gates. This match could bankrupt me! But more than this, I'm a moral creature. I don't like the idea of the fix being in for anything. What kind of a world would it be if everything was predetermined? Nobody would want to wager on anything." He looked at me straight in the face. "Doesn't it make you mad?"

"Not really." I sighed; I had resigned myself to my fate.

"Really?" said Phil the Raccoon.

"I admit," I said, "that throwing a wrestling match with the Messiah may not be *exactly* the way I would have chosen for myself. But isn't every existence in Creation a fixed match of sorts, a futile combat against insurmountable odds?"

"Oh dear, oh dear, oh dear," said Phil the Raccoon. "That's hardly the attitude to take."

"I am Death," I reminded him. "I'm not really meant to be very positive."

"It could be worse," said Phil the Raccoon.

"I don't quite see how," I replied. "After all, I'm dealing with an all-powerful being with a split personality."

"Well, look," said Phil the Raccoon, "give me twenty-four hours to come up with a solution. Maybe this doesn't need to happen."

"What do you mean?"

"Maybe you don't have to die, Death."

I looked at the small, bushy-tailed mammal gesticulating on the ground in front of me. Was this really all that stood between me and extinction? Was *this* my final hope?

Last Judgment

It was my last day on Earth. In fact, it was the last day Earth would ever have. Any minute now the rivers would begin to run red with blood, fire would begin to fall from the sky, and the whole prematch razzmatazz would begin. Twenty-four hours had elapsed since I had spoken to Phil the Raccoon, and since all would be lost in a matter of hours, what did I have to lose by humoring him a little? However, when I went to see him again, he was standing at the head of a huge crowd of creatures—humans, birds, fish, rocks— who were all talking wildly. As I approached them, their conversation slowly died down.

"Well, Death," said Phil the Raccoon. "I had to pull a few strings, call in some favors, and strong-arm a few of the smaller invertebrates, but me and the rest of Creation have been talking."

"About what?"

"Life is a mess. You're happy, you're sad, you're up, you're down, you're spinning wildly around not knowing what you're doing. Yet there's always been one constant. One thing we could always rely on, while all the rest of Life fell apart. And that's you, Death. You've always been there for us. Whether the big man upstairs exists or not, it's you who we *know* exists. We may have our differences, sure. I mean, sometimes you take us earlier than we think you should. But you always take us, and that's the point. We've always known where we stand with you, Death, or rather where we fall, and we appreciate that, from the bottom of our still-beating hearts. Am I right, fellas?"

There was a braying murmur of assent.

"In fact," said Phil the Raccoon, "we figure that you're an intrinsic part of Life. Whether it's the last beat of a heart or the final word in an argument, you're always there. Is a door any less the part of a house because you leave the house through it?"

There was a braying murmur of confusion.

"What I'm trying to say is—we don't want you to go. And we're not going to stand for it. For too long we've been the subject of arbitrary divine forces. I mean, look at Gerald here."

A flounder flopped forward. "Hey, Death," it said.

"I mean, having your eye migrate around your head?" continued Phil the Raccoon. "Can you imagine how that messes you up?"

"Scarred me for life," said Gerald the Flounder. "I wake up in cold sweats at night just thinking about it."

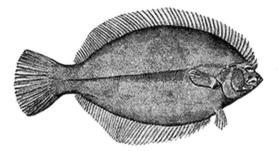

*Flounder: "You Lookin' at Me? No, Seriously,
Are You Looking at Me?"*

"Don't get me wrong," continued Phil the Raccoon, "there's nothing I like more than the infinite variety of Creation. But there's a fine line between 'infinite variety' and 'bat-shit crazy.' Anyway, what I'm trying to say is—what we're trying to say is—you never pull any of that nonsense on us, and we . . . we love you for it, Death."

The crowd broke into a round of applause. There was much hooting. Phil the Raccoon crossed his arms and swallowed. I noticed Gerald the Flounder had disappeared.

"Thank you, thank you all," I said. "I appreciate you saying all these kind words about me. But I'm afraid it's no use. God has decreed that you're all to be resurrected at the end of today and live forever in Heaven."

"Live forever?" continued Phil the Raccoon. "Are you shitting me? I can barely keep my alimony payments going as it is, let alone for all eternity."

There was a general murmur of agreement.

"And besides, who wants to live forever? Life may be brutish, ugly, and short . . . but so are we."

"I'm not," piped up a giraffe standing at the back of the crowd.

"All right then," snapped the Phil the Raccoon, "brutish, ugly, and tall. You see, Death, we appreciate Life for what is, in all its filthy glory. And we like having you around to tell us when it's over. You provide closure, you know?"

"Well, I'm glad you feel that way," I said, "but I'm not sure what can be done to stop it."

"Don't worry, Death," said Phil the Raccoon. "It occurs to me that, considering your working relationship with Life, a little solidarity is in order."

He then proceeded to tell me the most ridiculous plan I had ever heard.

Later that day, as the *Book of Endings* foretold, Phil the Raccoon choked to death on one of Gerald the Flounder's bones. But rather than sending his soul into the Darkness, I took it with me on a trip to Heaven.

Preparations for the Second Coming had begun. The bunting was out. Large posters read THY KINGDOM HAS COME and NO SMOKING. Newly installed bunk beds filled every possible nook and cranny. I noticed the stadium had been completed and was already starting to fill with angels. At its center was a roped-in ring. A tinny public address system was advertising the match.

"For one night only! The match to end all matches! The altercation to decide your salvation! Battling for your everlasting souls! In the white corner, the Mayhem from Bethlehem, the All-New Jew, Half-Man, Half-God, All Fighter! Jeeeeeeeee-zus Christ!"

Jesus Prided Himself on His Elaborate Ringside Entrances.

There was loud applause.

"And in the black corner," continued the voice, "the Reason for So Much Suffering in the World. Death. Former male prostitute."

There were a few scattered boos and then abrupt silence. Vendor angels were selling Jesus paraphernalia. Phil the Raccoon gave me a look of disgust, but I later caught him trying to buy a pair of stick-on stigmata. "For the kids," he told me. After all our planning, could I really trust him?

When we finally arrived at the Parliament of Heaven, it was almost empty. At the far end Jesus was packing a suitcase for His Second Coming. God was trying to sit on top of it in an attempt to get the lid down.

"Well, look who it is," Jesus beamed. "You're early. Better not be early tonight."

"Yes, Death," boomed God, "I hope you have not forgotten our . . . agreement."

"Ahem," coughed Phil the Raccoon.

"Actually, it's Amen," boomed God. "Who are you?"

"I'm Phil the Raccoon," said Phil the Raccoon, "and You're forgetting one thing, O Great One."

"I forget no things, you small furry creature," boomed God. "I know everything."

There was a pause.

"What have I forgotten?" boomed God.

"You think the living have just been wasting their time on Earth, just having sex and taking long walks and waiting for You to save us?" said the Raccoon. "Well, we haven't. We've been busy."

"I bet you have," beamed Jesus sarcastically. "Been chasing frogs, have we? Getting hit by cars? Being turned into hats? Oh, how busy you must have been."

"Ho, ho," boomed God. "Very droll, Jesus."

"Actually," said Phil the Raccoon angrily, "we've been holding meetings, and forming subcommittees. We've been debating issues and taking votes. We've been organizing!"

"What are you saying, you silly nocturnal flesh-eating mammal?" boomed God.

"The Earth is a closed shop, God," cried Phil the Raccoon, pulling out the soul of a dead whistle. "Creation is going on strike!" And with that, the Raccoon let out a mighty blast, and everything in

Creation immediately put down their tools, or claws, or proboscises and stopped what it was doing. The Earth stopped spinning on its axis, the clouds stopped moving, the winds stopped blowing, all the forces of nature ground to a halt in direct contravention of their divinely ordained duty. And the rivers refused to run red with blood, the birds declined to fall from the sky, not a flake of snow fell in the desert—Judgment Day was postponed! For seven days and seven nights, every creature, plant, and inanimate object sat down and sang. They sang for me.

"2-4-6-8, who do we appreciate," chanted the reeds in the rivers. "Death!"

"Oh, come on," boomed God. "This is ridiculous."

"10-12-14-16, who keeps Earth looking pristine," chanted the parrots in the trees. "Death!"

"I will not," boomed God, "I will not give in to this gross intimidation."

"56-58-60-62, who do we all go through," chanted the creeping things that crept in the tall grass. "Death!"

"Not you too, creeping things?" boomed God.

On the fifth day God sent in strikebreakers, replacement beings, and special new concepts hurriedly designed to get Creation moving again. There were many scuffles, but the new creations were ill-adapted to survival on Earth; they had not, after all, spent eons evolving upon it. The new plants God sent were swiftly uprooted by existing trees. New skulking things were crushed by age-old stomping things. New minerals reacted badly to the atmosphere and dissolved instantly. New languages failed to catch on and were swiftly ignored. Throughout all this, the chanting continued.

"1898988-1898990-1898992-1898994 who is waiting at the door," intoned the amoebas and mitochondria. "Death!"

What with the mayflies and lemmings staging die-ins of mammoth proportions, the metallic ores and sedimentary rocks refusing to be moved by even the most aggressive of tectonic forces, and the

Celestial Solidarity.

unending chanting of anything with a vibrating mucous membrane,
God was finally worn down. Phil the Raccoon and I were called to
Heaven for negotiations, but before I left I addressed Creation.

"Without you there would be no me!" I bellowed, pointing at
each and every member of Creation. They clapped wildly. "And with
me, there will be no you!" the clapping faltered somewhat. "Mark my
words, I will be seeing you all again, very, very soon!" There was
some disconcerted muttering, but slowly the world began to spin
again, and everything went back to normal.

In Heaven, we were met by God and a rather sulky-looking Jesus,
who was unpacking His suitcase.

"Very well," boomed God. "You've proved your point. But what
do you want?"

"First," said Phil the Raccoon, "we want Death to be reinstated as
Death."

"Yes, why not," boomed God. "In any case I've been having My
doubts about the Second Coming. I don't want people to think
We're selling out."

"Second, we want more and slower frogs," said Phil the Raccoon.
"Well, that's me done. Do you want anything, Death?"

"I want to call You God," I said to the blinding light. "Not Lord, not Master, not Lord God Sir, just God."

"Oh, all right," boomed God. "As long as I can call you Alice."

"Er, okay?" I said. After all, some concessions had to be made.

"And there's just one more thing," I said. "I want to see Maud."

"Whatever you say, Alice," boomed God, and Heaven suddenly disappeared.

I found myself back on Earth, in the middle of the twentieth century. Could I really be about to see Maud again? I thought about all the years that had passed since our glorious ten days together. Those ten days of forbidden joy in which no one died. Would she still remember them as fondly as I did? I wondered if she had changed. Of course, her physical exterior would be different, I had no doubt, but would Maud's nature be any different? Would she recognize me? It had, after all, been half a millennium since last we had seen each other. Would we know what to say to each other after such a long time apart? Would there be awkward silences? Would I be tempted by her again into Life?

I pulled out the *Book of Endings* from my cloak and was gratified to see that it had grown a giant appendix. My name was no longer visible. I noticed that instead of the Second Coming, a Second World War was now raging on Earth. You had to hand it to God— He had a sense of humor.

A phantom heartbeat sounded in my chest as I located Maud's name in the *Book*. It lay alongside many, many others. There would be no showboating this time for my beloved. I found her in a large concrete room, in the middle of Europe somewhere. It was filled with naked people. None of them looked very happy, not even Maud. I was slightly surprised by this. She looked skinnier than she had before; her cheekbones flashed in the dim light. Strangely, it looked as though she had been crying. I had never seen Maud cry before, although I was pleased to see that this only brought out the sparkle in her brown eyes all the more.

"Help me, Death. Don't let me die," she hissed upon seeing me. "Let me live, for the love of God, let me live."

I let out a sigh of relief. It was as if time had stood still. She was still playing the same old game, *our* old game! She was still the same delectable Maud!

"You've got to help me live, Death. Like you did before. The last time. You've got to let me live again."

She was good, I'll give her that. Utterly, utterly believable.

A thick gas began to hiss down from the roof of the room and Maud held her breath, her delicate red cheeks glowing in the dim light. As the other people in the room began to scream and kick up a terrible fuss, I saw her eyes frantically search for an escape route. It was truly as if she wanted to live! Suddenly she noticed an open air vent at the opposite end of the room and clambered her way over the dying to get to it, but as she tried to squeeze herself through it I grabbed hold of her foot and held her back, laughing at her feigned panic. She turned on me viciously. "I'm not playing this time, Death!" she choked. "I want to live!"

I smiled.

"No, no, Death. You don't understand. I don't *want* to die. Not this time. Not this time."

I didn't know quite what to say. It felt strange. There were none of her usual coquettish looks, no biting of her lip with excitement. Could she possibly mean it? I felt my existence spin on a coin edge. She was joking. She must be. She had to be. Right?

I reached out to touch her face, to try to get some sense of what she meant, but in that moment she turned pale, reeled backward, and started trembling. From her mouth foam flakes erupted, her eyeballs rolled in their sockets, and the blood deserted her face. Raising a loud scream, she wrenched her head to and fro, and then fell to the ground convulsing. It took some time before she was actually dead.

It was a good, classic death, one of her best, yet I felt strangely sad. I freed her soul and stood waiting for her with open arms. But she emerged shivering and refused to look at me.

"Maud, it's me," I blurted. "I wanted to see you so much. I was in a clinic and had to be taught to be bad again and then I stopped Gabriel from destroying the world and then I was almost phased out of existence but Creation went on strike and I was reinstated and then I asked to see you and here I am."

She looked at me with something like rage in her eyes, and the words froze in my mouth. The Darkness enveloped her rather shame-facedly, and she disappeared from view, but all the while her eyes stared at me. Stared at me with something that looked strangely like the opposite of love. I waited for a playful smirk to break on her face, a blown kiss to come from her lips, a wink to show in those lovely brown eyes, but there was none.

I never saw her again.

The End

And so history continued, much as it had before. The world kept turning, people kept dying, and I kept shipping souls off into the nether. It was good to be at work, good to be Death. The bright illumination of Life seemed to be extinguished within me, and all madcap thoughts of self-love and self-worth were banished from my mind. My world was dark once more, thick with fear, illness, and fatality. But every now and then, when a beautiful sunset took me by surprise, or a fluffy white lamb bounded across my path, the bright monster Life would rear up in me, flaming bright from the buried embers of my past, and I would sit down and scour the *Book of Endings* in the hope that I might find Maud therein. I still didn't know what to make of our last meeting. At times I thought I understood what she had been saying; comprehension seemed almost within my grasp. But such moments passed quickly, the Darkness would curl around my feet and I would feel deliciously empty again.

I was whirling across Earth without a thought in my head or a care in the world, when a fat cherub appeared in front of me with an irritated expression and a summons to Heaven. I hadn't been up there since the strike, but everyone seemed quite friendly. Peter said it was a shame about the fight being canceled and gloomily returned to giving his mother a sponge bath. Much of Heaven was empty. I soon found out where they were when a loud cheer emanated from the gigantic stadium that had been constructed to house my demise. Looking in, I saw Jesus, in a spangly leotard, hoisting the Holy Ghost above His head and slamming Him into the canvas. Jesus strutted around the stage, to much applause, while the Ghost lay on the floor groaning, clutching His side in a very convincing exaggeration of pain.

The Parliament of Heaven was empty too. God sat at the head of the hall by Himself.

"They seem to prefer the wrestling," boomed God, by means of explanation. "Is all miserable on Earth? Good, good. Listen, I need to ask your advice. Ever since Gabriel got back he hasn't been the same."

At that moment a naked Gabriel ran across the Parliament floor. His body was painted with blue stripes and he was making car noises.

"The thing is, he always did everything around here. I'm rather lost without him. I don't suppose you know anyone who'd be able to help?"

"Well, there is one person I can think of," I said.

I was greeted by a joyous Mother at the Gates of Hell, where she had returned to take up her old job. The automatic doors that had been installed had been corrupted by Hell's atmosphere and had started to let demons out on the sly in exchange for a good oiling.

It was quite a reunion. Mother lavished her attention on me, scalding me with hot cups of sulphur and dropping her famed iron scones on my feet, and Father almost remembered my name unprompted. In fact, it took some time before they would let me go in search of the person whom I had come for.

Reginald did not look good. In fact, he looked downright horrible. One of his wings had been torn off at the shoulder, and his left eye had been sewn shut with barbed wire. His teeth had been replaced with razor-sharp pebbles that stuck out at all angles. The top of his head was singed, and his halo had dropped over his head and was now strangling him. He tried to smile when he saw me, but this only forced his teeth through his cheeks. He let out a groan and began scratching frantically at his belly. I inquired what was wrong with him, and he opened up his tunic to reveal that hundreds of tiny imps had made a hole in his stomach and converted it into a disco, complete with mirror ball, illuminated dance floor, and tiny imp DJ.

"And it's always Saturday night," he sobbed. I flicked out the imps, tucked Reginald under my arm, and let the Darkness cover him. Soon we were on our way to Heaven.

It was a rather dazed Reginald who awoke to find himself seated at the left hand of the Father.

"Oh Master Death, thank you!" he sobbed. His wings and teeth had been repaired, his hair had grown back, and the disco in his belly had been converted into a chapel, complete with tiny angels praying in it. "I don't know how I can repay you. One more eon in that horrible, horrible place and I think I might have gone bad forever."

"Yes, sorry about that," boomed God, "but you should really strap up your sandals in the future, Reginald. Or should I say, Archangel Reginald."

Reaching into His eminence, He pulled out a halo brighter than all the others in Heaven and placed it atop Reginald's head. Reginald seemed to grow before my eyes, swelling in size. For the first time, he looked young and happy and at peace with the Universe. For the first time in countless eons, he looked impressive.

"Now," boomed God, "go and clean out the heavenly latrines."

"Wh . . . what?" said Reginald.

"The latrines, they've been blocked for ages."

"But Lord, would You not prefer I sang You hosannas?"

"No. Now, there's a mop and bucket in the cleaning cupboard."

"But Lord—"

"Do hurry up, Reginald," boomed God. "There's a good chap."

And so Reginald sloped off, a strange, broken smile on his face.

"And as for you, Alice," boomed God. "I'm sorry the thing with that mortal woman didn't work out. But I think We may be able to provide you with some suitable company. Now, there's a chance that you . . ."

As He droned on, my attention was diverted by the naked blue figure of Gabriel. He motioned at me not to make a sound. I saw he was trying to get to a thick green curtain I had never noticed before, which ran all the way behind God's throne. As God continued to talk obliviously, Gabriel grabbed one end of the curtain and, with an almighty tug, heaved it to one side. Behind the curtain hovered a giant shining divine orb of light.

"Who are You?" I asked.

"Oh, hello. I'm GOD," HE boomed.

"God?" I asked.

"No, GOD, all capitals."

"Don't listen to HIM," boomed God, suddenly realizing what was going on. "HE'S just a manifestation of Me."

"No, I am not," boomed GOD.

"Yes, YOU are, YOU even look like Me," boomed God.

"Lots of shiny things look like You," boomed GOD. "Spoons look like You. Are You a spoon?" HE turned to me, "Now look, I created Him."

"Lies!" boomed God. "All lies!"

At that moment Jesus came into the room still in His leotard.

"Dad?" he beamed worriedly, looking back and forth between the two divine lights. "DAD?"

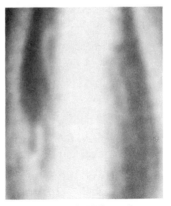

God? GOD? Spoon?

"Son!" the two blinding lights boomed as one.

I made my excuses and left.

In recent years, some strange things have been happening on Earth, or rather off it. I watched, in bemused fashion, as you started to put dogs into rockets and send them into outer space. I never quite understood what the purpose of this was—neither did the dogs—but I presume it was meant to be some sacrifice to appease the dark gods you supposed lived in the darkness of the cosmos. The human sacrifices weren't quite as successful, as the men, by and large, went back to Earth alive, and soon you started sending rockets into space with no living things on them at all, which seemed to me a bit foolish, as you don't want to make the dark gods angry if you can help it. However, it was one of these odd sacrifices of yours that brings me out of the past of my memoir and into the present.

I had forgotten the conversation I had had with God about Maud until fairly recently. One day, not long before beginning this book, I felt myself being drawn by an irresistible force off the planet Earth. I was pulled through space, past the moon and the dead meteorites and comets, until I approached a red planet with a cratered surface, rich in volcanoes and lava plains. I was on Mars.

According to the *Book of Endings,* a small spacecraft had been sent from Earth to land on the planet. It had descended onto the Martian surface using parachutes, rockets, and air bags, the last of which had suffocated and killed what seemed to be the only living life-form on the planet. I saw the Martian's puny body pressed deep into the planet's red dust.

When I freed its soul, it was rather confused as to what had happened, so I tried to explain. I told it about Earth, a planet teeming with Life, and the unfortunate accident that had occurred between it and the spaceship. But the Martian seemed angered by this and asked what it had ever done to the people of Earth to deserve such a fate. I told him that he had been killed purely by accident. He mumbled that he hoped there were humans in Martian Heaven so he could teach them some manners, and I was just about to pop its soul into the Darkness when I heard a cough from behind me.

"Actually, I think this one's mine," said a dreadful voice.

I turned around and saw a soft, dark, shapely figure standing behind me. It picked up the Martian's soul and whispered gently in its ear, and the Martian nodded its little head and shook hands with the figure, before being absorbed into the impossible Blackness that exuded from it.

I was agog. The being turned to me. The hue of her skin was the perfect whiteness of snow.

"Finally!" she said, blowing out her cheeks. "Tenacious little buggers, those Martians."

She looked at me and smiled. "Well, I'm done here. Do you need a hand back at your place?"

I felt a strange, light-headed elation. So it was true, I thought to myself. There really was Death on other planets.

EPILOGUE

Phil the Raccoon played a key role in forging Heaven's first union of the saved, campaigning for more salvation and shorter eternities. Long associated with demons from the underworld, he disappeared while eating frogs at a diner in Hell. His soul has never been found.

Urizel and his ever-turning sword of fire continued to guard the Eden Smelting Works until 2008, when he was made redundant. He was replaced by a small plastic alarm system that beeps.

Reginald never felt at home in Heaven. He returned to Hell after spending only three thousand years in Paradise and is currently undergoing ethical reassignment surgery.

Sunburn was finally dropped by the **Horsemen of the Apocalypse**. He is currently on a retainer for Club-Med Holidays.

Satan, following the collapse of the Soul Exchange in Hell, has proposed plans to merge Heaven and Hell under the auspices of Afterlife Inc., stressing Hell's booming population, and Heaven's stagnant growth.

Sin continues to guard the Gates of Hell. She is still married to Satan and continues to suffer from his neglect and cruelty. She is very happy.

Gabriel spends most of his time collecting string.

God and **GOD** agreed to submit to a paternity test to discover who was the true Father of all Creation. The results have yet to come back. GOD is currently only allowed to preside over Creation every other weekend.

Jesus continues to prepare for a new tour of Earth. In the meantime, He still reigns in Heaven, bitch!

Maud was never seen nor heard from again.

Death is still with us.

ACKNOWLEDGMENTS

D**eath** ***thanks*** a great many people, objects, and things that have given unselfishly of their existences to make this book possible. A certain few stand out for their special contributions:

Cholera, I never thought you'd make it, thanks for all your hard work over the years, you rule the mucosal epithelium.

Malaria, it's always a pleasure to work with you; you are simply the best.

Long Scarves Worn in Open-Top Automobiles, I had my doubts, but you had a point.

Not forgetting Zeppelins Filled with Hydrogen, Tortoises Dropped from Eagles' Claws, Sharp Toothpicks, Agricultural Accidents, Titus's Flea, St. Vitus's Dance, St. Titus's Dancing Flea, Red-Hot Pokers, Inflammation, Exflammation, Flammation, Laughter, Lies, Lead, Latrines, Lightning, Golf, Hot-Air Balloons, Hair Dryers, Electricity, Old Parachutes, Carbon Tetrachloride, Poison, Obsessive Fear of Being Poisoned, Robots, the Demon Core, Sharp Fences, Smallpox, Mediumpox, Largepox, Pneumonia (you too, Exposure!), Three-Day-Old Shellfish, Fugu, Indigestion, Leprosy, Gangrene, Low Lintels, Goat Hair in Pies, Sharks, Butts of Malmsey, Falling Pianos, Infectious Monkeys, Stampeding Buffalo, Runaway Trains, Potato Famines, and Kaiser Wilhelm II.

God, I know we've had our disagreements, but I wouldn't be nothing without You.

This book is dedicated to all those who have gone before and all those who are to come. That means you. Yes, you. No. Not him. You.

George Pendle thanks the various therapists, analysts, and religious leaders he consulted during the writing of this book. In particular, Jill Grinberg, Luke Dempsey, Lindsey Moore, Dr. Pepe Rockefeller, and Charlotte.

PICTURE CREDITS

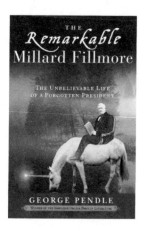